PRAISE FOR SASHA

"Sasha has done it again! I dev... ...r them to come out because I k... ...e should be on your must-read ... you are into sports romance."

"You want a sizzling soccer romance??! This is for you! I could not put this book down! I was hooked from the second I started reading!!"

"Sasha Lace has fast become one of my favorite authors! The world she exposes, the world she builds, has me glued to my screen from the first word to the very last!"

"This is everything that I love about contemporary romance: strong male and female main characters, romance with instant chemistry."

"A witty, flirty, and a little bit of everything else romantic story. The sizzle was awesome too. Read it in one sitting, it was such an easy read."

"30% in and Sasha Lace became a one-click author."

"I am loving that an author is giving women their shot in the world of sports romance!"

"Gabe needs to be added to your list of book boyfriends, he is handsome, knows what he wants and my heaven, knows his way around a woman. The spice in this was beautiful and fun. It was delicious."

"I left each chapter wanting more and more and MORE. Well written, fast read that gives readers everything they are looking for."

"As with any book by Sasha there was a point where I was reduced to a crying mess and wanted to throw my Kindle at a wall . . . which led to having to stay up all night to get to the HEA."

"Would I recommend this book? Yes! Would I recommend everything written by Sasha Lace? Yes!"

Playing for keeps

TITLES BY SASHA LACE

Playing the Field series

Playing for keeps

SASHA LACE

Text copyright © 2023, 2024 by Sasha Lace
All rights reserved.

Published by Montlake, Seattle

First published as *Keeping the Single Dad* by Sasha Lace in 2023. This edition contains editorial revisions.

www.apub.com

Amazon, the Amazon logo, and Montlake are trademarks of Amazon.com, Inc., or its affiliates.

ISBN-13: 9781662526169
eISBN: 9781662526152

Cover design by The Brewster Project
Cover image: © LadadikArt © lupengyu / Getty Images; © Taiga
© By Michael Reusse (alt) / Westend61 on Offset / Shutterstock

Printed in the United States of America

CONTENT WARNING

Grief (death of a spouse and death of a parent)

Alcoholism

Explicit sex

Blackmail

References to drug use and injecting drugs

For Heather
Thank you for your friendship and support on this
writing journey.

Chapter 1

LANA

Dad's glassy eyes met mine. He propped himself up in the hospital bed. "Lana? You don't have to be here. Everything's fine."

Blood smeared Dad's face and crusted the strands of white hair that fell over his lined forehead. His skin looked ruddy over the gaunt ridges of his cheekbones.

Sure, Dad. Everything looks super fine.

Mel gazed out of the window at the dark city skyline. My older sister hadn't spared me a glance since I'd walked in. She looked as put together as always—her red hair gleamed in the bright hospital lights, her chic ruffle-collared blouse and stylish pencil skirt hugged her slim frame perfectly—but tension radiated from her in waves.

Dad shook his head ruefully. "I was gardening, and I tripped over a gnome. A bloody gnome, of all things!" His Scottish burr was slow and slurring. Even after all these years in England, he'd never lost his accent. "I bashed myself on the wall."

He turned his head, and his overpowering stench of tobacco and liquor filled my nose. I did my best not to recoil.

Oh, Dad. Not again.

I can't go through it again.

Mel kept her gaze fixed on the window as she traced a finger over the rain-streaked glass. I had no idea what she was thinking when she went still and quiet like this. This had to be freaking her out, too. The fact that she'd bothered to call and ask for help was evidence enough of that.

Mel would always be a mystery. It was so late, but she still looked perfectly polished and ruthless, as though she'd just stepped out of the boardroom after having dismissed her entire staff without notice. I had no idea what she did at the job I'd swung for her at the football club that meant she had to be power-dressing after midnight. It was to do with contracts, or finance, or something involving spreadsheets. She'd explained it before, but it always went over my head, and now I couldn't ask without looking like an arsehole who didn't know what her sister did for a living.

Dad poked a cut below his eye and grimaced. My stomach sank. Five years of sobriety and now this. He'd had the odd slip and got back on the wagon, but he'd been doing well. Why now?

I held his clammy hand. "It's okay to tell us if you've been drinking."

"Not you, too." Grimacing, he snapped his hand away to prod the bandage wrapped around his head. "Your sister has already been on my case."

Mel turned to look at me for the first time since I'd stepped into the room. Her unimpressed gaze traveled over my outfit. A bridal veil flowed from a plastic jewel-encrusted tiara on my head. A black and pink sash emblazoned with the words "Same Penis Forever" was draped over my teal slip dress. Silver kitten heels completed the look. The bloody things were giving me blisters. I always felt more comfortable in football boots than fancy shoes.

Mel's critical appraisal made me feel self-conscious. I shrugged. "Skylar's bachelorette party."

"I see you've kept things classy," she muttered.

Of course Mel wouldn't approve of penis-related sashes. My sister had studied fashion in London before she'd had to drop out. She should have been in New York or Milan now, living a life of catwalk shows and starry galas, not working a corporate job at a football club, and definitely not stuck in an overcrowded hospital with her screw-up sister and alcoholic father.

Mel moved to Dad's bed and smoothed the blanket. "Remember what they say at Alcoholics Anonymous. Relapse is part of the process. Recovery is not linear, it's a cycle. You think about what triggered this and you learn."

Mel had the thin, strained voice she used when she was about to explode and snap over the slightest thing. God. I hated that voice. I hadn't heard it in so long. Memories of all the times we'd had to deal with Dad's drunkenness flooded my brain. At his worst, he'd disappeared and slept rough on a park bench. He'd been so much better since then. Why now?

Mel shot me a sidelong glance. "I shouldn't have bothered you. I didn't realize you had something on. You can go back. I've got it under control."

Nope. It had been a while since we'd done this dance, but I hadn't forgotten the steps. Of course my older sister wanted to be the martyr and bear the brunt of a relapse.

Dad rolled his eyes. "Got what under control? Me? She's always been a worrier, this one. Not like me and you." He reached for my hand and squeezed it. "We know how to have a good time, don't we, lass? A chip off the old block."

He gripped my hand tight and brought it to his lips. "I haven't seen you in a while. Any word on *the call*?"

Not this again. Could we have one conversation where Dad didn't ask about *the call*? As if he wouldn't be the first person I'd tell. I'd been waiting for *the call* to play football for England since I was twenty. It still wasn't impossible at twenty-six, but every year that flew by made it less likely. The stupid tiara on my head felt suddenly too heavy. I slipped it off and pulled out the little plastic penis earrings that Miri had insisted we all wear.

I kept my smile breezy. "Not yet."

He let go of my hand and turned his face away. "Not to worry. Still time. Some players are . . . late bloomers." Dad cleared his throat. "Anyway, don't either of you worry about me. When Logan Sinclair leaves this world, it won't be at the hands of a bloody gnome."

Mel sighed. "Let's get him home." Her disparaging gaze fixed on the veil I held low in my hand. "I'll take it from here. You can get back to whatever you were doing."

"I'm here now, aren't I?" My voice came out sharper than I'd intended. "I'll help you get him home and then I'll head back."

She tossed her shiny hair haughtily. I got it. Mel had always been better than me at all this stuff. She was the golden girl and I was the screw-up. Mel had kept us going after we'd lost Mum. Everything had fallen apart when Mel left for university.

I'd tried not to disturb her perfect life, but then Dad's drinking spiraled. He'd go missing for days, forget to pay the electricity bill or get the groceries. I kept showing up for lessons and football practices with a smile on my face. I'd lost one parent; I didn't want to be taken away from the other one.

In the end, everything unraveled. I fell in with some older kids in the area. From the outside it looked like I'd gone off the rails, and maybe I had, but I hadn't meant to ruin Mel's plans. I was just a stupid teenager doing stupid things that I regretted now. I'd needed the escape.

When my sister came home after that first term at university, she didn't go back. Mel sacrificed her dreams to save a sinking ship. I'd never be able to shake this feeling that Dad and I were the anchor weighing Mel down.

4

Dad threw his arms open and burst into song at the top of his voice.

I straightened the sash over my dress. "At least someone is having fun."

Mel approached Dad in her detached, no-nonsense way, as though he were a wild beast in transit and she just needed to find the right spot to aim the tranquilizer dart. "Well, come on then. Don't just stand there. Let's move him. If you're sticking around for a change, make yourself useful."

Chapter 2

ALEXANDER

"Daddy!"

Brodie flew into my arms. Pain crackled the length of my spine and blazed across my right hip. The fitness test at the football club today had nearly destroyed me. Brodie squeezed me tight and the throbbing in my back intensified. If I wasn't careful, it would go into a spasm again. I pushed my son away gently and worked to keep a grimace from my face. I hadn't seen Brodie since yesterday. We'd never spent a night apart. I'd missed him terribly.

"Bit posh here, isn't it?" My sister, Rachel, peered around the fancy restaurant at the Beaufort Hotel.

Mirrors sparkled on every wall and the gold accents on the black furniture reflected the light in a dazzling display. The gentle tinkle of silverware and the low hum of conversation filled the air.

I pulled a chair out to let Brodie sit. "Would you expect anything less from Gabriel Rivers?"

I'd expected Gabe Rivers—*the* Gabe Rivers, one of the richest men in England and football royalty—to be a prick, but his reputation did him a disservice. He was down-to-earth and charming.

He'd insisted I stay in his fancy hotel. Only a fool would turn down a free dinner and a four-poster bed for the night.

Rachel's smile widened as she slid into a chair next to Brodie. "They must be serious about signing you if they're rolling out Gabe Rivers to schmooze you."

"Gabe's a good guy. They all seem like good guys. It's a young squad. Most of them are in their early twenties. The captain is half my age."

Rachel picked up an elaborate silver saltshaker and examined it with a faint smile. "They don't have your experience."

No, but they have fresh legs and spines that don't creak.

I smoothed the thick tartan wool of my kilt and sat. Usually, I only wore the kilt for special occasions. I'd never worn it outside of Scotland. The Calverdale United social media team had insisted upon full regalia for the promotional video. In the end, it was ridiculous. It wouldn't have surprised me if they'd pulled out bagpipes and haggis.

I winced at the prices on the fancy menu and sent my sister a *can you fucking believe this?* glance over the top of Brodie's head. After humble origins, I'd been playing football long enough to afford anything, but I still didn't appreciate being ripped off.

Brodie bounced excitedly on his chair. If only I had the energy of a seven-year-old . . . and the exercise recovery time.

"Daddy, who's your second-favorite pirate?"

"I don't even have a first-favorite pirate."

The nutmeg freckles on Brodie's nose bunched. "Why not?" He leaped from his seat and swished his imaginary sword in an arc through the air. "I'm going to be a pirate when I grow up, either that or a dog walker."

An elderly woman at the table next to us fingered the pearls around her neck and shot Brodie a withering look. I had no time for people that had an issue with kids in public spaces. Brodie had as much right to eat his outrageously overpriced meal in here as anyone else. He just did it with more relish. The poor kid had been through so much. I chose my battles these days.

"Come here." I smoothed his thick yellow hair between my fingers. "When the time comes, you'll make an excellent pirate or dog walker. Or do both. Pirates must outsource their pet care. How else do they go on those long voyages? You could be a dog walker for pirates. They might pay you to look after the parrots, too."

Brodie's toothy grin filled me with warmth. Our overpriced food arrived and we tucked in. The only time Brodie was quiet was when he was eating.

Rachel sipped her wine. "So? When do you start?"

"I have a contract meeting tomorrow. If the lawyers agree then it's good to go."

Rachel smiled. "We can't wait to have you both down here. The girls are so excited to have their favorite cousin around."

Brodie straightened in his chair. "Can I stay with Auntie Rachel tonight? Please. Please."

Rachel hitched her shoulder. "It's fine with me as long as your dad doesn't mind."

That would mean two nights apart in a row. Brodie squeezed his hands together and gave me puppy-dog eyes. I didn't want another night apart, but as if I was ever going to say no to that look. Anyway, this was good. Great, actually. This was Brodie being independent. He'd been so anxious and clingy. For a while, I couldn't even shower without him in the bathroom. This was a good thing.

I brushed crumbs from his shirt. "If you like, pal, but you're missing out on the fancy rooms they've got here."

Brodie shrugged. "Auntie Rachel's house is fancy."

Rachel chuckled. "I wish."

We finished our meals and when it came to the bill, the waiter wouldn't let us pay. Gabe Rivers wasn't just letting me stay in his fancy hotel, he was also feeding me. Definitely a good guy. I held out Brodie's coat for him.

Rachel squeezed my shoulder. "A night off Daddy duties. You should treat yourself to a drink at the bar."

"I don't drink in the season."

"One pint won't hurt." She raised a mischievous eyebrow. "You never know, you might meet a beautiful stranger to spend the evening with."

I couldn't help my incredulous snort.

"Why is that funny?" She gave me a tentative smile and watched Brodie as he skipped ahead of us through the restaurant. "It's been five years. If there's one thing I've learned about life, it's that you can hold multiple feelings at once. You can grieve your wife and also keep yourself open to meeting somebody else. Evelyn wouldn't have wanted you to be alone. She wanted you to be happy, Alex."

"I am happy."

"Are you?"

I watched Brodie stabbing the air with his imaginary pirate sword, and my heart swelled. "If Brodie is happy, then I'm happy."

The last thing Brodie needed was disruption. We'd fought so hard for normality. I'd never bring someone into our lives who might walk away. It was impossible to date in my line of work anyway. So many women wanted to hook up with a footballer for the lifestyle. How could you know who was genuine? Easier not to bother. Brodie was all that mattered.

I craned my neck to the dimly lit bar beyond. Soft piano music trickled out. A hot bath and bed were calling to me after the fitness test, but Rachel was right. It had been so long since I'd sat and enjoyed a quiet pint. Maybe I could get wild and have a bag of salted peanuts. I couldn't turn down the opportunity of a night off-duty.

9

I squeezed Brodie in a hug and kissed the top of his head. "Be good for Auntie Rachel."

"If I'm going to be a pirate, will you get me a real sword?"

Not this again. "No swords in the house."

His face dropped. "I need one."

"I can't buy you weapons."

"A dog then?"

"We'll talk about it later."

"That's a yes." His huge grin lit his face, and he jumped up and down. A pang made my heart ache. He looked so much like his mother when he smiled.

"It's not a yes."

"It's a yes."

My sister shepherded Brodie toward the foyer. His excited squeal drifted over the rumble of the milling guests. "I'm getting a puppy!"

Chapter 3

LANA

Tinkling piano music needled my skin. The PR team had set up this meeting at Gabe's pretentious hotel. I wished I'd pushed back and suggested somewhere more casual. The journalist placed her recording device on the table with a gentle click and pushed the red button. I should have canceled tonight. Dad's relapse wouldn't stop hammering my mind. At least he hadn't been alone today. There was no way Mel would leave his side now.

I turned my attention back to Karen Delaney. The prospect of an interview made my heart pound. The press had hounded Dad for years, and they'd written a couple of bitchy gossip pieces about some of my friends in the squad. It was all pointless bullshit about fashion and who was fucking who. The men's team could wear anything, and fuck whoever they wanted, and nobody batted an eyelid. The double standard annoyed the hell out of me. It was too easy to say the wrong thing by accident. So easy to get in hot water with the team or get myself canceled.

"Lana Sinclair." Karen smiled. "It's a pleasure to meet you."

I tried to muster some enthusiasm in my response. "Lovely to meet you, too."

It wasn't. I always tried to dodge media engagements, but in the end the management had forced me.

"Congratulations on an amazing session."

Her smile was syrupy sweet. Bleached-blonde hair spiraled in curls around her heart-shaped face. She looked like a harmless mum waiting at the school gate. I smoothed the smart Balmain dress I'd swiped from Mel's closet and squeezed some lime into my virgin mojito to buy myself some time. How best to respond? I wanted my confidence to come across, but I couldn't risk looking smug or she'd tear me to pieces.

I settled for a noncommittal smile and nod. "Thanks."

She nodded and scribbled something in a notepad.

Shit. What was she writing?

Her too-interested gaze landed on my drink, making me suddenly self-conscious. It had been stupid not to get a soda. Now she'd be writing an article about me getting drunk during an interview.

I took a sip of the cool, minty concoction. "It's just a mocktail."

She nodded, but her smile was unconvinced. Fine. I shouldn't have even had to explain it. Of course she would believe whatever she wanted. An article about me was really just a way to write about Dad. It fitted the narrative that Logan Sinclair's daughter was also a handful. She could think what she liked. I couldn't care less about people too lazy to look closer.

"It's been an interesting couple of years. Calverdale Ladies made it into the Women's Super League, but it's been a battle to stay on top."

Good. Let's focus on football. The only part that matters. "We've had a great season. We're competing against world-class players and—"

"There are rumors of a rift with Skylar Marshall? You were captain while she played in the US, and now you've had to step down." Karen inched the recording device across the table, and her smile spread wider. "That must sting?"

I fought to keep my face level, but a heavy feeling gnawed at my gut. I'd let my best friend down so badly. I'd broken girl-code by kissing her ex. She said she'd forgiven me, but we'd hardly hung out since she'd returned from playing in LA. I'd been an idiot for getting sucked in by Sean Wallace. I wanted to do better. The last thing I needed was an article dredging up dirt about us. As for the captaincy, Skylar was welcome to it. Unlike my friend, I'd never wanted to be a leader. Too much responsibility. I just wanted to play the game I loved, to the best of my ability.

"Skylar Marshall is not only my friend but one of the greatest footballers I've ever known. As my captain, she has nothing but my respect and support."

"It can't be easy to pass the baton back?"

"Easy as pie. We have some amazing matches ahead of us—"

"How is your father?"

My smile faltered. "What?"

"The papers used to call Logan Sinclair the bad boy of football. Some people say the apple hasn't fallen far from the tree. You've got a reputation for being a wild child. How do you feel about that?"

Some people.

People like you, who can't mind their own business.

It didn't matter how much Dad had changed, the press had dogged him his whole life. Sure, he'd had a slip last night, but we'd work through it. All anyone wanted to talk about was the excess. Nobody wanted to talk about how much work he'd done to improve himself.

"People can call me whatever they want. All that matters is what I do on the pitch. My private life is private. As is my father's."

Karen's smile widened, and she scribbled in the pad again. Chatter and tinkling silverware filled my ears. I pinned my hands together in my lap to stop myself from fiddling with my ear-rings. This woman was making me too nervous. What was she writing? Had I sounded too arrogant? Screw it. I had to be truthful. Authenticity was the only way.

Karen smiled, blandly. "Some photos have come to my attention. Your father appears to be going through a . . . difficult time. It would be terrible if one of our competitors got hold of a story like that. You know what the gutter press is like."

A shiver crept across my shoulder blades. "What are you talking about?"

Karen tilted her head and studied my face. "Last night? Reports suggest Logan wound up in hospital after an all-night drinking session. We've got pictures of him urinating in an alley and ranting in a pub."

I took a deep breath, the way Skylar's psychologist fiancé had shown me. Reece had been helping me to work on my temper. Punching this woman would feel incredible at this moment, and then I'd regret it.

"I don't know what you're talking about. Dad is fine."

Karen gave an exaggerated sigh and picked up the recording device. She clicked it off and put it in her briefcase.

"Look, I'll level with you, off the record. This is a tough break. I don't want to do this to you." She tapped a sharp crimson fingernail on the table and lowered her voice. "Women in sport should be celebrated, not torn apart for a bad outfit choice. Celebrity is tawdry, I'm afraid. Your dad is a sporting hero and the only thing the British public love more than tearing a woman apart is watching a hero fall. It's all passé and predictable."

Karen inclined her head, a watchful intensity in her expression. "I have to turn in a story by the end of the week. Perhaps you have something more interesting for me? Maybe you overhear things in the locker room. I'd rather write about a current football star than a has-been." Her face brightened as though she were doing me a huge favor. "No offense."

Ice circled my mouth. What the hell was this? She wanted me to sell out another player to save my dad's neck? No way. She was messing with the wrong girl if she thought I was a snitch.

I folded my arms. "I'd never sell out a single one of those girls. The team is my family."

"You misunderstand. I don't care about the women's team. The women's team doesn't sell papers." She leaned in with a warm smile, as though we were just two old friends discussing something harmless like makeup tips. "I'm only interested in the men's team."

It didn't matter if it was the women's or the men's team. We were all footballers playing for Calverdale. I was friendly with most of the guys on the team. Hell, I'd hooked up with most of them. I wouldn't sell them out. Still, I'd have to be careful. Despite her overfamiliar demeanor, she didn't seem the type to bluff.

"I'll get a lawyer. This is blackmail."

"That's a shame. I was hoping you'd be more sensible." She didn't look at me as she packed her briefcase and placed a business card next to my glass.

Not acceptable. Dad was so sensitive. I couldn't let the press drag him through the dirt when he was already at rock bottom. He was mortified about his behavior last night. He'd agreed to go back to AA, but it was going to be tough. I couldn't let her walk out of here.

I stood. "Wait. Write a story on me. Say whatever you want, but leave my dad alone."

A lump rose in my throat. This could kill my career. If I wanted to get picked to play for England then I needed to look like a solid, stable choice. An article about Dad wouldn't help matters, either. We'd all look bad. Still, if it meant protecting him, I'd cope with whatever came to pass.

Karen pressed her lips. "I told you, male footballers sell papers, not women. Give me something better, or we go to print with your father."

"Please. You can't do this. It's not fair."

"No." Her small smile was almost apologetic. "It's not."

She lifted her handbag higher on her shoulder and strutted away.

Chapter 4

Lana

I signaled the bartender for another mocktail. These were the times when I wished I drank alcohol. I needed to shake off this sense of dread after Karen's onslaught, but alcohol had never done me any favors when I was a teenager, and I'd seen Dad drunk so many times it had put me off drinking for life. I pulled out my phone and scrolled with trembling fingers. My thumb hovered over Mel's number. The way she'd looked at me last night drifted to mind. She was always so mad at me, whether or not I'd done anything wrong. My sister would give me so much shit for this. She'd blame me, as if it was my fault Karen Delaney had set her sights on ruining my life. I scrolled on.

Maybe I could talk to Skylar? Not that she'd have any time for me. She'd been joined at the hip to Reece ever since she'd come home from LA. What was I supposed to do? My loyalty to Dad came above all else, but the team was my world.

"Seven pounds for a pint? Is this some kind of joke?" A Scottish voice drifted to my ears.

The short, sharp vowel sounds reminded me of Dad's Glaswegian accent. I turned to take in the towering beast of a man standing a way along the bar. He was at least a head and shoulders taller than everyone around him. In his blue tartan kilt, he looked like a Highland warrior, with broad shoulders and long, strong legs. Silver streaked his dark hair and dusted his temples. Despite his formidable stature, his eyes were soft and kind.

He caught my eye. "I knew it was pricey down here, but this is daylight robbery."

Even though I was in a terrible mood, I couldn't help but chuckle at his incredulous look. It reminded me of Dad. No matter how much money Dad made, he'd always hated getting ripped off. That was one perk of knowing the billionaire owner of the Beaufort. I didn't have to pay for the rooms or the drinks.

"That's normal for this place." I signaled the bartender. "Here. Let me get it for you. I'll put it on my tab."

"You don't have to do that." He held his palms up in mock surrender. His hands were huge—strong and long-fingered. No rings either. Interesting.

"It's on the house. I know the owner and I can assure you he can afford it."

Curiosity flickered in his eyes. "You know Gabriel Rivers?"

"Yeah. I know Gabe."

The bartender put the pint of beer on the bar in front of the dashing Scotsman, who flashed a warm smile. "Thank you. That's kind of you."

"No problem."

He took a long drink. Froth clung to his top lip for a moment before his tongue traced the edges of his full mouth. I couldn't take my eyes from the movement.

"How do you know a celebrity, then?"

I opened my mouth to tell him that Gabe was my boss at the football club, but some devilish impulse made the words wedge in my throat. The last person I wanted to be was Lana Sinclair. Lana

Sinclair had an alcoholic father she couldn't manage, a sister who thought she was a total idiot, and a viper-in-kitten-heels journalist from hell blackmailing her. Lana Sinclair was up to her eyeballs in shit that she couldn't deal with. Wouldn't it be better to be someone else for a little while? Someone composed and in control. Someone responsible and mature. Someone more like . . . Mel.

"I'm here from out of town on business with Gabe. Finance stuff." I waved a dismissive hand. "I won't bore you with the details."

"What's Gabe like to work with? Is he a good guy?"

A good guy? Is there any such thing? "He's great. Don't believe anything you read in the papers."

The gigantic Scotsman gave me a smile that set my pulse racing before he slid onto the stool next to me. How tall was he? He had to be around six foot five. Six foot six? It was a good job we were sitting down. Even in Mel's vertigo-inducing Louboutins, at five foot two I'd be getting a cramp in my neck right now if I had to talk to him standing up.

He drew his lips in thoughtfully. Beautiful full lips for such a rugged-looking man. "Gabe surprised me. Just goes to show you shouldn't judge a person without getting to know them."

I raised my glass and clinked it against his. "Amen."

Amusement flickered in his eyes as they met mine. "Amen."

Everyone was always so committed to misjudging me. People looked at me and saw whatever they wanted to see. Mel saw a teen-age screw-up who had made her give up her dreams. Dad saw a chance to relive his glittering career. My friends saw a carefree party girl. I'd never shared any of the things going on at home with the team. Maybe it had become a habit from spending all that time when I was younger convincing the outside world that everything was fine. Some horrible scratchy feeling inside always stopped me from being honest. It felt like such a betrayal.

Even my best friend didn't get me. I couldn't blame her. Skylar didn't even want me as her maid of honor because I'd fucked up and kissed her scumbag ex-boyfriend. And why? Sean Wallace had been a let-down. All men were a let-down. None of them ever took me seriously or treated me with respect. They all saw what they wanted to see too. No one cared to see anything beneath. The truth was, even I didn't like to see beneath most days either.

I smoothed Mel's tight dress over my thighs. I'd dressed up like a contestant on *The Apprentice* to impress Karen Delaney. Fat lot of good it had done me.

I flicked my long auburn hair over my shoulder. "Are you staying here?"

"Aye."

"Are you staying here alone?"

His gaze slid down my body before darting back to my eyes. "Aye. What about you?"

Good. I knew what that look meant. I needed a way to feel better. This giant sexy Scotsman would do the trick. "I'm just passing through."

He watched me with a look that seemed to electrify the surrounding air. "What's your name? I'm Alexander."

Alexander.

It was delicious to hear his name in that deep Scottish voice. I could listen to him reading a post-match analysis and it would still be as sexy as hell. I opened my mouth to tell him my name, but the same impulse that had made me lie about Gabe gripped me. I couldn't bear to be Lana. Not tonight. Not after everything that had been going on. For one night at least, I could be someone else. It was easier that way.

My heart pounded as the lie slipped from my lips. "My name is . . . Melissa. Everyone calls me Mel."

He took another sip of his pint, and once again the movement of his full lips was hypnotic. "You look young. How old are you?"

"Do you think?" I forced a flattered laugh. "I'm thirty, but thank you."

That lie slipped out easier. Maybe the more you told, the easier it got. "What about you? How old are you?"

"Old enough to know better." His low, lilting accent held as much humor as it did authority.

"I like men. I don't waste my time with boys."

"Is that so?" A small smile flickered over his lips. "Tell me more about yourself, Mel."

He wanted to know more? Shit. What was I doing? I didn't lie. That kind of stuff always came back to bite you in the arse, but this day couldn't get any worse. What did it matter? We were just two strangers in a bar. It was fun. I'd never see him again. I'd started this stupid ruse, why stop now?

"My favorite food is pizza, but the proper kind you'd get on the street in Italy."

"Oh? You're a food snob?" Laughter danced in his eyes.

Yes. Thank you. Mel is an absolute food snob.

"I just have a . . . refined palate. My favorite color is blue. I like the smell of petrol. I'm a cat person, not a dog person. When I was five, I—"

"You don't like dogs?"

I tried to remember all of Mel's bullshit reasons for preferring cats to dogs. We'd argued about it so many times.

"Dogs are messy. The hair gets everywhere. It's unhygienic."

He took a thoughtful sip of his pint. "That could be a problem. I'm never going to get on with someone who doesn't like dogs. We will fundamentally never be able to agree on anything."

"There are reasons not to like dogs. What if a dog bit you when you were a kid?"

20

"Fear of dogs is acceptable." His voice was teasing. "I won't quibble if you have some deep-rooted dog-related psychological trauma."

Something in his calm, gruff manner soothed me as much as it made my skin tingle. Was he into this? No point playing games. As casually as I could, I slid my hand along the smooth cool bar. My little finger grazed his. My heart jolted, and I inhaled sharply at the contact. For a dreadful moment, I thought he might jerk his hand away, but he held perfectly still. The lightest graze of our fingers made warmth bloom up my wrist.

His gaze riveted to my face. "I'm talking about a groundless dislike of dogs. I can't get on board with that."

"Cats are independent. They look after themselves."

"See, that's the part I don't get." His little finger slid tantalizingly back and forward over mine, spreading a delicious heat through my body. "You let a cat out of the door, and then you know it's out there on the streets. I would worry the whole time. You can never tame a cat. How do you know it's going to come home?"

"A cat chooses its owner. It will come back if it likes you and it's getting what it wants from you."

He eased closer on his stool. His strong thigh brushed my leg. "Right, but a dog will adore you until the end of time and you don't have to do anything to earn that love."

My nose filled with his subtle cologne, hints of wood smoke and black pepper. His huge, solid presence pressed so close was so bracing. I had to fight not to breathe him in. "A cat knows how to love. It's just more discerning than a dog."

"A dog only knows how to love unconditionally. We all need to be loved like that, don't you think?"

An unexpected ache burned my throat. "Have you ever loved anyone like that?"

He slid his hand away. His somber expression held me entranced, the amber tones in his brown eyes like whisky held to the light. Why wasn't he touching me anymore? I found myself checking his hands again. Definitely no rings. "Are you married?"

He drew a breath. "No."

"You're single?"

"Yes."

"Sure?"

"Am I sure I'm single?" His laugh was deep and full-hearted. "Yes. I'm sure."

My hand tingled from where he'd touched me. My body ached for more. I took a breath and slid down from the stool. Even standing on tiptoe, I couldn't reach his ear to whisper. "I'd love to see inside one of these fancy rooms."

He could say no. This was a bold move even for me, but I'd had my fair share of hookups. Men were only good for one thing, and most of them weren't even that good at that. Dad's relapse and Karen Delaney's threats had messed with my head. I needed this distraction. Even if I looked a fool, throwing myself at this man-mountain. It was a way to make this terrible evening better. Besides, I'd never seen a mountain I'd been more eager to climb.

I pressed myself closer, relishing the heat of his hard, muscular body. The fresh, clean scent of his cologne filled my nose again, and this time I couldn't help but breathe him in. I took his huge hand in mine and turned it over to trace the lines on his palm. "No strings. Just fun and done."

I watched his throat bob as he swallowed. Maybe the stupid cat thing was a deal breaker. Chatter and the tinkling music from the piano filled my ears. Was he going to say no?

I flashed a smile and hoped it looked seductive. "So, what do you say? Will you give me a tour of your room?"

He watched me in fascination before he interlaced his huge fingers with mine. A giddy sense of pleasure filled me.

Leaning down, he whispered into my hair. "Aye, sweetheart. I'll give you anything you want."

Chapter 5

ALEXANDER

As soon as the elevator doors slid closed, we were on each other. I'd envisioned my evening would contain all the extravagance of a pack of salted peanuts and a pint before bed, not a devastatingly beautiful redhead plastered to me. Her soft mouth met mine in hot, forceful kisses that made me breathless.

Our tangled figures reflected from every angle in the sparkling mirrored elevator as we soared upward, groping each other furiously. I'd forgotten what it was like to give in to desire. Forgotten what it was like when my senses came to life like this. We pawed at each other like horny teenagers behind the bike sheds. Our pants and groans drowned out the soft drone of piped music.

Her hand grazed my erection through my kilt. The shock of an intimate touch after so long made me jolt. So this was really happening? Not some elaborate daydream. I held her at a distance.

She pressed her back against the mirrored wall. "What is it?"

"They have CCTV in these things."

"So?"

"So, I don't fancy some security guy in an office getting over-excited about this."

"Really? I couldn't care less." She jerked me roughly back to her lips. "Let's give them a show."

"Maybe we should slow down."

Her hands dropped low to squeeze my backside. "Why?"

My body flooded with heat. A rough groan escaped my lips. Fair point. Why slow down? Her lips met mine again, and I succumbed to her kiss. The elevator pinged, and the doors slid open. Still kissing, we stumbled out together, rolling along the walls, down the corridor. I fumbled in my leather sporran for my key card. She squeezed between me and the gap in the door. Her smooth palms explored the planes of my back under my shirt.

Somehow, I got the door open, and we burst inside. At this rate, we'd lucky to make it to the bed. I lifted her into my arms. Her strong thighs wrapped around my middle, and I kicked the door closed behind me. Entangled, we stumbled into the room, shedding my shirt as we went. Her lips seared a path down my throat, and my body tingled with the kind of charge that usually only came with saving an important goal. I put her down on her feet by the side of the plush kingsize bed. Her cool hands slipped up my thigh and under my kilt to graze my hard length.

She chuckled softly. "Nothing under the kilt. You're a true Scotsman, then?"

"Aye, lass. This is a kilt, not a skirt."

I slid my hands under her tight dress, up smooth nylon, seeking the waistband of her underwear to rip it down. Maybe I could have taken my time, but her kisses were as lusty and urgent as mine.

My mouth felt bruised from her demanding kisses. Not that I was complaining. I'd take anything this woman had to give. "You're sure you want this?"

"I'm sure."

She guided my hand beneath her underwear. My fingers brushed wet heat between her thighs. I couldn't stop my groan at how ready she was for me.

She smoothed her hands over my arms. "You must work out."

I traced the beautiful line of her jaw with my lips. "I have to keep in shape for work."

"What do you do?"

There were always women desperate to hook up with someone in the public eye. No matter who it was. Things might get complicated if she knew I was a footballer. "Does it matter?"

"No." Her lips traced a sensuous path down my chest and she dropped to her knees. "I know what you do, anyway. You're a firefighter. That's why you have a problem with cats. You have to spend your whole day pulling them out of trees. I have all these fantasies about a firefighter."

She lifted my kilt, and her fingers wrapped around the base of my shaft. Her hot mouth closed around me, stealing the breath from my lungs. She worked my length. Pleasure tightened my every nerve. I couldn't last for long if she was going to do this.

I pulled her to her feet and lifted her, hauling her over my shoulder. She gave a startled laugh and whacked my back.

"What are you doing?"

"I'm rescuing you. I've spent my day getting sweaty, sliding down poles, and saving lives. Now, I'm here to set your body ablaze."

Her laugh rumbled through my back. "I didn't realize firemen were such dorks."

"It's true. We are all notoriously incredibly brave and heroic dorks."

She moaned softly as I laid her down on the bed. For a moment, the sight of her strong, shapely body in pale-blue lace underwear held me still. Her wild red hair tumbled against the golden pillow like a scattering of autumn leaves. She glowed with youth and vitality. So beautiful. It had been so long since a woman had taken my breath away. An odd prickling made my chest tight.

Melissa's gaze panned over me. For the first time, a shadow of uncertainty flickered in her confident demeanor. "Is everything okay? Do you want to stop?"

I drew a breath, trying to clear my head and ignore my pang of guilt. It had been five years. If not now, then when?

"No." I fingered the strap of her bra and reached behind to unclasp it. "I'm just admiring the view."

She tossed her bra to the side. Her full breasts puckered with smooth blush-pink nipples. Perfection. She watched me with a lustful expression as I freed myself from my kilt and stood bare. I lowered my body over hers. She gasped and pushed my shoulders to force me downward.

I couldn't help my chuckle at her eagerness. I felt the charge between us too, but I wouldn't be rushed. It had been years since I'd had a woman writhing beneath me. I'd take it slow. Tease her. I dipped my head to her breasts, sucking each swollen bud in turn, before pushing them together to take both tight pebbles into my mouth at once. She moaned as I kissed the constellations of freckles that dotted her throat.

"You have perfect breasts," I murmured.

My hands roved over the curve of her hips, dancing up her inner thighs. She arched up to meet me. I planted hot, open-mouthed kisses down her sternum and licked around her belly button. She watched me, sighing with pleasure, and wriggling beneath me. A current of lust surged through me. She was getting impatient. Me too.

I kissed and stroked through her underwear, crumpling lace under my lips, purposefully avoiding where she needed me to touch her most. I was desperate to taste her, but not yet. We'd been so hot and heavy in the elevator, but if I had one night with a flame-haired goddess like this, then I'd savor her. Otherwise, this would be over in two thrusts.

Purple bruises smattered her legs. I traced a finger over the marks. "What are all these bruises?"

"Work."

I traversed the soft lines of her waist and hips with my mouth. "Things get rowdy in the office?"

"The office?"

"You said you worked in finance."

Her eyes slipped away. "Right. Finance."

Something about her tone gave me pause. "Do you really work in finance?"

"Does it matter?"

No. Not now. She could tell me she supported Celtic over Rangers, and I'd be hard pressed to stop now. She gasped as I rolled her over and kissed the back of her legs. Her spine arched when I trailed my lips over her perfect, peachy backside through pale-blue lace. I smoothed my hand over her ass. Delicious. It was all I could do not to bite it. My fingers itched with some strange urge, and I couldn't help but lift my palm and give her a gentle, playful smack. She chuckled, but her laughter faded to a moan as I slowly slid her lacy G-string down her legs and went back to kissing where the soft creamy skin of her thighs met her backside.

Lying on her front, she squirmed upward, shifting fluidly like a cat and lifting her hips for me. I nudged her legs apart with my knee and positioned myself behind her. She twisted to flash me a hooded look over her shoulder.

Spreading her, I buried my face between her legs, tasting her for the first time. My nose bumped against her delicate glistening folds. An agonized groan left her lips as I tongued and probed the wet heat between her thighs. Reaching behind her, she fisted her

28

fingers into my hair, directing me. I hadn't done this for so long. I'd always loved going downtown, even if I was out of practice. The little noises and juddering movements that a slow, firm lick could elicit made me unbearably hard.

It was easy because this woman wasn't shy about getting what she wanted. She bucked against me, riding my tongue and doing my job for me. Her moans and gasps only spurred me on. I gave her perfect backside another playful smack, and she laughed with pleasure. She responded so strongly to my touch. I'd wanted to take my time, but I needed to be inside her.

I came up for air and wiped my mouth against my wrist. "We need a condom."

She scrambled off the bed and grabbed her handbag off the floor. I could barely take a full breath at the prospect of how it would feel to slide home.

She freed the condom from its packet and raised a devilish eyebrow. "Allow me."

She smoothed the tight latex over my shaft. Heat seared from her touch. If I could last more than three thrusts this was going to be a miracle. A religious man would have said a prayer.

"Turn around. Get back on your knees."

Amusement danced in her eyes. Pleasure coursed through me at her eagerness to obey my command. I grabbed her hips, pulling her into position. We both groaned as I lined myself up and pushed into her tight, wet heat. She bucked and clenched around me. Heat flooded my body. I held perfectly still—the sensation so intense, I could easily unravel. She bucked again.

I sucked in breaths, sweat dripping down my temples. "Don't move."

She froze.

The strength and vitality in her bare body made me weak. The need to release was unbearable. I couldn't have guessed I'd be doing this tonight. How had I got this lucky? This woman was incredible. She tightened around me and rolled her hips again.

I gripped her in place. "I said keep still."

She flashed me a glance over her shoulder, watching me with a wicked glint in her eye. That look only made it worse. She bit her lower lip. Her eyes lingered on mine as she rocked her hips, deliberately grinding against me.

A groan escaped me, and I slid my hands down the length of her supple back. "I told you not to do that."

"Whoops."

I squeezed my eyes shut because the cocky smile on her lips was about to send me over the edge. She rolled her hips, riding me. I gripped her and thrust into her in slow, maddening strokes, taking back control. I'd played in a World Cup, for goodness' sake. That took concentration and stamina. I could show this woman a good time.

She lowered onto her elbows and bucked faster. Together, we found a tempo, and I let myself enjoy her rather than worrying about it being over too soon. Pleasure bloomed over my skin like crackling electricity. My body trembled with my efforts to hold myself back.

With a firm push at the base of her spine, I pressed her down flat on the bed. We collapsed together. The length of my body covering hers—her back warm and smooth under my chest—as I worked, driving into her in a steady rhythm. She squirmed beneath me, panting and moaning. I put every scrap of will into holding off. A desperate need for release made my hips snap harder but I wouldn't give in until I'd satisfied her. Ladies first, always.

A cry left her lips. She shuddered underneath me. Her body melted against mine and her gasps were so sexy they sent me over the edge with her. Pure explosive pleasure tore through me. I collapsed, hot and exhausted. Our bodies fused together with sweat.

Footsteps sounded in the corridor outside. The guests at this fancy hotel had probably heard our indecent cries down in the bar. I said a silent prayer that no one would make a complaint that could get back to Gabe Rivers. A deep sense of peace and awe filled my chest. I hadn't had sex in so long. I'd forgotten what I'd been missing.

Melissa wriggled and rolled out from underneath me. Yawning, she stretched her arms high above her head. "Well, that was a first."

Alarm went through me. "That was your first time?"

She burst out laughing. "No. That ship sailed a while ago. Usually, I only come if I'm on top. That was the first time it's been different."

I couldn't stop the smile that crept onto my face. "You enjoyed that?"

She rolled her eyes, but her face brightened with amusement. "Men and their egos. Yes. It was amazing. The best I've had for a while. You blew my mind. The earth moved. You've set the standard for firefighters everywhere."

She was teasing, but a warm glow of pride lit me. Despite being out of practice, at least I hadn't lost my touch.

Her gaze dropped to my groin, and she nodded her approval. "You have that curve. It hits the spot. You've got a special peen. Good for you." She raised a playful eyebrow and kissed the tip of my nose. "You're one of God's favorites. Use your gifts wisely."

I couldn't help my laugh. Who was this woman? I'd never met anybody so direct. She jumped out of bed and gathered her clothes from the floor, before she disappeared into the adjoining bathroom. Water hammered in the shower and filled my ears. What now? Even before I'd married Evelyn, I'd always been in long-term relationships. I'd never done casual. Was this going to be weird?

Melissa emerged from the shower, fully dressed. She pulled her long red hair into a damp ponytail.

"Well," she smiled, breezily. "That was nice. Thanks."

Was that it? "You could stay longer? I could order room service. We could have a drink?"

"No. Thanks." She fiddled with the clasp of her handbag and smoothed her smart dress.

She looked so fresh-faced and beautiful. Words I hadn't meant to say spilled out. "Could I take you out for dinner sometime?"

What was I doing? I couldn't date. It wasn't fair on Brodie. I'd moved down to England from Scotland to give him roots and get him settled. The last thing he needed was his dad suddenly getting a girlfriend.

A line appeared between her neat brows. "What? Like a date?"

I should have backtracked, but more treacherous words fell from my lips. "If you like . . ."

She hesitated for a moment. My misgivings clamored in the silence. England was supposed to be a new start. Brodie needed stability. I didn't date. The first time I'd had sex in five years and I was ready to abandon all my principles and fall at her feet. Sure, it had been mind-blowing sex, but I had to get a grip. This woman was a stranger. A wildly beautiful and captivating stranger, who had made me feel alive again for the first time in longer than I cared to remember.

She regarded me with a puzzled look, as though I'd asked her to solve a complicated math equation, and not join me for a coffee.

Her frown deepened. "You're asking me out on a date?"

Was it the accent? Maybe she couldn't understand what I was saying. "Yes. I'm asking you out on a date. I'd love to take you out for dinner, or we could just get drinks if you prefer . . ."

Damn it. I wasn't even supposed to ask once. Now I'd asked twice.

An overbright smile lit her face and she clambered over the rumpled mess of sheets toward me. "Fun and done, remember?" Her lips were cool on my forehead as she landed a neat peck. "That was great, though. Good work." She gave a mock-serious salute. "Peace out."

Peace out? I opened my mouth to question her, but she sauntered nonchalantly to the door. She swung the door open and vanished without looking back. I collapsed back down on the bed, not sure whether to feel relief or disappointment that she hadn't taken me up on the offer of a date.

So much for a quiet pint and a bag of peanuts. What the hell had just happened?

Chapter 6

Lana

I knocked on the door to Dad's house. Moonlight bathed the tiny patch of lawn. A car alarm wailed somewhere. Once, we'd lived in a castle near one of Scotland's most remote and beautiful lochs. Yellow roses had climbed the walls and the water was so cold it stole your breath. It couldn't be further from the small run-down house I stood in front of now. I knocked again. The door swung open. Mel's steely eyes were red-ringed. I hadn't seen her cry since Mum's funeral.

"Are you okay? Have you been crying?"

Sniffing, she narrowed her eyes and swiped her nose with the back of her hand. "Is that my dress?"

Busted. I wrapped my trench coat tighter. "What? No. Can I come in?"

"It's late. Dad's asleep." Her gaze dropped to my shoes and her frown deepened. "Are those my Louboutins?"

Damn it. She was pissed, but it's not like I could have done the normal sisterly thing and asked to borrow her stuff. She'd have bitten my head off. "Are you going to just stand there or are you going to let me in?"

She folded her arms. "You can go home. I'm staying with Dad."

"I want to see how he is."

"He's fine. He went to AA without a fuss. I'm moving in to monitor him."

Of course Mel would want to be in control of everything. Then she got to moan that I wasn't doing enough. I couldn't win either way. At least I ought to offer to help.

"Fine. I'll move in, too."

She raised a haughty eyebrow. "What's the point of us both being here? I've got it under control."

"Right, but can I at least stay tonight?"

She stared at me, before hitching a shoulder. "Fine, but I want my shoes back, and my dress."

Mel's style might have been French minimalist but her temper was French Revolution: bring out the guillotines, take no prisoners. I followed her down the hallway, stepping over boxes full of Dad's junk. Football trophies and memorabilia spilled out of a crate. Some of them were mine from when I was a kid but most of them belonged to Dad. I picked up a heavy bronze football and spun it in my hands. The metal that had once gleamed was dull and coated in dust. All Dad had left of his glorious football career was a box of old trophies. It was a miracle he hadn't tried to sell them, like everything else.

In the kitchen, a hideous odor of rot and rubbish made me gag. Takeaway boxes and empty beer bottles littered the small table. Rubbish was piled on every surface and the sink overflowed with filthy plates. How had he got into this state and neither of us had noticed? I'd been so busy at the club. This had gotten out of hand. I should have been better.

Mel dusted her hands together and surveyed the mess. "I've finished cleaning the bathroom and the living room. The kitchen is next."

"Five years sober. Why now?"

Mel stiffened. "It was the wedding anniversary. I forgot to call him, I assume you did, too?"

Heavy silence wrapped around us. A grim, restless energy seized me. An hour ago I'd been having the best sex of my life, and now I had to deal with this look on Mel's face and a kitchen that looked like it had been swept up in a hurricane twenty miles away and deposited here.

Mel scanned the half-empty fridge before taking out a pizza and throwing it in the bin. She regarded me with as much disgust as she had the rotting pizza. "Where were you tonight?"

I filled the sink with hot water and set to work on washing the dishes. "I had an interview with a journalist."

And a roll in the sheets with a gigantic sexy Scotsman.

"Very fancy." Her mocking voice grated me.

"Not really. She's blackmailing me."

"What?"

Silence swirled around us. My heart pounded so hard, I felt it in my throat. Mel wouldn't understand.

"Blackmailing you, how?"

I kept my back to her as I chipped at a porridge-encrusted pan. "This stuff is like cement when it dries."

"You can't tell me you're being blackmailed and not give me the details."

I sighed and plunged the pan back in to soak. "She wants me to tell her secrets about the men's team. If I don't, then she's going to run a story about Dad falling off the wagon. She's got some photos of him pissing outside and ranting."

A pause. My mouth went dry. I didn't dare turn around and look at her face.

"Are you serious, Lana?"

Her words landed in my gut like kicks. No doubt she thought this was my fault. I wasn't going to stand around and get lectured about my failings. For once, this actually wasn't my fault. "I'm going to the all-night grocery. We need dishwashing liquid."

I tried to glide past her, but she caught me by the elbow. "What are you going to do?"

"I don't know. Maybe I should call the police. I mean, it's illegal, isn't it? You can't go around blackmailing people. What do you think I should do? Maybe you could speak to someone at the club?"

Mel paled and pressed her lips flat. "You want *me* to speak to someone at the club?"

"You're corporate. It will be better coming from you."

The words sounded pitiful even to me. It wasn't fair to put this on Mel, but she'd always been better at problem-solving.

Mel raked a hand over her face. "I haven't got time for this. I'm so busy with work. I'm doing all this overtime, and now you expect me to sort this out for you? I'm tired of it. I have to look after Dad. I shouldn't have to baby you, too."

A guilty feeling pressed my shoulders down. Mel was right. I didn't need her to fix it. This wasn't Mel's responsibility. This had been dumped on me, so I needed to sort it out. Mel would expect me to screw it up. She'd always been the sensible one. I'd step up. I'd prove I could sort this out.

"I've got it under control."

Mel frowned. "Are you sure?"

"I'm sure."

"Fine, but I suggest you do what she wants. Tell her anything. Do whatever it takes to keep Dad out of the papers. Nobody is going to win in a fight against the tabloid press. They are too powerful. This is the worst possible timing. Your priority needs to be getting Dad back on track."

Sell out my friends and let Karen Delaney win? No way. There had to be another option. "I'm not a rat."

"You're looking at it wrong. Feed her a few things. What does it matter?"

"And what if the team finds out I'm leaking stories?"

"Nobody needs to know."

There had to be a solution that didn't hurt my team. I took a breath and headed for the door. "I'll think of something."

"Are you sure you've got this, Lana?"

How many times? "Yes. I'm sure."

"Get it dealt with quickly. Your family needs you."

"The team is my family, too."

A shadow darkened her face. "I'm talking about your *real* family."

The team was my family. They'd all been nicer to me than anyone around here ever had. The rotting smell in the kitchen suddenly overwhelmed me. It was like we'd stepped back in time. Dad was broken again. I'd got in a mess. Mel could swoop in to save the day. She probably got a kick out of it. Watching us screw up reminded her of her superiority. How she'd coped with the fallout from Mum's death, and we hadn't.

I tried to remember the deep breaths that Reece had shown me. Getting angry wouldn't help either of us. Actually, screw that. Putting Mel back in her box would help me a lot. "Look at you. You love all this, don't you? Super Mel never messes up. She's always responsible, always on time, always—"

"Oh, stop. Some of us have to live in the real world. It's not all running around kicking a ball and partying with celebrities."

"I live in the real world."

She pinched the bridge of her nose. "Please. I don't want to argue after the day I've had. Are you going to deal with this or not?"

"I told you. I'm going to deal with it." My voice came out an octave higher than usual.

She turned away, but not before I caught her bottom lip trembling. Guilt and weariness washed over me. She'd been with Dad here all this time. That was all I ever felt in this house. Guilt that I was failing Dad. Guilt that I was as offensive to Mel as a pizza ten days past its sell-by date. At least I'd had a pleasant distraction this evening. I'd needed it. Needed the release. My mind drifted back to the Viking of a man I'd left naked in a four-poster bed at the Beaufort. After that earth-shattering orgasm, I'd almost considered his offer of a date. Weird that he'd even asked. I'd never had a hookup who wasn't content to pretend it had never happened.

I moved past Mel to the door. "I'm going to get more dishwashing liquid."

"Don't bother. Go home. I'll sort out the mess here." Mel's uncompromising gaze met mine. "You only have one mess to sort out, and for Dad's sake, you better do it fast."

Chapter 7

LANA

The next morning, I squeezed in next to Skylar on the hard wooden bench in the locker room. Memories of my gigantic sexy stranger filled my mind. He'd probably be on his way back to Scotland. Oh well. Fun and done. It had been an itch I'd needed to scratch.

I tried to tune back in to Claire's team talk.

Skylar leaned in next to me. Amusement laced her whisper. "Is that a hickey on your neck?"

My fingers fluttered to my throat. I'd tried to cover the purple marks with makeup this morning, but clearly I hadn't done a good job.

Skylar nudged me in the ribs. "Had a good evening, did you?"

"Wouldn't you like to know?"

Claire clapped her hands together. "Good work this morning. From those of you who bothered to turn up on time . . ." She raised an unimpressed eyebrow in my direction.

After getting back from Dad's so late last night, I'd accidentally slept through my alarm this morning.

I held my hands up. "Sorry. Traffic was terrible."

Claire smoothed a hand over her white-blonde bob. Her pale-blue eyes gleamed more glacial than ever. "Get showers. Do what you need to do. I'll see you back here this afternoon."

I rose, but Claire signaled me and pointed to her office. "We need to talk."

Great. Nothing good ever came after that sentence. Claire had been gunning for me for ages. I'd been in her bad books ever since starting a stupid bet a while ago. I regretted it. Sometimes I just did the stupidest things. It had meant to be fun to see who could shag the hot new team psychologist first. Nobody could have predicted that Skylar would fall head over heels in love with him. I hadn't meant to hurt his feelings, either. I'd apologized profusely, and I'd done my time cleaning the stadium toilets after match days as punishment. Everybody had got over it, but Claire had never been the forgiving type.

Claire closed her office door behind us and gestured to a chair. She sat opposite me, behind her desk, and steepled her fingers across her lips. Shit. Claire was not happy.

"We're in the Women's Super League. I shouldn't need to tell you that at the end of this season, one team will go down." Her voice was calm, but her eyes flashed dangerously. "Nobody gets to coast this season. Nobody is safe."

So she was going for the melodrama. I was ten minutes late. Not a big deal. "I'm sorry. It won't happen again."

Claire pressed her lips. "Nobody gets to turn up late. We're a team. We play together and we train together. Training doesn't work unless everybody is here. You miss training, you mess it up for everyone."

I peered out of the window, above Claire's head, to the training ground outside. Of course it impacted the team, and for that I was sorry. The team were my family. I'd only been thinking about Dad. Shame ground in my gut. "I apologize. It won't happen again."

"You're benched for the next game, and you need to think about your conduct. We're restructuring the team and that means making tough decisions. You need to do better if you want to keep your spot."

My blood turned to ice. Benched? I couldn't afford to miss a single game. You never knew which game would have scouts on the lookout for the next picks to play for England. If I had a chance of playing for my country, then I needed to be on the pitch for every game to get noticed. This was an overreaction.

"Are you kidding me? You made me captain when Skylar left and now you're benching me?"

"This kind of thing can't go unpunished. I don't want everyone thinking they can turn up late."

So, Claire was taking the opportunity to make an example of me instead of being lenient. Every single match counted if I was ever going to get spotted. Claire would jeopardize my chance to play for England over something so trivial? A sudden anger lashed through me, and there wasn't a psychologist in the land who could have coached me to keep my voice calm.

"I got us here too, you know. Do you think we'd be in this league if it wasn't for me?"

"Nobody is debating your talent. It's your behavior off the pitch that's the problem."

"What behavior?"

She couldn't still be mad about the thing with Reece? How many times did I have to apologize? He'd let it drop, and so had Skylar. Claire's eyes dropped to my neck, and I resisted every urge to cover the hickey with my hand. So what? I was allowed to have fun. It didn't hurt anyone, and it didn't mean I wasn't serious about the team. If Claire thought that, then screw her. She could judge all she wanted. I had no regrets about last night.

Claire folded her arms. "We're in the Women's Super League. This is world-class football. The younger players look up to players like you for guidance. You have so much potential, Lana, but sometimes I wonder if you take any of this seriously."

Adrenaline coursed through my body, but I fought to take deep breaths the way Reece had taught me. I took this team seriously. Football was my life. It was the only thing I'd ever been good at. The only thing I'd ever wanted to do. If Claire chose to ignore that, then what the hell could I do to convince her? Why should I *have* to convince her?

I folded my arms across my chest and dashed any hope of talking through the Karen Delaney situation with Claire. She was no better than Mel. She'd just think I was screwing everything up, too.

Still, I couldn't help the annoyance that made my heart pound. "This is unfair."

"Who said life was fair? Prove that you deserve your place on the team, and you have nothing to worry about." She waved a dismissive hand. "Now, get out there on the pitch. You're doing ten laps."

"Ten?" I couldn't keep the outrage from my voice.

I'd been training all morning, and she wanted me to do a five-kilometer run? Screw that.

Claire tilted her head. Her icy blue eyes bored into mine. "You're right. I'm being too lenient. Make it fifteen."

I kicked a clod of grass as I stormed out of the building and onto the training pitches. This was bullshit. Sure, I liked to party, and I was late sometimes, but I'd put everything into this team. I'd scored so many of the goals that got us into the Women's Super League. Now Claire expected me to prove I was worth keeping around? To think I'd considered going to Claire for help with Karen Delaney. It would just give her another excuse to kick me aside.

"Lana?"

Mel's voice held me in my tracks. I swiveled to see my sister on the sideline. She looked immaculate in a fitted navy suit with gold buttons and the Louboutins I'd reluctantly handed back.

"What are you doing here?"

"The men's team have a new signing. I'm here for a contract meeting."

"Right."

An awkward silence fell. When I'd put in a word about a job for my sister with Gabe, I hadn't considered that I'd have to see her more. Mel had bounced around between jobs after finishing her law studies at the local college. She'd never seemed happy with any place she'd worked. I'd only helped her to get a job here because I'd thought the staff perks might put a smile on her face. I was wrong. It would take more than free gym membership and casual Fridays to make Mel smile. Unfortunately, I had no idea what it *would* take.

At least I didn't see her much. The sound of the mower on the pitch filled my ears. Mel opened her mouth and closed it again. I didn't even attempt to make conversation. I never knew what to say to Mel if it wasn't about Dad, and we both knew better than to talk about him at work.

Mel cleared her throat and glanced at her fancy watch. "I should go. I don't want to be late."

Relief flooded me. Yes. Please go. Put us both out of our misery.

"Fine. I've got laps to do."

She flashed a tight smile. "Right."

"Right."

She peered over my shoulder. "Ah. Here we are. This is my next meeting. He looks lost. I'd better help him."

Mel waved to a figure in the distance. "Over here."

I locked eyes on the man-mountain in a smart suit. My breath froze in my lungs.

What the actual fuck?

The man I'd spent the night getting naked and sweaty with, and never wanted to see again, was heading toward us.

Melissa reached out to shake his hand. "Alexander McAllister? I'm Melissa. I'm a lawyer at the club. We're in this meeting together. I'll take you."

Alexander's gaze flashed to mine, and I watched the play of emotions on his rugged, handsome face—shock, confusion, panic, and finally horror—before he smoothed his expression. "Melissa?"

"Lana."

A line appeared between his brows. "Pardon?"

Heat flooded my face. "My name is Lana."

I had to hand it to him. If he was freaking out as much as I was, it didn't register in his polite appraisal. No one could guess that less than twenty-four hours previously this man had been buried so far between my thighs I'd wondered if he was ever going to come up for air.

Mel hitched her designer bag higher on her shoulder. "I'm Melissa. This is my sister, Lana. Lana plays for the women's team."

He hid his confusion, but his brain must have been doing cartwheels. It didn't help matters that Mel and I shared a lot of characteristics—the same light red hair, pale freckled skin, and green eyes.

Mel's glossy ponytail bounced as she inclined her head in my direction. "Alexander is the new Calverdale goalkeeper."

A bloody goalkeeper! No wonder he was a giant and his hands were so huge. If he was signing for the top team in the Premier League, he was a good one. Why hadn't I heard of him?

Alexander frowned and transferred his solid gaze back to me. "You're not Melissa? Your name is Lana?"

Mel checked her watch again and gave a low impatient hum. "We need to get going."

My mouth was dry, but I forced out the words. "That's right. My name is Lana."

Melissa flashed a thin-lipped smile. Patience had never been her strong suit and nor had concealing her irritation. "Shall we move this along? This meeting is about to start."

Was he going to say anything about yesterday? Melissa would rage if she knew I'd pretended to be her. My heart pounded.

Alex held out his huge hand, his manner professional and polite. He didn't have the slightest hint of the kind and gentle smile that had graced his full lips last night. "Nice to meet you, *Lana*."

I shook his hand, his palm cool against my clammy one. A tingling warmth crept up my neck. Less than twenty-four hours ago he'd been licking a ring around my belly button. I fought with everything I had to look calm. What must he have thought of me? I'd fed him a pack of lies last night and pretended to be the woman standing next to me. Why wasn't he calling me out? Then again, he'd played along with the firefighter thing. Neither of us was innocent.

Somehow, I managed to find my voice to speak. "Where have you transferred from?"

"I played in Scotland. I've transferred from Rangers."

Well, that made sense. That was why I didn't know him. I didn't really follow Scottish football. Hadn't my dad spoken about an Alex McAllister once? Was this the Alex McAllister that had played with my dad when he was up in Scotland? No. This couldn't get more awkward. I better not have spent an evening fucking one of my dad's old teammates. Even I wasn't that unlucky.

"Did you play for Rangers when Logan Sinclair was captain?"

"Yes." He frowned. "Do you know Logan?"

The drone of the mowers on the pitch grew loud. I was wrong. Turns out things could get way more awkward.

"Logan Sinclair is our father." Melissa pivoted and beckoned for Alexander to follow. "And now I must insist we go."

Alexander swallowed. From the look on his face, he found the idea of screwing his ex-captain's daughter as unpalatable as I found screwing a friend of my dad's. This was awful. I wanted to run back into the training suite and never come out again.

Alexander cleared his throat. "How is Logan? It's been a while . . ."

Sad. Drunk. Broken.

Melissa pasted on a fake smile. "He's . . . great." She clapped her hands together and put a hand on Alexander's broad back to escort him. "Time is of the essence. There are loose ends to tie up with the contract."

"Of course." Alexander inclined his head. "See you around, *Lana.*"

I returned his polite smile as best I could.

Not if I see you first.

Chapter 8

ALEXANDER

Heat blasted from the radiators in the brightly lit conference room. Sweat dripped down my neck. The low hum of the lawyers quibbling over tedious contract details washed over me. I let my gaze wander over the red-haired Calverdale lawyer sitting opposite me at the long table.

Melissa looked similar to the sister I'd spent the night with—the same delicate, pretty features and pale, creamy skin—but this woman didn't have the same mischievous sparkle in her eyes and lips on the verge of a laugh. This Melissa was smart and prim in a fitted suit, and her demeanor was serious to the point of severe. She looked more like a headmistress at an exclusive boarding school who had a sideline in dominating City bankers with bullwhips and chains. This wasn't the Melissa I'd spent last night with. What the hell was going on?

Gabe flashed me an indulgent smile and whispered under his breath, "Sorry about this. You know what lawyers are like when they get lawyering. The boring parts will be over soon and we'll get you signing on the dotted line."

"No problem."

He flashed me another sidelong glance. "Everything okay for you at the Beaufort?"

"Perfect."

"Good. Let me know if you need anything, won't you?" He raked a hand through his hair and raised an eyebrow. "And avoid the mushroom soup."

Last night, Lana had told me she knew Gabe Rivers. Why hadn't I probed her on it? What the hell had I been thinking, having a one-night stand? I'd been so blinded by a beautiful young woman whispering in my ear that I'd done something reckless. Now I'd have to see her every day. Logan Sinclair's daughter, for goodness' sake! My old captain. My suit jacket felt suddenly tight around my shoulders. How could I work alongside her?

Gabe leaned in. "Looks like we're all ready for you to sign. Do you need more time to think or are we doing this?"

Was this crazy? I was uprooting my life with Brodie, taking him away from all his friends, to come to England. Most players my age had hung up their football boots. Retirement didn't mean I couldn't still forge a career in the industry. There were options like coaching or the media. Maybe a different path would be better. God knows my body needed a break. Bumping into my one-night stand couldn't be a good omen. What were the chances of such rotten luck? Maybe this was all a huge mistake.

Sweat clung to my temples. "Could we open a window?"

"Of course." Gabe got up smoothly and glided across the room.

Maybe this wasn't the worst thing in the world. I could clear the air with Lana. Maybe I could ask her out for a drink and get to know her properly? Heat stroked my neck. I pulled at the collar of my shirt. No. That was a ridiculous idea. It would unsettle Brodie. Never mind the fact that she'd lied to my face and pretended to be someone else.

All the reasons I hadn't dated in five years still held true. Just because I'd had one night of mind-blowing sex didn't mean I could get involved with a woman. The fact that she was Logan Sinclair's daughter was too weird to contemplate. He'd taken me under his wing when we'd played for Rangers. Did he live around here? Did Melissa see him much?

Not Melissa, but Lana.

I didn't know either of these women. Why had Lana given me her sister's name? It hadn't felt so natural talking to a woman in such a long time. Was any part of that conversation true? Had she been taking me for a fool the whole time? I had to know.

I cleared my throat. "Can I ask a question?"

The lawyers stopped quibbling and fell silent. Melissa flashed a tight smile. "Of course. Anything you like."

"What's your favorite color?"

She stared back. "I'm sorry?"

"I'm curious. You've asked me a lot of questions. It's only fair that I ask you a few, isn't it?"

A tense silence enveloped the room. I was being weird, and Melissa didn't want to play ball. She was clearly a very different person from her down-to-earth, easy-going sister.

Melissa flashed Gabe a hesitant glance and smoothed her shiny ponytail. Her unimpressed green eyes met mine. "My favorite color is blue."

"Right, and your favorite food?"

She pressed her lips. "I fail to see how that's relevant."

"Humor me."

Her hand fluttered to smooth the ruffled collar of her blouse. "Pizza, but proper street pizza that you'd have in Italy. Not the cheap frozen stuff."

The realization settled heavy. These were the same answers Lana had fed me. "Are you a dog or a cat person?"

A tiny line appeared between her perfectly arched brows. "I don't like dogs. Very unhygienic."

"Right."

Another silence wrapped around us.

Next to me, Gabe chuckled darkly. "Do we all get to answer these questions, or just the lawyers?"

"No. That's enough."

So, it wasn't just a fake name; Lana had been pretending to be her sister. I'd felt so close to her in the bar and she'd played me for a fool. It shouldn't have mattered. Fun and done. We weren't supposed to see each other again.

Melissa pushed a thick wad of paperwork across the table toward me. My fingers were clammy as I flicked through the pages. I couldn't focus on a single word. Change was unsettling, even when it was for a good reason.

Gabe slid me a sidelong glance. "You can take it home and think it through if you like?"

Rob flashed me an easy smile from across the table. He'd be an excellent manager. This was still a great move for me. It wasn't my time to stop. Not yet. I still had at least one good season left in me. I couldn't let a little awkwardness put me off.

"No. It's fine. I'm ready to sign."

Rob and Gabe shared a grin. Gabe clamped a hand on my shoulder. "We're looking forward to welcoming you to the team."

"Thanks. I'm looking forward to joining."

At least, I was.

I signed the contract. The conference room erupted into a hub of activity and sound as people got up to congratulate me.

Melissa flashed me a tight smile as she held out her palm. "Did I pass your test?"

I shook her hand, her skin smooth against mine. "Test?"

"All those questions?"

51

"I apologize. That was something to . . . get to know who I'm going to be working with."

Melissa's green eyes met mine. "Good luck with joining the club." She studied me thoughtfully, reached into her jacket, and withdrew a business card. She put it flat on the table and scribbled something on the back. "Please call me if you have any more questions." She fiddled with her briefcase, a faint rose flush coloring her cheekbones. "My personal number is on the back."

She nodded and headed stiffly to the door. She didn't move the way her sister did. Lana moved like an athlete, sleek and confident. Filthy images from last night filled my mind. Lana lying on the bed, bare and trembling with anticipation. I could almost hear the little gasps she'd made when I'd been between her deliciously toned thighs.

Spicy cologne filled my nose as Gabe leaned in to whisper, "If you're going to flirt with my staff, how about doing it on your own time and not in the middle of a contract meeting?"

I almost dropped the pen I still gripped so tightly. "I wasn't flirting."

"I should hope not." Laughter danced in his bright eyes. "Let me give you some advice. If you're interested, keep the questions to a minimum. No woman wants to feel like she's a contestant on a quiz show. Just ask her out for coffee."

My jaw tensed. "That wasn't flirting."

Gabe patted me on the back to guide me out of the conference room. "Good, because I don't know what that was. But if that's your flirt game, we're going to need to do some work."

Chapter 9

LANA

I drained my lemonade and reached for my coat.

Skylar's eyebrows shot up. "What? No. You have to stay for one more."

"I need an early night. I'm behaving myself. Claire is on my balls."

Skylar grinned and smoothed a hand over her lilac hair. "Claire is always on everyone's balls."

Animated conversation and music filled my ears. The pub was livening up. It was a good vibe but I couldn't shake this tense, nervous energy. The one-night stand I never wanted to see again was signing for the club, and I still had Karen Delaney's threats hanging over me.

Melissa expected me to sort out this mess with Karen, but how? I couldn't sell out my teammates or damage the club's reputation. Stories in the press made us all look bad. The club meant the world to me. When Gabe had taken over, he'd stopped at nothing to give us what we needed to succeed. Together, this team had achieved everything we'd set our sights on. Claire had chosen me to captain while Skylar was away. Claire had been good to me, even if she wasn't always happy with my conduct. The whole club had been good to me. I owed them my loyalty. So, where did that leave me? Burying my head in the sand wouldn't cut it.

Skylar glanced at her watch. "I'm going to have another. I need to enjoy my last few weeks of single life."

"Getting cold feet?"

She laughed. "Never."

"I'm never getting married." I mock shuddered. "A man can tie me to the bedposts, but not the kitchen sink."

"Reece loves it when I go out and have fun." Skylar quirked a sardonic brow. "As long as it doesn't involve him."

"And you're happy with that? The two of you are quite . . ." I paused, looking for the most diplomatic way to phrase it. ". . . different."

Skylar had been a new person since she'd shacked up with the former team psychologist. I didn't get it. He was reserved and bookish, and Skylar was popular and outgoing. On the surface, they were incompatible. How he'd locked down a woman like Skylar was anybody's guess. He must have a huge dick. One of those "geek in the streets, freak in the sheets" types. It was the only viable explanation.

Skylar twiddled with the umbrella in her strawberry daiquiri. "I'm into gardening now. Reece has been teaching me."

I patted my mouth in an exaggerated yawn. "Sorry, I fell asleep. Were you saying something?"

She laughed. "No, I'm serious. It's fun. Gardening is great exercise."

"There are better ways to exercise with your fiancé."

She raised a suggestive eyebrow. "Don't worry. We're getting all kinds of exercise."

"Good. I don't want you getting old before your time."

Her phone buzzed on the bar and she turned it over, scanning the screen with a smile. Blue light lit her face as she texted a string of emojis. She was happy. It made my heart sing to see that smile on her face. Skylar had been my favorite person ever since I'd joined the club and she'd taken me under her wing, the way she did every newcomer. I'd never met a man I cared about even a fraction as much as I cared about my best friend.

"Is that Reece checking up on you? How is the doc, anyway? Reading to his parsnips?"

A smile curved Skylar's lips. "I'm texting Miri. She's helping with last-minute wedding prep."

Oh. I kept my disquiet from my expression. Skylar had asked Miri to be her maid of honor. It made sense. Miri was our striker and married to Gabe, our director. Gabe had brought her on to the team shortly after he took it over, and she'd fitted in like she'd always been here. Miri also happened to be Reece's sister, so she was about to become Skylar's new sister-in-law. It was the right call for Skylar to pick Miri, but I couldn't help but feel a bit salty about it. Skylar was my best friend. Maybe she would have asked me if I hadn't kissed her egomaniac ex. I wished I could turn back the clock. I'd been such an idiot to get sucked in by Sean's golden hair and puppy-dog eyes. The man was as toxic as he was hot. The bastard ought to have come with a health warning.

Skylar drained her drink and turned her attention back to the bustling bar. "What do you have to do to get served around here?"

"Has Claire mentioned anything to you about restructuring the team? She reckons I'm not taking it seriously enough." A bitter laugh escaped me. "As if this team isn't my entire world. I have to stop all of it: partying, late nights . . ."

Skylar narrowed her eyes. "Why didn't you say? I wouldn't have asked you out tonight if I'd known . . ."

Because I want it to be how it was before I stabbed you in the back.

Because I wanted to be your maid of honor and you asked Miri.

I turned my face away. "Someone has to stop you from getting too boring, don't they?"

Silence fell between us. Karen Delaney drifted to my mind. I had to tell Skylar, even though I knew what she'd say. Calverdale always came first with Skylar. She'd tell me to protect the team, but it wasn't that simple. Who would be in Dad's corner, if not me?

A TV on the wall above the bar blasted out the sports news. Sean Wallace's arrogant face appeared. There really was no escaping this man. He was all over the news lately. The men's team was taking street kids from Brazil and training them with the squad in some big charity initiative. Sean was fronting the campaign, which was a joke, considering he was the least charitable person I'd ever met. He'd gotten bent out of shape once when I bought coffees for the guys that slept rough near the stadium.

Skylar's gaze drifted to the big screen, and she rolled her eyes. "Gross. He's only doing it for attention. He couldn't care less about those kids." She chewed her lip and shot me a glance. "Have you seen much of Sean lately?"

I had the sudden urge to do something with my hands. I grabbed a coaster and picked at the edges. "No. I haven't, and I don't want to."

Skylar drew circles on the bar with her finger, her voice soft. "He was a prick to me. I was in denial for so long, but that relationship was toxic. He's a bully, Lana. He hurt me all the time—"

I snapped my head to look at her. "He hurt you? If that bastard laid a finger on you, I'm going to—"

"Not physically. It was mental. He was seeing other girls behind my back, and if I questioned him about it, he acted like I was crazy. He called me horrible names. I felt so bad about myself with him. It's only now that I know what it's like when a man treats you well." She fixed her gaze on the screen and Sean's smug face. "Sean has everyone fooled into thinking he's this amazing guy. If people knew the truth about him . . ."

My hand tightened around the coaster that I'd half shredded. "Why is he like this?"

Skylar chewed the skin around her thumbnail and lowered her voice. "If I tell you something, do you promise not to tell anyone?"

"Of course."

"He got nastier and nastier. Sometimes he would fly into these rages. He had this doctor he used to see, but he was private and weird about it. I didn't question it at the time, but sometimes I wonder if he's been taking something . . ."

"Drugs?"

"Steroids, maybe. I don't know. He's always been fit, but he's bulked up the past year."

I leaned in, catching a whiff of her watermelon perfume. "Have you told anyone?"

"No. It's not for me to snitch on him. We're not friends, but I don't want to ruin his life."

"You don't still have feelings for him, do you?"

"As if. I've moved so far on that I'm on a different planet." Skylar chuckled. "Thank God. If things hadn't gone so wrong with Sean, then maybe I wouldn't have met Reece. I'm grateful. I don't let Sean take any of my headspace these days. You shouldn't either." She traced her finger over the bar. "Did you sleep with him or was it just . . . ?"

"No. It was just flirting . . . a few kisses . . . nothing else."

"You didn't miss out, believe me." She glanced over her shoulder and lowered her voice. "It's different with Reece. He's very . . . attentive in the bedroom."

"Attentive, huh? No wonder you're marrying him."

Skylar covered her pink cheeks with her palms. "That's not the only reason I'm marrying him."

I raised a sardonic eyebrow. "No. Right. Of course. There's always gardening."

Skylar's eyes sparkled with amusement. It was so good to see her happy with Reece. My eyes drifted back to the screen, and Sean's smug face, and a wicked thought drifted into my consciousness.

Sean Wallace. The perfect scapegoat.

If I could give Karen dirt on Sean Wallace, then it would keep her off my back. Nothing too bad; just enough to protect Dad. I didn't even need to tell her about the drugs stuff. There was enough shit with his fooling around. I had loyalty to Calverdale, but to Sean Wallace? No. I didn't have a scrap of loyalty to that bastard. He'd treated me like rubbish, but, worse, he'd hurt Skylar.

I knew things hadn't been great with him and Skylar, but I hadn't realized how deeply he'd hurt her. Sean Wallace could be an unlikely answer to my prayers. The man was made of Teflon, anyway. Whatever the scandal, he was nonstick.

I pulled away from Skylar and gave her a smile. "I wouldn't worry about someone like Sean Wallace. One day, he'll get run over by the karma bus, and it won't be pretty."

"Maybe." Skylar slipped down from the stool and pulled on her coat. "Come on. You need an early night." She quirked a wry brow. "Word might get back to Claire that we've been enjoying ourselves, and you know how much she hates that."

Chapter 10

LANA

The next morning, I arrived at the training ground early and swung past Claire's office so she could see me. I would fit in a workout before practice and then this afternoon I'd call Karen Delaney and throw Sean Wallace under the bus. Unpalatable as it may be, this had to be done. It was Sean or Dad.

In the gym, sweat dripped down my neck, and my feet pounded the treadmill. The men's team filtered in through the side door by the weights area. I slowed my sprint to a jog. If the men were training, then I needed to get out of here. I grabbed my water bottle. My gaze fell on the imposing, dark-haired man stretching his long, sturdy legs on the mat. Alexander. Heat stroked the back of my neck. I'd known I'd have to see him again, but so soon?

His gaze locked with mine, but instead of doing the decent thing and ignoring me he strode straight toward the treadmills. What the fuck? Why the hell was he coming over? This was in direct violation of all the rules of a one-night stand. Hadn't it been awkward enough with Melissa? I had half a mind to run away, but screw that. It wasn't me trying to make it awkward. I was happy to ignore him and pretend it had never happened.

He planted himself in front of me. His enormous, solid presence eclipsed everything around him, forcing me into his orbit. A gray T-shirt clung to his muscular frame. I tried to keep my guilty gaze from drinking in his impressively tall, sculpted body.

He glanced around the gym, and his voice dropped low. "Can we talk?"

How about no? We'd agreed to fun and done. Of course I didn't want to talk to him. I'd let loose in that hotel room precisely because I didn't think I'd have to look this man in the eye again.

I kept my voice low, thankful that everyone was in the weights area. "We have nothing to talk about. Fun and done, remember?"

"That was before I knew we'd be in the same building. Can we at least clear the air so it's not weird?"

"It's only weird if you want to make it weird."

I stepped down from the treadmill and moved to the mats to stretch.

Alexander fell in step alongside me. "You told me a bunch of lies."

"I don't want to do this now."

"I just want to know why."

On the mat by the mirrored wall, I bent over to touch my toes and stretch out my back. "What does it matter? I can't turn back the clock."

Alexander's eyes tracked the movement as I straightened. "What else did you lie about? Was any of it true? Are you really thirty? Is your favorite color really blue?"

I rubbed an ache in my back. "I'm twenty-six, and no, blue isn't my favorite color."

"Twenty-six?" He paled and raked a large hand over his face. "I would never have laid a finger on you if I'd known how young you are."

"Why? How old are you?"

"Forty-two."

"That bothers you?"

"Yes. It bothers me." He stared back at me. "I'm sixteen years older than you."

So? The least disturbing thing about this situation was the age gap. I'd never been with anyone over thirty, but his dusting of gray at the temples and the lines around his mouth and eyes gave him a look of wisdom and strength. Men were allowed to grow older and still be sexy. Society only liked to make women feel bad about aging. Regardless of his age, he was still hot as holy hell and he fucked like a piston, so what did it matter?

"Why? Why pretend to be your sister?"

I'd just run off all my excess energy and he was getting me all riled up again. What could I say about this situation that didn't make me want to cringe to death? "I told you I don't want to have this conversation right now."

He folded his arms and sighed. "Then when?"

I grabbed my water bottle and towel and sauntered toward the women's dressing room. How about never?

"Where are you going? We both work here now. We're going to see each other all the time. I had half a mind not to even sign that contract. This isn't me. I don't hook up with women and then ignore them. I can't ignore you."

The desperate edge to his whisper held me frozen. Still, this wasn't my problem. He'd have to deal with it.

"I don't care if you ignore me. In fact, I implore that you do the decent thing and ignore me." I rested a hand on the door to the women's changing room. "Fun and done, remember?"

I went inside before I had to listen to his reply.

After a beat, his head appeared around the door. "Is there anyone in there besides you?" he hissed.

"No, but that doesn't mean you can come in."

He moved inside quickly, ducking his head. He hovered by the door, his eyes wide and imploring. "Are you really Logan Sinclair's daughter?"

"Yes."

He reached round to rub the back of his neck, and his arm bulged with muscle. "He was my captain."

"So? It's fine. There's no reason for us to have further interactions."

I pulled my sweaty T-shirt over my head and off.

Alexander's dark eyes widened in alarm. "What are you doing? Stay dressed. We haven't finished talking."

"I've finished. You're the one in the women's changing room uninvited. It's nothing you haven't seen already, anyway. You were into it the other night."

His heated gaze dropped down my body then he twisted to face the lockers. He pressed his palms over his eyes.

"We were two consenting adults having fun. We forget it happened and get on with our lives."

He turned to face me again. His guilty eyes slid down to my breasts nestled in my sports bra before they darted back to my eyes. "This is just my luck. The first woman I slept with in five years, and this happens."

Five years? There was no way this man hadn't had sex in five years. He was incredible in bed. The best I'd ever had in . . . forever. If he was telling the truth, it was an absolute waste of such natural talent. Scandalous, in fact.

"Why so long . . . ?"

The dim pulse from the gym drifted into the silence between us. A torrent of memories flooded my mind: *The weight of his solid chest on my back, pressing me into the mattress. His deep, lilting voice crackling over my body. The manly scent of his sweat.*

The chemistry had been off the charts. He'd been so command-ing and authoritative. He'd taken control when he wanted but I'd taken it back when I needed, like a perfectly choreographed dance. We'd understood each other sexually. It was a rare thing. I'd never had that with a man before. He must have felt it too, because he'd asked to see me again. I'd never met a man who wasn't happy to pretend a hookup had never happened, especially a footballer. What was up with this guy?

He stood there, tall and solid like a towering tree, and so ruggedly handsome it made my fingers itch to drag him into the shower for round two.

He sighed and leaned back against the wall. "I suppose we'll just have to be polite and carry on as normal?"

I took a step closer. He held perfectly still. It would be so easy to kiss him. Would he stop me? He wanted me, no matter his pro-testations about my age. Did he still think I had *perfect breasts*? He'd given my body so much attention: licking, sucking and showering kisses.

My heart pounded in the way it always did before I was about to do something reckless that I'd regret. It had been fun the other night. Maybe round two wasn't a bad idea. It would make the day a bit more interesting. This was the answer to his question about Melissa. My sister was sensible and considered. She never did stu-pid, impulsive things. Of course it would make sense that I'd pre-tend to be her. I reached for the zip that ran down the front of my sports bra and undid it slowly. My breasts sprang free.

"What are you doing?" His voice barely broke a whisper. "Put those away."

"If you're going to stare, you might as well have a proper look."

He kept his eyes fixed on mine. His voice was a low murmur. "Anyone could walk in here."

"Exciting, isn't it?"

My skin prickled with pleasure as I fondled my nipples, bringing them to hard peaks.

His huge hand flexed at his side, but he made no move to touch me. He swiveled away from me, fixing his gaze on the sinks. "Cover yourself. Do it now."

"Or what?"

Silence swirled, and in it a thread of something exciting and dangerous wove between us. Anybody could walk in. It was fun to push him and see how he'd react.

His voice held a rough edge. "Cover yourself."

"What if I don't like to do what I'm told?"

"Do it now. It's not a request."

"Or what?"

He took a breath. "Or I'm in danger of taking you into that shower and picking up where we left off." His gaze was so dark and serious, it sent a tremor through me. "And you don't want me to do that."

Heat pooled between my thighs. "Why not?"

"Because this entire building is going to know what's going on in here."

"Not if we're quiet."

He ran his tongue over his full lower lip. "I can promise you, we won't be quiet."

My body flooded with tingling warmth. Still, he was right. We were at work. Things were getting carried away.

I pasted a smirk on my lips. Slowly, I pulled up the zip on my bra. "Well, you'd better run along. Wouldn't want to make things . . . awkward."

A line appeared in his dark brow. He inclined his head and wrapped his huge hand around the door handle. "Tell me the truth. Why pretend to be your sister?"

An unwelcome heat crept into my cheeks. Not this again. Wasn't it obvious? He'd met Mel. He must have seen why I'd want to be her. My sister was smart, sophisticated, and in control. Everything that a man could want. Everything I didn't feel.

"Would you have taken me to your room if you'd known I was twenty-six?"

"No, but it wouldn't have mattered to me what you did for a living or what your favorite color is. What is your favorite color, by the way? Not your sister, but you . . ."

I wouldn't have answered except his gaze was gentle and under-standing. I suppose I owed him some honesty after so many lies. "Green. The bright kind, when the sun dapples leaves."

Like Mum's eyes.

"And your favorite food?"

"Pad thai. I got addicted to it when I went backpacking."

"You like to travel?"

"When I can."

"Are you a cat or a dog person?"

"I prefer dogs to humans. You always know where you stand with a dog. A dog doesn't judge. They love you unconditionally. No matter what."

He gave me a grudging nod. His low, lilting voice was smooth, but insistent. "Have you ever been loved like that?"

Sudden heat burned my throat. Where did he get off asking me questions like that? No way.

I stared him down. "Why haven't you had sex for five years?"

A look of tired sadness passed over his face. He opened his mouth and then closed it again. "I shouldn't be in here. I'm glad we . . . cleared the air."

He wanted honesty from me, but he wasn't willing to give it. A typical man, then. "Goodbye, Alexander. I'll see you around. Try not to make it weird."

◆ ◆ ◆

Showered and dressed, I packed my kit into my carryall. My conversation with Alexander had left a bad taste in my mouth. I shouldn't have had to see this man ever again. Now, I'd have to see him every day. Something strange had happened in that locker room. One minute we'd been talking, and the next I'd been goading him to touch me. I'd put myself out there, and all he'd wanted to do was bombard me with questions. Where did he get off, cornering me like that? Alexander thought the age gap was a big deal, but he was the one acting immature about it.

He was mad at me for lying to him. It was nothing compared to how mad Mel would be if I didn't sort out this mess with Karen Delaney. This was all a distraction from my real problem. I pulled Karen Delaney's card out of my bag and dropped it onto a wooden bench.

I didn't want to sell out anyone from the team or get the club into trouble. I disliked Sean Wallace, but he was still a Calverdale player. Then again, all the men at this club were the same. Even Alexander wasn't that different. Sure, he actually bothered to talk to me again after a hookup, but I didn't like anything he had to say. He'd had questions for me, but he couldn't be honest with me in return. He'd made me feel so guilty for lying to him, when he had his own secrets. He hadn't even told me he was a footballer.

Every man at this club that I'd hooked up with had pretended I didn't exist afterward, but the worst of them all was Sean Wallace. He'd given me a huge sob story about how broken-hearted he was, and how into me he was, and I'd bought every word of it. If I had to sell out this club, then better that it be him.

I found Karen Delaney's card and fired off a text: It's Lana. What about Sean Wallace? He's not as squeaky clean as his reputation.

66

The phone buzzed instantly with a reply from Karen: What have you got?

I hovered with my thumb over the keypad. It wasn't too late not to do this, but what choice did I have? Mel was right. Dad was too vulnerable right now. A story in the press would threaten his sobriety. It was either sell out the club or sell out my family. It was a terrible thing to do, but at least it was just Sean. That man had it coming. I had to be careful to keep things anonymous, and not to involve Skylar. It wouldn't take much digging to find other women willing to dish the dirt on Sean.

I sent back my reply. Sean Wallace is a cheating scumbag and a bully. He's also crap in bed. Keep mine and Skylar's name out of it and I'll give you some juice. Plus, all this charity work is bullshit. He just does it to make himself look good.

The phone pinged with a response. Meet me. We need to talk.

Chapter 11

ALEXANDER

My lungs burned, and white noise roared in my ears. I did everything I could to stand straight and not fall to my knees on the pitch. The training session had been brutal. Ten years ago, I would have aced it, five years ago even, but since I hit my forties every muscle and bone in my body wanted to make sure I knew how hard it was working.

A hand landed on my shoulder. Sean Wallace flashed a goading smirk. "Not bad for an old-timer."

Old-timer? The cheeky bastard. I'd played alongside Sean's father years ago. Adam Wallace had been insufferably arrogant, too. *Like father, like son.* Sean was one of the youngest captains in the Premier League. I'd seen jumped-up kids like this all the way through my career. The guys that believed their own hype. They were usually prodigies at a young age and every second of their lives they'd had their heads filled with how wonderful and talented they were. He had his smirking face in magazines, so he thought he was God's gift. I had plenty of comebacks, but I didn't want to speak and give him the satisfaction of seeing how breathless I was. Also, he was my captain. It didn't matter whether I liked him, I still had to respect him.

I stretched my arms above my head, and pain shot the length of my back. I couldn't help my wince.

Sean scanned me with a curious expression. "The physios are in this afternoon. Get yourself a massage, mate."

I smoothed a smile on my face. "Thanks, pal. I will."

He nodded and extended his leg in a hamstring stretch. "My dad said to pass on his regards."

"How is Adam?" *Still an insufferable arsehole, I take it?*

"He's doing great. Taking it easy and enjoying his retirement. No point running yourself into the ground, is there? At some point you have to call it a day and hang up your boots."

What was that supposed to mean? Was he goading me, or was I being oversensitive? If he was anything like his dad, then he was trying to wind me up. It wasn't easy joining a young squad. Rob had insisted my age wasn't a factor. They wanted me for my experience. These kids were all talented, but none had played at international level. Now that I'd met the lads, it made me wonder if Rob was looking for someone to rein them in. They were a young squad. Untested but cocky. Wild and unruly.

Lively shouts and laughter drifted on the breeze. Sean's gaze shifted over my shoulder to where the women were training. Lana ran drills with the others. Her red ponytail bobbed as she sprinted with effortless grace, keeping the ball at her feet. The sight of her half naked in the women's changing room forced itself into my mind. My fingers had burned to get a handful of those beautiful, firm, uptilted breasts again. My thoughts skittered back to the silkiness of her taut nipples on my tongue.

Sean followed my gaze. "I'd watch out with that one, mate."

"I'm sorry?"

A nasty smile pulled at his lips, and he whacked me on the chest. "Great rack, but I wouldn't get too attached if I were you. She's fucked most of this team. She's trying to collect us like football cards in an album."

My temper sharpened my voice. "You don't talk about women like that around me."

"Relax. I'm kidding." He held his hands up in mock surrender, but the smug smile didn't disappear from his lips.

My gaze flew back to Lana, and jealousy gnawed away at me. Did these two have history? Had this cocky wee bastard been pawing all over her in the past? Had she moaned for him the way she'd moaned for me?

Sean inclined his head to the goal. "Come on, then. Get in there. I can tell my old man I got one past Alexander McAllister."

I'd like to see you get one past me, you arrogant shite.

Sean trotted to stand opposite me at the ten-yard line. I patted my gloved hands together and prepared myself. He might have been a prick, but he was also a phenomenal talent. Sean blasted the ball at me. I dived. The ball hit my chest, knocking the breath from my lungs. Still, I'd kept it from going over the line.

I jogged to Sean and handed him the ball. "Nice try."

His eyes narrowed, and he snatched the ball from me. "It was a goal."

"No. I got there for it, pal."

"No. You didn't, *pal*." A sudden chill hung on the edge of his words.

He glared at me, his nostrils flared with fury. I knew better than to go up against a hothead like Sean Wallace. It wasn't as if we'd ever know the truth of it without watching a playback.

"Fine. It was a goal if you say so, pal. No problem."

"Are you taking the piss?"

A small group of players gathered closer. Sean chuckled, icily, but no one else made a sound. The shouting from the women's team on the pitch next door rushed to fill the tense hush.

I kept my face level. I didn't want a falling-out with my captain before we'd even played our first match. "This is just training. It doesn't matter."

"It fucking matters to me." Sean glowered at me like a toddler having a meltdown.

I'd dealt with plenty of toddler meltdowns, but I doubted I could placate Sean Wallace with the promise of an ice cream sundae. I didn't know what this man needed to stop being such a prick. A swift kick to the balls probably wouldn't go amiss.

Aiden, one of the young strikers, put a hand on Sean's shoulder. "Why don't you take a minute, mate?"

Sean shrugged his teammate off, picked up the ball, and booted it far into the distance. With one last withering look in my direction, he stormed off. The team stared off at him in stunned silence, before chatter broke out. What the hell was that?

Aiden sighed and picked some mud from his kit. "Don't take it personally. Didn't you see the news this morning? He's had some kiss-and-tell story come out. It doesn't make him sound good."

Josh, one of the midfielders, tugged at his football jersey. "That's putting it mildly. I doubt if he'll ever get laid again. A load of women have come forward to testify what a lousy shag he is."

That wasn't good. The team was only as strong as the captain. Sean Wallace needed to get himself together, or we'd all be a mess. Everyone knew you had to ignore the stuff in the news. Press attention was part of the territory. I kept my nose clean and out of the tabloids these days. I had a son to think about. Besides, I was so boring there was nothing to print about me. My partying days were behind me.

Aiden toed the ground with his football boots. "Don't listen to any of the crap Sean says. He's threatened by you."

"By me? Why?"

Aiden smiled. "Are you kidding? Because you're a legend. You were my favorite trading card when I was a kid."

I laughed. "Now you're making me feel old."

These guys hadn't even hit their prime yet. They had muscles that didn't protest the next day after a workout, and knees that didn't creak. The lucky bastards probably didn't get hangovers either.

"The point is, none of us have played in a World Cup. Sean knows that. He'll try to wind you up, but don't let him." Aiden nudged me in the ribs. "You definitely saved that goal. We all saw it."

Josh bounced a ball between his thighs. "It's Dan's birthday tonight. It's a good chance to meet the rest of the guys. It's going to be carnage . . ."

That was the last thing I needed. An evening with a bunch of twenty-year-olds getting drunk out of their skulls. I'd lost interest in all that years ago. "I promised my son I'd take him bowling tonight, and I don't drink in the season."

Aiden smiled. "Me neither, mate. I'm on the lemonades. You should still come for one at least?" His eyes drifted to the other pitch. "Most of the women's team are coming, too. It'll be fun."

My gaze found Lana again. I couldn't help but watch her, whether or not I wanted to. This woman was no good for me. When she'd stood in front of me half naked, it had taken every ounce of self-restraint not to touch her. She hadn't cared a bit that somebody could walk in on her topless in that locker room. She was divine, but off limits. Too young, and too reckless. I wasn't about to spend a night in her company. I'd leave the partying for the youngsters.

"I'm out, pal. Sorry. Daddy duties."

◆ ◆ ◆

I left before the end of the training session to see if I could catch Sean alone. The guy was an arsehole, but he was my captain. The team had to get along. If I'd learned one thing about being part of a team, it was that it was better to address a problem head on and try to find a way through it. I'd do what it took to smooth things over.

The locker room was empty. I rounded the corner to the showers. Sean sat on a bench with a towel around his middle. His arm was crossed over his body at an odd angle. It took me a moment to notice the small syringe in his hand. A fine needle pierced his skin as he injected himself.

His face twisted with anger. "What the fuck are you doing, creeping around?"

Glass glinted in the bright locker room lights as he swiped a couple of little bottles and shoved them into a green bag. He zipped the bag and crossed to his locker to stash it. "Vitamin injections. I'm trying to boost my energy levels. You should try it."

I held perfectly still. It could have been vitamins, or it could have been something else. Either way, I didn't want to make it my business. Shit. Why did I have to choose this moment to walk in here?

"Vitamins, huh?"

"I have a doctor who prescribes them. I can give you his name or . . ."

"It's fine. I wanted to clear the air. Do you want to talk about what just happened?"

With his broad back to me, Sean rummaged in his locker. "It's no big deal. We're fine." He tightened the towel around his middle and raked a trembling hand over his ashen face. A bead of sweat rolled down the side of his temple.

"Is everything okay, pal? Do you need to sit down?"

He swiped his hand across his forehead. He peered in the mirror attached to the inside of his locker, studying himself with an indefinable expression. "I don't want any beef, either. We're fine. I've just had a stressful morning. They've printed a load of bollocks about me in the news. It's messed with my head. We're good. I'm sorry about all that out there."

I nodded. I hadn't expected him to apologize. Maybe he wasn't that bad after all.

He gave himself one last preening glance before he slammed the locker shut. "Are you going to fuck off now and let me have a shower in peace?"

Fine by me. I held my hands up. "Of course. I'll leave you to it."

Chapter 12

LANA

The burnt toast and cigarette stench of Dad's house filled my nose. I'd spent all afternoon scrubbing the walls with disinfectant, but a vile odor still clung to the wallpaper. Dad sat at the kitchen table, his red dressing gown draped loosely around his bare shoulders and round belly. A cigarette dangled in his yellowed fingers. At least he was wearing boxers under that robe. I had to be thankful for small mercies.

I plucked the cigarette from Dad's fingers. "None of that."

His head shot up. "I can't drink, and I can't smoke now, either?"

"You need to get ready. Kickoff is in an hour."

I ran the cigarette under running water and threw it in the bin.

Mel breezed into the kitchen. She dusted her hands together and surveyed the freshly scrubbed surfaces. "I'm making dinner. Vegan casserole."

Dad's mouth dropped open. "Vegan? Now I know you're both trying to upset me."

Mel's lip twitched. It was the closest she'd come to a laugh in a long time. She had always enjoyed inflicting pain on people. Controlling Dad was about as much fun as she was going to get.

I cleared my throat. "Are you sure you don't want to come to the match with us, Mel?"

My sister raised a perfectly arched brow. "You want me to come and watch a football match with you?"

"Why not? You work at a football club. Aren't you curious to see the guys on the pitch?"

She wrinkled her slim nose. "A load of men running around chasing a ball in a stadium full of hooligans ranting and fighting? I can't think of anything worse."

I swallowed my irritation. Some of us like running around kicking a ball. Better than being the most uptight, boring human being alive.

She rolled up the sleeves of her smart tailored blazer and set to work wiping the counter I'd already cleaned. "Is Alex McAllister playing tonight?"

"I don't know. I should think so. He's signed now, hasn't he?"

A smile lit Dad's gaunt face. "You mean Alex Mac? The Alex Mac who played for Rangers? What's he doing down here?"

Mel planted a steaming mug of tea on the table in front of Dad. "He's signed for Calverdale."

Dad beamed. "Good for him. He's a great guy."

"I could invite him round. Maybe the two of you could catch up about the old days?" Mel fiddled with the buttons of her chic blouse. "What was he like back when you played together?"

My ears pricked at Mel's odd tone.

"A great goalie. Good team spirit. Always reliable."

Mel examined a chipped mug in her hands with studied disinterest. "He's . . . nice. He was asking me a lot of questions . . ." A pink flush stained Mel's cheeks, and she twisted the thin gold chain around her neck. "Anyway, I'll see if he wants to come over for a catch-up."

Was Mel blushing? She was usually so poised and controlled. I hadn't seen her cry or show any emotion since Mum's funeral and even then she'd hidden away when I'd tried to hug her. What questions? Alex wasn't interested in her, was he?

I pulled Dad up out of the chair by his elbow. "For God's sake, Dad. Go and get dressed. We're going to miss kickoff."

He shot me a wry smile and shrugged me off.

Mel watched him leave the room, then flashed me a look of barely concealed irritation. She kept her voice low. "Did you sort out the problem with the journalist?"

I waited until Dad's footsteps thudded on the landing above us before I replied. "I gave her a story about Sean Wallace."

The story had appeased Karen for now. She said she'd tear up the stuff about Dad, but how could I trust her?

Silence swirled around us. I waited to see if Mel would congratulate me or offer any encouragement, but she stared back at me blankly.

"I don't know what you're thinking of, taking Dad to a football match. There will be booze everywhere. All that temptation . . ."

"It'll be fine. We're in the VIP stand. It's just friends and family of the team. He needs something to lift his spirits."

She pressed her lips flat, unconvinced.

I couldn't help but ask the question that gnawed my gut. "Why were you so bothered about Alex McAllister?"

A wrinkle appeared between her eyebrows. "*Bothered?*"

"You want to invite him round here?"

She smoothed her sleek ponytail. "For Dad. It will give him a lift to see an old teammate."

"Right. For Dad."

She frowned. "What's that supposed to mean?"

"Dating a coworker? How unprofessional. That's not on brand for you."

She snorted incredulously. "I'm not dating anyone."

"But you like him?"

"What business is it of yours?"

She was right. It was no business of mine. Alex could do what he wanted, except it was weird to think of him going after Mel. Mel wouldn't be interested in a man like him. He was too nice for a start. Maybe he had a huge litter of Dalmatians that had caught her interest.

Mel studied my face for a beat too long then shook her head in feigned surprise. "Him? I should have known. The ink hasn't even dried on his contract yet, and you've got your eye on him. He's a lot older than you." Her frown deepened.

What had given it away? I would have denied it, except Mel's mocking look made mean words spill from my lips. "So? It doesn't seem to bother him."

A lie, but I wanted to hurt her. God knows she'd made me feel like crap enough times. A shadow flickered in Mel's eyes. Maybe she'd really liked him. Maybe she'd really had her heart set on that perfect Dalmatian coat. Mel never brought anyone home. I knew nothing about her dating life. We'd been so close when we were little. Now, we were always at each other's throats.

I hid my discomfort at Mel's glare with a laugh. "Judging me, Mel? Now, that *is* on brand for you."

Mel busied herself wiping the table around Dad's plate. "I feel sorry for you. All these casual flings. If you never give anyone a chance, you'll never form a true connection."

"A true connection? Don't worry about me. I get plenty of *connection*. Everyone's the same. Everything good always ends in goodbye. Men are out for what they can get. At least this way I'm in control."

Her eyes roved over me. I expected her to come back with an angry retort but she looked unusually earnest. She bit her lip and her eyes slipped away. "Not everything ends in goodbye. I'm still here. So is Dad."

The memory I tried so hard to keep at bay pulled at my mind. *A wash of blue lights against the bedroom window. I'd crept out of bed and sat on the stairs to listen to the two somber police officers at the front door. I'd known something terrible had happened before either of them opened their mouths.*

Mum had been on her bike when she was struck by a car. That was the day that destroyed us. Once we'd been a normal family. One moment changed everything.

My heart ached, but I pasted a smile onto my face. "I'm fine. I'm the last person you need to worry about."

Mel shook her head, and she was looking at me again like some out-of-date food product that she'd need to find the swiftest way to dispose of. "Look after Dad tonight. Try to be responsible for once in your life."

"I can be responsible."

She flicked her ponytail over her shoulder and turned on her heel. "I'll believe that when I see it."

Chapter 13

LANA

Dad's eyes lit up when he saw how close we'd be sitting to the pitch. He smiled and patted my knee. "Front row seats. Perks of having a footballer for a daughter."

The low roar of the crowded stadium wrapped around us.

"It's going to happen, you know." He took a bite of his hot dog and munched happily. "One day you're going to be holding the World Cup in your hands."

Not again. I patted my hands together for warmth. "We'll see."

He snapped his head to look at me. "I still have faith in you. You just have to want it enough."

Of course I wanted it. Just because you wanted something didn't mean you got it. Every footballer dreamed of playing for their country. Dad didn't get that this was an even bigger deal in women's football. He'd always played in front of packed stadiums whether he was playing in a World Cup or not. It was different for women. So many football fans wouldn't have any interest in women's football, but when we played on the world stage, the whole country sat up and paid attention. Everybody got behind the English Lionesses. I wanted so badly to be a part of it. I just didn't have any control over the decision.

Sean was the first to emerge from the tunnel. He led his team across the pitch in a neat line of pale-blue jerseys to rapturous chanting from the stands. The crowd loved Sean. They only saw the golden hair, the blue eyes and that handsome face. I'd only seen that once, too. I'd been a fool.

Alexander appeared last, towering head and shoulders above every other man on the squad and dressed distinctively in goal-keeper orange. It was strange that any man could cosplay as a neon highlighter pen and still look hot as holy hell. A tremble ran through me. The nerves were getting to me, and I wasn't even play-ing. This match should have been an easy win for Calverdale, but today all eyes would be on the new goalkeeper.

"There's Dad!"

Further along the row of hard plastic blue chairs, a little boy jumped to his feet. A pale-blue Calverdale scarf wrapped around his neck. Excitement lit his features.

The boy leaned over the railing to shout across the pitch. "Good luck, Dad!"

Weird. Only a handful of the guys on the team had kids, and I knew them all. The question left my mouth, unbidden. "Which one is your dad?"

A queasy feeling gripped me because I could guess the answer before it left his lips.

The little boy beamed with pride. "The goalie."

Alex had a son? The boy looked around six or seven. He had Alex's strong jaw and dark eyes, but instead of Alex's dark hair, the boy's mess of yellow curls gleamed bright in the sun like daffodils. The woman sitting next to the boy guided him to sit. She caught me watching and flashed an indulgent smile. I returned her smile even though my mind whirled. Alex had told me he was single.

81

No wonder he'd been happy with one night. The lying, cheating bastard had a partner and kid tucked away. The guilt ground in my gut. This poor woman. I didn't want to be a woman that did that to another woman. I still couldn't live with myself after Sean, and he'd already broken up with Skylar.

The whistle blew for kickoff. Sean got possession of the ball and sprinted off down the outside line. He moved in a blur. Dad finished his soft drink and dusted his hands together. "I'm going to get another drink."

Alarm went through me. I couldn't let him go to the bar unsupervised, even for a soft drink. Too much temptation. Mel would kill me.

I held out a palm to keep him at bay. "Don't worry. I'll go."

"I can manage."

I leaped up. "Let me. I'll get it for free. Perks of being staff."

"I'm sure I can stretch to a lemonade."

"Already? The match has barely started. Do you want to at least wait until halftime?"

He folded his arms and stared me down with a belligerent glare. "I'm thirsty now."

Bloody hell. It was like negotiating with a child. It had been so long since I'd felt like somebody's kid and not a parent. I kept my voice calm and gave him a meaningful look. "You shouldn't go to the bar on your own."

He wrinkled his nose and eyed a group of guys behind us who were all clutching plastic cups full of beer. "One drink. Everyone else is drinking."

"It's never one drink. You know that." I kept my voice soft, despite my rising agitation. Mel had been right. I shouldn't have brought him here. I'd wanted so badly to believe he would be okay.

An excited roar went up from the opposition stand as the other team got possession of the ball. Their striker broke free and sprinted toward the goal. Alex crouched and braced his gloved hands ready to make the save. He didn't look fazed. This is what goalkeepers did. If a striker missed a shot on goal that was one thing, but if the goalkeeper didn't make a save, then people got pissed off. A goalkeeper could never win a match, he could only ever save it.

Alex's strong, massive presence filled the goal like a warrior god. He was absolutely mesmerizing. He also had a family he hadn't told me about. Guilt settled like a cannonball in my belly. The striker hoofed the ball toward the goal and Alex dived. The ball sailed past his fingertips into the back of the net. Alex landed heavily in the mud. A wall of sound hit us from the opposition stand. Damn it. He'd nearly got to it.

A shout erupted from the seats a couple of rows back from the VIP stand. "Alex Fucking McAllister! How could he let that one in?" A bald, red-faced man in a black puffer jacket stomped on a plastic cup.

I twisted in my seat and kept my voice polite. "Would you mind your language? There are kids here."

The guy snorted. Sweat glinted on his bald head and dripped down his wide neck. "It's a fucking football stadium, love. What do you expect?"

Agitation rippled across my shoulder blades. What would Reece say? Breathe. Just this breath. Anger was information. I had a choice on how I reacted to it. I could give this man what for, but he'd just color the air blue and make things worse. Instead, I took the high ground. "I'm respectfully asking you not to swear when there are so many children around."

The man glared back at me and raised his hands in mock surrender. "Whatever you say, love."

I turned back around. The woman who had come to support Alex flashed me a grateful smile. Who was she? A girlfriend? A wife?

The hypocritical bastard had got so wound up about my lies, when he'd told the biggest lie of all. Single my arse.

Should I tell her? Didn't she deserve to know she was with a cheating piece of shit? Not here. Not in front of the kid.

The bald guy behind piped up again. "This team is a fucking shambles, and this new goalie is a joke. He was already washed up at Rangers. God knows why they've brought in someone so old. They need young legs."

Alex's little boy frowned and pressed close to the woman at his side. "Are they talking about Daddy?"

The woman eyed the thugs behind wearily and whispered, "No. Just ignore them."

Another snap of irritation made me leap to my feet. "You don't know what you're talking about. Alex McAllister has got more experience than that entire team combined. He's the only one of them who's played at international level."

"Who are you, love? His fucking fan club? What's a woman know about football?"

His companion, seated next to him, elbowed him and burst out laughing. "She plays football, you fucking idiot. That's Lana Sinclair. She's on the women's team."

The bald man snorted and waved a dismissive hand. "They're worse than the fucking men's team. You only went up the table because you've got that celebrity prick pumping so much money in that you can't fail."

My mouth dropped open. How dare he? There was a blur of movement at my side. I watched in horror as my dad scrambled over the plastic chairs up to the higher row of seating. Dad's fist landed in the bald man's face. The man's head snapped back and the drink in his hand went flying. Cool liquid splattered my cheeks and filled my nose with its malty odor. Shouts rang out as beer rained down on the crowd. Blood streamed from the bald man's nose. Oh God. I scrambled up to the upper row of seats.

The man lunged at Dad. Time became too fast and unreal. I threw myself in front of Dad. White-hot pain shot through my nose as a fist collided with my face. A constellation of glowing dots exploded behind my eyes. My head snapped back. Copper laced my tongue. I pressed my hands over the intense throb in my face. Dad threw himself on top of the guy and they scrambled on the grimy stone floor.

Another guy wrapped his arms around the man who'd attacked Dad, holding him at bay. Shaking, Dad got to his feet. Then someone was tugging my sleeve, dragging me away. My vision darkened. Hot liquid streamed from somewhere over my eyes. The bastard must have been wearing a ring. I held my jacket to the wet gash on my forehead. I'd wanted to lift Dad's spirits with some football, not start a bloody brawl. What a mess.

Mel was going to give me so much shit for this.

Chapter 14

Alexander

Pain blazed right between my shoulder blades. I rolled my shoulders but it did little to soothe the ache. The match yesterday had taken it out of me. I strode through the labyrinth of corridors on the ground floor of the training suite, heading toward the physio. As I rounded the corner, a solid body bashed straight into me. Lana. Her workout clothes hugged her tempting athletic physique. Her auburn hair tumbled carelessly down her back—a flowing cascade of autumn leaves.

Beautiful.

Swelling and a fresh purple bruise marred her right eye.

"What happened to your eye?"

She met my look of concern with a brutal glare.

"Fuck you." She dodged past me.

Baffled, I watched her storm down the corridor. "Excuse me?"

She paused, swiveled around and stomped back to me, wagging her finger in the air. "Actually. No. You shouldn't get away with this so easily." She ripped out the words impatiently. "You need to know what a prick you are."

My confusion deepened. "I'm sorry?"

Hands on her hips, she planted herself in front of me. "I'm onto you. You should be ashamed of yourself. I sat next to your girlfriend in the stadium yesterday. You have a kid, for God's sake. I asked you if you were single. You're a liar."

The stadium? She must have meant Rachel. I held up my hands in surrender. "No. You've got it wrong. My sister took Brodie to watch me yesterday. That's why I moved down here to England. I wanted Brodie to be with his cousins. I told you the truth about being single. My wife . . . passed away . . . five years ago."

My throat burned to talk about it so casually. Sometimes, five years felt like an eternity, sometimes more like five minutes. That was the thing with grief. Time moved on but the pain didn't lessen. More and more shit just piled up in your life, so you had less time to think about how much your heart ached.

She regarded me with a speculative gaze, searching for the truth in my words. "So, when you said you hadn't . . . for five years . . ." Lana's face clouded with uneasiness. "Look, I'm sorry. When I saw your son, I assumed . . . I got it wrong . . . I didn't mean to bite your head off."

She smiled tentatively. Her pretty eyes glimmered with the light spilling in from the tall windows that lined the corridor. Her vitality and confidence were so captivating. She stood tall and proud, as though she had an absolute certainty of who she was and her rightful place in the universe. I hadn't been so self-possessed at that age.

"I can see why you would have thought that about Rachel." My gaze drifted back to her bruised eye. "You didn't tell me what happened to your face."

"It was nothing." Awkwardly, she cleared her throat. "I should go. I have to run laps." She lifted her chin and met my eyes. "You can keep me company. I always run better with a buddy."

No. Bad idea. I didn't move to England for this.

There were so many reasons not to spend time with Lana, but did she have anyone else to talk to?

The silence thickened. She tossed her hair over her shoulder. "I mean, you don't have to if you don't want to . . ."

"It depends. Are you going to be Lana or Mel?"

"Lana. Although you'd have more fun watching Mel run." Her lip twitched. "The vibe is three-legged gazelle on a tightrope."

"That's quite an image."

She stepped closer. Unwelcome excitement coursed through me.

"It's a fact. They should put her in a nature documentary." Her voice filled with humor. "She's high maintenance and impossible to please. Just wanted to give you a heads-up in case you were thinking of asking her out. I wouldn't waste your time."

"Jealous?"

Her pretty eyes widened with faux innocence. "Me? Never."

She leaned lightly into me and her sweet citrus scent filled my nose. Her smile was so charming.

"I'm not thinking of asking your sister out. She's not my type."

Lana pulled her long hair into a ponytail. "What is your type?"

The air crackled with tension. The chemistry between us was so off the charts that even a simple conversation always veered into flirting. I had to shut this down.

"No comment," I said.

"Fair enough." A faint light twinkled in the depths of her eyes. "Now, let's see if you can keep up with me . . . again."

The wind whipped my face as we ran laps around the pitch. Lana ran next to me, red ponytail bobbing up and down. We ran lap after lap on wet grass, until an ache took root in my side, and I had to slow my pace.

I sucked in air, trying to hide my breathlessness. "Why are we doing laps, anyway? Didn't you already have training this morning?"

She stretched her strong sculpted arms above her head. "Claire gave me laps again. She is on my back all the time. I was late this morning. The team has been under pressure since we moved up. There is talk of restructuring." A shadow darkened her face. "I'm in Claire's bad books at the moment."

It had been the same way with Logan. He'd often been in trouble with the management. Logan had been a sensitive soul. He'd always taken everything so personally.

"Any decision about the team is a business decision. If Claire is going to keep the team in the league, she has to make strategic choices."

She muttered angrily under her breath. I couldn't help the smile that pulled at my lips. Lana had inherited her father's quick temper. He'd been at the height of his career in that first World Cup together, and he'd mentored me. Logan had been a decent fella back then. What was he up to now? Enjoying his retirement, hopefully.

"How is Logan, by the way? I should pop in and see him. We're long overdue a catch-up."

She shot me an alarmed look, and I winced, realizing how weird that would be. What would we catch up about?

Hey, Logan, great to see you. What have I been up to? Oh. Well, nothing much, although I did sleep with your much younger daughter.

"What was my dad like back then?"

I paused, choosing my words carefully. Logan had been off the rails. He'd always be the one to drink anyone else under the table. "He was a great captain. Everybody respected him."

She nodded, woodenly. Sadness returned to her eyes. The ache in my side blazed brighter. I bent over with my hands on my thighs. "So, how are you going to get back in Claire's good books?"

She rolled her eyes. "I shouldn't have to try. My form has been great this season."

"Being part of a team isn't just about talent. It's about attitude and behavior, too. What are you doing to show your commitment to the team?"

She wrinkled her nose. "You sound like Claire. What more can I do?"

"There's plenty. The club has outreach programs. You can volunteer. I go into schools and talk to the kids and play with them. You could inspire young girls and show them what is possible. Talk is cheap. If you want Claire to know you're committed to this team, then show her through your actions."

Her expression filled with curiosity. Not everybody enjoyed getting advice. Maybe she wasn't ready to hear it. I hadn't meant it as criticism, but she could easily misconstrue my intentions. Perhaps I shouldn't have said anything at all. It was just a habit to try to fix people's problems. I was so used to coaching Brodie.

She flashed a tentative smile and rubbed the back of her neck. "You think I could do something like that?"

"Of course. I think you'd be great."

Her smile widened. "Thanks." She glanced at her watch. "I should get going. We have more training this afternoon, and I don't want to be late. I'm on my best behavior. I have to be a good girl." Playfully, her gaze slid over me. "It's not easy being good all the time. I prefer to be bad."

She stepped forward. Anybody could see us, but I couldn't move away.

"Was that really the first time in five years? How was it, getting back in the saddle?" Her minty breath fanned my neck as she stood on tiptoe to whisper, "You were great, you know. That was the hottest sex . . ."

My skin tingled where her lips nearly grazed my throat, and my senses flooded with the way it had felt with her. *The press of a warm body against mine again. Skin on skin. Her sensual, drugging kisses.* Her touch had brought me to life in a way I hadn't been for so long.

"You're too good to waste that kind of talent." There was a trace of laughter in her voice. "Don't wait another five years, will you?"

I needed to shut this down. I held perfectly still, barely breathing.

She stepped back abruptly, and gave me a wave over her shoulder as she sauntered away.

"See you around, Big Mac."

Chapter 15

LANA

Claire was waiting for me in the changing room. Her icy gaze met mine. "Gabe's office. Now."

"What? Why?"

She didn't wait around to reply. I raced after her down the corridor. Music poured out of the gym, grating my nerves. Claire stormed ahead past the cafeteria.

I jogged to catch up. "What's the problem?"

She retrieved her phone from the pocket of her jacket, tapped the screen, and presented it to me. I watched the brief video clip while my brain scrambled to put it into context. It was a video of me in the stands at the stadium, ranting at the man yesterday before the fight had broken out. Shame made my gut feel like lead, but it could have been worse. At least it was me in the clip and not Dad.

"Is that it?"

"You don't think that's bad enough? Look at your conduct. You're a representative of this team."

"That guy was swearing in front of kids. I had to put him in his place."

"It's gone viral. People are saying you're out of control."

Shit.

She stopped at Gabe's office and knocked on the door. Gabe swung the door open and gestured to a chair the other side of the desk, next to Claire.

"How are you?" Gabe's amiable gaze flew to my bruised eye.

Great. Never better. I love it when Claire marches me around like a naughty schoolgirl sent to the headmaster. I resisted the urge to prod my swollen eye. The bruise looked ugly. I'd given up trying to cover it with makeup.

"I'm fine. Some idiot was trying to start something at the match yesterday. It wasn't my fault. You know that, don't you?"

Claire and Gabe shared a look.

Gabe laced his elegant fingers in front of his lips. "I've got PR on my balls about this. You'll have to talk to them and find a way to smooth this over. The guy isn't going to press charges, but it's cost us. Regardless of where the blame lies, this doesn't look good for the club."

I gritted my teeth. "It was the guy who started it. He was swearing and carrying on. There were kids in the crowd."

Claire's level gaze settled on me, even though her words were meant for Gabe. "Lana is already on a warning for her poor timekeeping."

Why had she dragged me here like this to scold me over something so trivial? "This wasn't my fault."

Claire inclined her sleek head. "You're on the bench for the next match."

Benched? Again? No way. I couldn't afford to miss another game. I threw my hands in the air. "You can't do that."

Claire raised her chin with a cool stare in my direction. "I suggest you get your act together or you'll be on the bench permanently."

Panic swished inside me like a bucket of iced water. She wouldn't do that, would she? I threw Gabe an imploring look. "Come on, Gabe. You had stuff on you in the news all the time. You know what the press is like. This will blow over. It always does."

Gabe rubbed a hand over his jaw. "Claire makes decisions about the team. Not me."

Claire turned her face to the window and peered out onto the training pitches. "I have to think about the team. There are younger players watching every move the older ones make."

So, she'd make an example of me again? She couldn't do this to me. I'd messed up, but I couldn't sit it out on that bench. It wasn't fair. "When Skylar left, I stepped up and kept the team going. We wouldn't even be in this league without me."

Gabe smoothed his tie. His eyes slipped away. "Nobody is disputing your talent."

A snap of anger made my nostrils flare. "This is bullshit and you know it. Spit it out, Claire. You're still mad about that thing with Reece, and the bet. That's why you keep coming down so hard on me. What more do you want me to do? It was so stupid. I've apologized so many times. Reece and Skylar have forgiven me."

"If I'm hard on you, it's only because I want to get the best from you."

By putting me on the bench? By taking away my chance to get scouted?

Gabe gave an uncomfortable cough. He didn't want to deal with this. He knew I'd moan to Miri and Miri would give him shit about it when he got home. Good. Somebody needed to listen to me. I was struggling outside of work; I didn't need Claire riding me.

Claire gave me an indifferent nod. "Go home now, Lana."

My body shook, and I sucked in a breath. So much for keeping calm. "You're suspending me?"

"No. Just cool off. We'll talk sensibly when you've calmed down."

My nails cut half-moons in my palms. "Oh, don't worry. I'm calm. You're the one making rash decisions."

"Enough." Gabe raised an unimpressed eyebrow. "Claire is right. Go home and cool down."

Everything about Claire's calm, poised demeanor reminded me of Mel. Maybe I hadn't been behaving how I should because of everything going on with Dad and Karen, but they didn't have to come down so hard on it. How could Claire question my commitment to football? I had no idea how to make her understand how serious I was about this team. It was her job to see it. Why should I have to convince her? She was just like Mel—only prepared to see all the shitty things she believed about me.

Silence swept the neat office. There was no point arguing. I had no energy to fight people who had already made up their minds about me. I could never win with Mel. Claire was no different. Everybody was always so committed to misjudging me.

"Fine. Whatever." I swung the door open and left before I embarrassed myself with tears.

Chapter 16

ALEXANDER

I rolled my shoulder, attempting to loosen some of the tension after the deep-tissue massage. Physical therapy was supposed to make me feel better, but I swore the physios enjoyed inflicting pain. I rounded a corner. A flash of vivid red caught my eye before I banged into something solid.

Lana stepped back with an expression of surprise. She looked ethereal in the half-light spilling in through the tall windows; her flowing auburn hair shone with undertones of gold. This woman was so beautiful, it was hard not to stare. She was also so young, so I really shouldn't have been staring. Then I noticed the tears glimmering in her eyes.

"Is everything okay?"

She glanced down the hallway, grabbed me by the hand, and pulled me into the small empty room where I'd just had a massage. She shut the door behind her and locked it. A frown pulled at my brow. That door had no business being locked.

"What's wrong?"

"Everything. All of it." She threw her hands up in the air. "I'm just so sick of everyone. I can't get anything right with anyone. My sister . . . Claire . . . I'm so fed up . . ."

A shadow passed over her face. It was the same look her father had always worn, as though he were furious at the world. What was she angry about?

"Slow down. Tell me from the start."

Her eyes froze on me, and her gaze sharpened. "I'm tired of talking. I want to feel something different."

With one fluid motion, she pressed her hard body against me. A hot shiver of need made me stiffen. My heart lurched, madly. "What are you doing?"

She didn't look at me as she grabbed a bottle of massage oil and coated her hands. She spoke in an odd yet gentle tone. "I need you, Alex."

The air became scented with a sweet heady aroma of sandal-wood and balsam, like a walk through a pine forest in the rain. My senses reeled. "What do you mean?"

She gave an impatient shrug. "I have all this churning inside. I need to feel better."

"Then let's go for a drink and talk."

Her gaze dropped to my lips. A flame danced in her eyes. "No. I don't want to talk." Her brittle smile softened slightly. "Can I touch you?"

I swallowed. The correct answer was no. There were so many reasons why the correct answer was no. "Why don't we go and get a cup of tea? If you need someone to talk, I'll listen."

"I don't want to talk. Do you remember what you said to me in that bar? You said you'd give me anything I want." She stepped forward and clasped her body to mine. "I want you. I feel like shit. Please make me feel good."

"Then let's get that tea. I'm sure whatever is going on, we can work it out."

"That's not how you help me."

My backside hit the edge of the massage table. Her soft lips came to mine, slowly. She gave me time to back away, and I should have done, but I was weak for this woman. Her kiss was hot and irresistible, soldering us together. An aching need clutched me. I'd missed this so much. This feeling of closeness. Skin on skin. The warmth of a lover's touch. I should have pushed her away but my tongue glided against hers, deepening the kiss.

Her lips branded a path over my neck, and she spoke between urgent kisses. "I don't want soft or gentle. I need it like I'm some stranger you met in a hotel bar and you'll never see again. Do you understand?"

Anticipation crackled like electricity through me. "Not here. We're at work."

"The door is locked. We'll be quiet."

"We can't be quiet. What if the physio comes back?"

She peered around the small room and her gaze landed on a stereo in the corner. She moved to fiddle with the dial. Soft, soothing music poured out into the dimly lit room. It was hardly music to fuck to. This was absurd. We couldn't do this. I had to walk away.

"Lana, I'm sorry, but this is . . ."

She pulled off her pale-blue jersey, unzipped her sports bra, and freed her firm, full breasts. My heart jolted.

She watched me intently. "Can I touch you, Alex?"

It would have taken a strength I didn't have to deny her. "Yes."

Her hand slipped under the waistband of my gym shorts. Her slick, oil-coated fingers wrapped around the base of my shaft, and pleasure jolted through my body. She pumped her hand up and down in a tortuous slippery motion. A groan left my lips. My head fell back, and my fingers tightened around the edge of the massage table.

She worked my shaft, making my body scream with a desperate tension in need of release. I grabbed her wrist, stilling her. "We shouldn't be doing this at work. People will gossip."

She snapped her hand away. "Stop?"

"I can see you're upset. Don't you want to talk?"

"No. I want this."

Taking my hand, she guided me to where my fingers burned to touch. I fondled her breasts, bringing her nipples to rosy peaks, before sucking each tight bud into my mouth. Heat flooded my body. This wasn't reasonable, but it felt so good.

She pulled my T-shirt off over my head, and her breasts crushed against my chest, skin on skin. Her lips seared my neck in a flurry of hot kisses. She leaned in to whisper in my ear, "I need you. Are you going to take what you want? Don't go easy on me."

Her slick fingers tightened around my shaft as she worked me again, picking up her speed. Her lustful expression shredded the last scraps of my self-control. I spun her around and pressed her down flat on the table. I ripped her leggings down, followed by her underwear. She wriggled her peachy backside in anticipation. I smoothed my palm over the perfect milky skin of her ass and traced the hollows of her strong, supple back. My lips found a path over the bumps of her spine.

She spread her legs. A thrill shot through me at such a beautiful sight. She reached around to guide me to her entrance.

I stroked the birthmark at the base of her spine in slow circles. If I hadn't been so desperate to sink inside of her, I would have filled her ears with compliments.

Instead, I saved my voice for the essentials. "We need a condom."

She squirmed her backside against me. "I'm on the Pill."

"You're sure you want this? We could just go and talk—"

"No more talking." She threw a glance over her shoulder, and her expectant eyes met mine.

A rush of arousal made my heart pound. I took hold of my cock and pushed into soft wetness. I was so slick from the massage oil that I filled her in one fevered thrust. She gasped and bucked against me. Holding her hips, I drove into her. She pressed her face flat against the table and bucked against me as I drove into her from behind.

I didn't take my time to be slow or tender. That wasn't what she wanted. She'd come to me for this.

"Do you like that?"

Her lips parted and her eyes rolled back. "Mm hmm."

"You're going to tell me if I'm going too hard?"

"You're not. I need it harder."

Her slick heat coated me, and I thrust with abandon. Her moans carried over the soft piped music. She grabbed my hand and brought it to cover her mouth. I gave her the pounding she craved, one hand digging into her hips, and the other muffling her agonized gasps. My view was incredible, but I wanted to see her face when she came. She gave a shocked yelp as I pulled out, picked her up, and laid her down on her back on the massage table. I lifted her legs high and over my shoulders. We both groaned as she welcomed me back inside. I outlined the circle of her breasts, tracing my thumb across her perfect nipples while I pumped into her in quick, sharp strokes.

Her legs tensed and she shook as she hit her peak. I held off, savoring the way her body clenched greedily around me in waves of pleasure. Release tore through me. I fell forward, using the massage table to hold me up so I didn't flatten her. My breath escaped me in sharp pants. Sweat chilled my skin. Fuck. It was hard to keep up with a twenty-six-year-old athlete. Blood pounded my temples.

The soothing music grew loud again. Lana wouldn't meet my eyes. All the passionate intimacy that had just wound between us slipped away like sand through my fingers.

Gently, I pulled out. I moved to the sink and got a cloth to wipe her down.

She grabbed the cloth from me, brusque and businesslike. "I've got it."

A grim, heavy feeling crept into my bones. What if somebody had walked past and heard us? Soon, we'd be the talk of the entire building. Lana gathered the clothes strewn on the floor, and we both dressed in silence.

Her smile was fleeting. "Thanks. I needed that."

She tried to dodge past me to the door. I grabbed her elbow gently, holding her still. "Wait. I need to know that you're okay. I didn't go too hard, did I?"

"Of course not."

"You'd tell me, wouldn't you?"

"Yes." Her eyes held a faraway look. Was she regretting what we just did? How had I let that happen? She was upset. She'd said she wanted this, but I should have tried harder to get her to talk.

"I'm taking you for lunch and you're going to tell me what brought you in here in this state."

She smoothed a stray hair back into place. "No, thanks. I'm good."

"It wasn't a request. I'm not letting you walk away after that. I want to know what's wrong."

Her eyes flashed as though we were playing a game and I'd just changed the rules. "You might be Daddy when you've got me bent over a table, but don't think you get to tell me what to do when we're fully dressed."

Was that it? She'd come in here for sex, and now she was out of here? How could she be so casual about it all? When I was young, you saw someone you fancied in a bar and bought them a drink. The dating

101

world was so different these days. I didn't understand it. I'd never cared to understand it. None of this should have been happening.

"Is that it? You're done with me?"

She paused with her hand around the door handle. "Fun and done. That's the deal."

"We didn't make a deal."

She folded her arms tight across her chest. "In the hotel room."

"Don't you think things have changed since then?"

"We've hooked up twice. It's nothing."

Nothing.

This was the first woman I'd been intimate with since Evelyn. I hadn't cared to admit it to myself because it was so weird that she was so young, but all of this was a big deal. A huge deal.

I found a disinfectant spray, wet a cloth at the sink, and set to work cleaning the massage table. "Things have changed. We were strangers the first time. Now, we know each other."

Her eyes filled with belligerence. "You don't know me. Not really."

An unwelcome tension stretched tight between us. Had any man ever taken the time to get to know her, or had all her relationships been like this? No-strings sex. She snorted but there was something else flickering in the depths of her bright eyes. What was that? Panic?

"What if I want to know you?"

Confusion invaded her stare. "Why?"

"Because sometimes you look sad and like you need a friend. I want to be your friend."

The awful soothing music grew loud in the silence. I fiddled with the stereo until the hush rang out too loud.

She shrugged, but her voice was hoarse. "I'm fine. I have enough friends."

My heart contracted. She was so young to sound so sad and world-weary. She tossed her ponytail over her shoulder, unlocked the door, and left without another word.

Chapter 17

LANA

I pressed my forehead to the locker in the changing room. My skin flashed hot from the shower, and my jersey stuck to my clammy body. Despite scrubbing my hair, the scent of balsam oil clung to me. Memories of Alex's deep voice crackling over my skin filled my mind. Big Mac was good—even better the second time round. Still, there couldn't be a third time. I'd been weak. The meeting with Claire and Gabe had sent me into a meltdown. I'd needed to stop the roaring in my head, and once again Alex had been there at the right moment as a pleasant distraction.

"Benched? What the fuck, Lana?" Skylar's exasperated voice startled me out of my reverie.

Skylar dumped her carryall by the lockers. "I heard you're not playing on Saturday. I need you on the pitch. What did you do now?"

I turned my attention back to my locker. Of course Skylar would assume I'd done something. "Talk to Claire. It's her decision."

Skylar pounded her fist against the locker. The harsh clang against metal made my teeth grit. "This is bollocks. We can't do it without you."

"Get used to it. If Claire gets her way, she's going to put me on the transfer list."

Skylar's eyebrows shot up. "What?"

This is where it was heading, wasn't it? Claire wanted me out of here. "Claire's pissed off about the argument I had in the stadium. It was some idiot kicking off, and it got out of control. It looks bad for the club."

Skylar fiddled with the silver bar in her eyebrow then tossed her purple hair in a gesture of defiance. "If you go, then I go."

Despite the situation, I couldn't help but chuckle at the stubborn tilt of Skylar's chin. "Don't be ridiculous. This doesn't affect you. It's my mess. They'll get someone in to replace me."

"No one could ever replace you." Skylar placed a hand on each of my shoulders and pressed her forehead to mine. "We'll sort this out. I'm not going to lose you, okay? We got into this league as a team and we stay a team through thick and thin."

A sudden lightness filled me. Sometimes it felt as though things with Skylar would never go back to normal, and then there were times like this. She still had my back. I sighed and tied my damp hair into a ponytail. I couldn't leave this team. I'd never find another captain like Skylar. We'd been through so much to get here. How could I prove to Claire that I was worth keeping around? I had to make this right. Alex's words drifted to my mind. He'd talked about showing my commitment through actions. Maybe there was something I could do.

"Do you know anything about the club outreach work? How would I get involved in that?"

Skylar laced her purple football boots. "There's a guy that runs it. Geoff, I think. You can ask him."

"I might give it a go. What do you reckon?"

Skylar beamed and squeezed my shoulder again. "Sounds like a plan. I've got your back all the way. Don't give up. I'm not letting you go. I can't do any of this without you."

Chapter 18

LANA

A barrage of children's laughter hit me on the approach to the school gates. I pulled my coat tighter and hovered at the entrance to the playground. The little brick school lay beyond a tall iron fence. A rush of unexpected nerves surged through me. Part of me wanted to turn around and run. Talking to a bunch of kids shouldn't have terrified me this much. It could even be fun, although I couldn't shut off the worries.

What if I don't know what to say?

What if this is a disaster?

"Lana?" The deep Scottish voice sent a tremor through me.

Alex towered over me. He eyed me with trepidation and pulled his team jacket tight against the wind.

Not Alex. As if I wasn't already on edge enough. "What are you doing here? Are you stalking me?"

Alex peered through the school gates at the noisy chaos in the playground. "I'm running a PE session. The outreach team sent me. This is my third visit. For all I know, you're the one stalking me."

I couldn't help but laugh. "In your dreams."

He pressed the intercom at the gate. A low hum. Then, a beep and a click. He pulled the gate open, and I followed him into the playground. Kids swarmed around us from every angle, like piranhas scenting flesh.

Alex shot me a sidelong glance and chuckled. "Try not to look so nervous," he whispered under his breath. "Kids sense fear like attack dogs."

Shit. Was that true, or was he teasing me? I tossed my hair over my shoulder. "I'm not nervous."

"Good. You'll be great."

We wound our way through groups of children toward the school office. Alex raked a hand through his hair. "No matter what's going on between us, let's keep things professional while we are here. We're representing the team."

"Nothing is going on between us."

He frowned. "Right."

We entered the school hall full of kids, and I pasted a smile on my face. I was here to inspire girls to play football, not to worry about Alex Mac. This was a chance to demonstrate that women could do anything that men could.

Okay.

I've got this.

Maybe, it could even be fun.

Another football blasted into my middle, knocking the air from my lungs. This was not fun. We'd split the kids into boys' and girls' teams. I glanced across the hall at Alex, who was happily practicing his skills with a group of well-behaved boys. My girls were wild. They were more intent on hoofing the ball at each other than practicing kick-ups. Just my luck to get a bunch of little hell-raisers while Alex got the cherubs playing harps. These girls could be perfect if they could concentrate for five minutes.

"Right." I clapped my hands together. "Let's have a practice match. We'll split into two teams."

A hand shot in the air. "Have you got a boyfriend, Miss?"

I tried to keep the annoyance from my face. *What business is it of yours?* "No. Let's save questions until the end."

"Why haven't you got a boyfriend?" The girl stared back at me. Her defiant tone held a subtle challenge, but I wouldn't allow it to faze me. I'd spent a lifetime dealing with Mel. That was preparation for anything a bunch of feral kids could throw at me.

"I have no time for boys because I'm too busy playing football." I handed out the colored bibs for the girls to wear.

"Can't you have both?"

The tall girl eyed me suspiciously as she took her bib. She was a head and shoulders taller than the other children, including the boys. Good. I'd put her in goal.

"Yes. No. I don't want to. Let's focus on the task. I'm going to split you into two—"

"Is Mr. McAllister your boyfriend?"

Oh my God, kid, really? What was with this child? I'd definitely put her in goal, as far away from me as possible. I followed her gaze to Alex, and the boys that surrounded him in a neat circle and hung off his every word. I couldn't help but watch him. He was a natural with these kids. It shouldn't have surprised me, since he had a son. How old was Alex's son? A little younger than this class? It must have been tough raising him alone. These kids were hard work, and I'd been here less than half an hour. Alex must have the patience of a saint to put up with one around the clock.

The girl clapped her hands together and sang in a high-pitched voice, "Miss Sinclair and Mr. McAllister up a tree. *K-I-S-S-I-N-G*."

Heat climbed the back of my neck to the tips of my ears. "Stop that."

Instead of stopping she went again, louder this time. Another couple of girls joined in. The embarrassing chorus echoed around the high ceilings of the school hall. Alex glanced over and raised an amused eyebrow. At least someone was entertained.

I threw my hands up in exasperation. "Does anybody even want to play football?"

Alex drifted back to my side, accompanied by the teacher.

Another small girl put her hand up. "My brother says girls can't ever play as good as boys."

I snorted. "Your brother sounds basic."

Alex coughed to smother a laugh. "What Miss Sinclair means to say is that it wasn't kind for your brother to say that, and it's wrong."

"Of course it's wrong. Girls can do anything boys can do, and most of the time we'll do it better."

The little girl beamed. "Jacob *is* basic. Can I tell him you said that?"

"Absolutely. You should tell him." I peered around the group, sizing up my opponents. "Anyone else think football is just for boys?"

The girls huddled and conferred. I jumped in before having to listen to any more annoying backchat.

"Because football is definitely not just for boys. People used to think that it was, so you're going to have to fight to show them what you've got. It shouldn't be like that. You shouldn't have to fight, but this is life. Women have to fight for a seat at the table, and women had to fight just to step on the pitch. If it means something to you, then you never give up."

I prowled in a circle around the huddle of girls, who had all miraculously fallen silent.

"You're going to need to be brave and strong. If you don't have fire in your belly, then you may as well stop now, because there's no point. But if you're not a quitter, if you have this fire inside you that is burning you up, then you keep it lit because one day, if you work hard, you'll get to be part of a team. You'll get to walk onto the pitch with your team, knowing you've got each other's backs, no matter what. Knowing that you fought with everything you had, for the honor of being there."

Every set of eyes in the hall burned into me. I'd forgotten myself. Was I getting too carried away? A sudden sadness made me want to crumple. I'd been one of these little girls once. Football had always been my whole world. How could Claire bench me? My path into football had been easier than most. My dad had been a famous footballer, but still I'd had to fight to be taken seriously. I'd endured all the jokes at my expense. When men weren't trying to get into my football shorts, they were making fun of me. I wouldn't stop fighting to stay on my team. I'd made mistakes, but I'd given everything to this game.

Alex's hand brushed mine. Heat seared from his touch. "They're listening." His voice was low and gentle. "Keep going."

I turned to receive my audience's rapt attention. "It's hard being a woman in a man's world, but you know what? You can be proud of yourself for that, because if a man tells you that you can't do something, then you don't listen to a word. Every time a door slams in your face, you kick it down. Every time someone tells you no, you tell them to f . . . flip right off. This is a woman's world. It's yours for the taking. Don't let any man tell you differently."

The girls gazed at me in stunned silence. The tall girl that had been bugging me started clapping. Then everyone was clapping. The hall reverberated with applause. Shit. Were they clapping for me? How had I managed to turn this around?

A little girl with glasses and long dark plaits grabbed a ball. "I want to be a footballer."

Muttering broke out among the girls. Another little girl put her hand in the air. "Me too."

"And me."

"I want to."

I gathered the girls together. "Right, girls. Let's show them what we've got. We're going to kick their—"

"*Footballs.*" Alex watched me with a rueful smile. "We're going to kick all the *footballs.*"

"Right. That's right. We're going to kick all of their footballs. Girls versus boys. What do you say?" I chucked the ball in Alex's direction.

He caught the ball smoothly. "Okay, but I'm not going to go easy on you."

"Good. I never want you to go easy on me."

He raised a dark brow and cleared his throat. "Right. Let's spread out, then."

Chapter 19

ALEXANDER

Squeaks from kids' trainers reverberated all around the school hall. I'd run a couple of sessions at this school before, but I'd never seen the children belting around like this. Lana had got them so fired up and focused. She'd seemed nervous walking in here, but it hadn't taken her long to find her feet. This woman was a natural.

Lana would make an incredible coach one day, if she wanted to go that route. I'd tell her when we got out of here. That was if she'd give me the time of day for a conversation. I had the feeling she'd been avoiding me at the club. We hadn't spoken since the encounter in the massage room. Clearly, it had meant nothing to her, but I couldn't put my mind to anything else.

The spark between us had shocked my heart back into action. There were so many reasons that I couldn't go *there* with this woman. Not to mention that she'd made it obvious she didn't want to go there with me either. Lana only wanted casual. Even if I could get past my other reservations, there was no getting around that. I had to think about Brodie. If I ever made the decision to start a relationship, it would have to be something committed. I couldn't risk Brodie getting attached to someone who would walk away.

Lana didn't even want to stick around for coffee afterward, let alone hang out with my kid.

Lana stood next to me, transfixed by the game, as though nothing had happened between us. This wasn't the right place for a discussion. She wanted to forget about the sex. If I was sensible, I'd want that, too. If only I could get her out of my bloody head.

A cry of excitement dragged my attention back to the action. The real reason I'd come here today. I was supposed to be coaching these kids, not obsessing over a woman much too young for me. This wasn't me. I loved these visits, and I owed the kids my undivided attention. A boy hurtled toward the goal with the ball at his feet. The tall girl, who Lana had selected to put in goal, braced herself to make the save.

"Oh God," Lana whispered under her breath.

The boy smashed the ball at the net, and the girl dived left, her hands outstretched as they reached for the save. For a heart-stopping moment, I thought she wouldn't get to it, but she caught the ball before it went over the line. It was an amazing save. She leaped straight back to her feet with the ball clutched proudly to her chest and a triumphant smile on her face.

Lana whooped and punched the air. "Let's go!" She cupped her hands over her mouth and shouted. "Amazing effort. Absolutely brilliant save. You superstar!"

The girl beamed with pride and booted the ball back into play.

Lana nudged me in the side. "That's how it's done. You could get some tips from these girls."

Her teasing smile made my pulse pound. "I've never seen these girls play like this. I think you might have put a future England captain on her path with that speech."

Her trainer squeaked as she dragged it over the floor. She snorted and dropped her gaze to the ground. "She'll probably get the call before I do."

"The call?"

"To play for England." Her eyes darted to mine before they went back to the children.

I should have been watching the game too, but I couldn't take my eyes off Lana. She always had a cocky smile on her face, but sometimes I caught her looking like this, sad and lost, and it made me wonder whether that smile was just a brilliant piece of armor. Was she worrying she wouldn't get her chance to play for her country? It would be a terrible shame if she didn't. Lana was an incredible talent. I'd heard she'd even been captain for a while.

"You've still got plenty of time."

She sighed. "You sound like my dad."

"It's the truth. I know so many players who got called up at your age."

She kept her gaze fixed on a little red-haired girl who sprinted down the outside line. "How old were you when you first played for Scotland?"

The answer wouldn't help. "Twenty."

Her mouth tightened into a thin line. "Right."

"But that means nothing. Every team needs young players, but they also need experienced players. Every team needs its leaders to look up to."

She fiddled with the silver whistle around her neck. "I was captain when Skylar went to LA. You can ask any of the girls on the team and they'll tell you I'll fight for them. It hasn't made any difference. No one cares what I do on the pitch. The scouts don't notice me."

"The women on the pitch know that you've got their backs, but how does anyone else know? You have to show people."

"How am I supposed to do that?"

Her eyes flashed with fire. Obviously, I was touching a nerve, and needed to tread carefully. I kept my voice low and tentative.

"Through your actions. By really showing yourself. Every team needs the person who is going to fight for them in the trenches. We all want the player at our sides who will never let us down. If you're doing all that, then that's great, but when you're out there on the pitch, and the TV cameras are rolling, you need to make it known that you're *that* player. If there's any trouble on the pitch, you're the one running over to sort it out."

She narrowed her eyes. "You want me to play up for the cameras?"

"Of course not. You just do what comes naturally. Have the steel to make sure the women around you don't lose heart, and then show it. If someone goes down with an injury, you be the first person at their side. If there's a foul, get over there and defend your teammate. Show that you won't let anyone get bullied. No one can deny your talent, but this is about the finishing touch. You demonstrate that willingness to be the person who everyone wants on their team. Look at you here, doing this. You're showing your commitment. It might seem like a small act, but it won't go unnoticed."

She caressed her pretty lips with the silver whistle, thoughtfully. I tried to stop myself from getting distracted by the action.

"That makes sense. A lot of sense, actually. These are the conversations I'd love to have with Claire. She just doesn't get me. Everybody just assumes because I'm Logan Sinclair's daughter . . . you know the reputation he had . . . the parties . . . the women . . ." A small smile pulled at her lips. "Before Mum. She didn't stand for any of that. Dad always said it changed everything when he met her."

She cleared her throat and snapped her attention back to the match. I'd never met Logan's wife, but I remembered the change when he finally settled down. She must have been an incredible woman to tame a man like that. I didn't know what had happened, but I had the sense she wasn't around. I wouldn't pry. If Lana wanted to tell me, she could do it in her own time.

"Your dad was an amazing player, but he had a . . . temper. Logan always finished a season with more red cards than goals."

She flashed me a stern glance, and I immediately regretted my words. That had been the wrong thing to say. She was protective over her father.

I held my hands up. "No offense. Your father was the best captain I've ever had the honor of playing with. When I turned up for my first day of training, I was terrified. I was a green boy from Glasgow, surrounded by all of my heroes, and no one was more legendary than the great Logan Sinclair. The lads wanted to banter and wind me up, but Logan put me at ease. He might have had his issues off the pitch, but he was a kind and decent man. It's not fair when people make assumptions about us that aren't true. People will always have their opinions."

Lana rolled her shoulders back. "I'm sick of other people's opinions."

"Then ignore them. They aren't your business. Just be yourself. Always. Not your sister. Not your father. Be Lana. Show yourself through your words and your actions."

"What if people don't want to see Lana?"

Her voice was so sad and small, it made my heart contract. Lana had incredible talent. She'd fired up these kids with her passion and dedication to the game. If only others could see her the way I did. If only Lana could see *herself* the way I did.

"Who wouldn't want to see you?"

She dropped her voice to a whisper. "You didn't want to in that bar. You wanted Mel. Someone mature and put together. Someone smart and sensible. Not me."

This wasn't the place for a conversation like this, but we were out of earshot of the kids. I stepped closer and matched her whisper.

115

"You didn't give me the chance to see you. It was you I was attracted to. I liked your smile, your sense of humor, the way you saved me from getting ripped off on a seven-quid pint."

She arched her eyebrow and whispered under her breath, "And my perfect breasts?"

"Yes. I like them, too. We men are simple creatures, but you don't have to worry about any of the other stuff. You're always enough. If someone thinks differently, forget about them. Keep your focus on your own game. That's the part you can control. Besides, I've met Mel. She doesn't like dogs, she won't entertain frozen pizza, which me and Brodie practically live on, by the way, and she's kind of . . . scary. I'd take Lana any day."

She laughed. "Yup. Mel is terrifying. I lost one of her gloves last month. I get cold sweats thinking about what she's going to do when she notices."

A whoop rang out as the girl in goal dived for another shot and saved it.

Lana shook her head in awe. "This girl's got it."

"This is where we can help. We make sure she gets what she needs if she wants to progress. I'll have a word with Cal in the Junior Academy. We'll get him down here. Make sure she has the opportunity for some decent coaching."

She shot me a tentative smile. "Have you ever thought about coaching?"

I'd thought about it. Most players my age would already be on the next stage of their career. It was possible to train and get accredited while you still played. Gabe had already mentioned it, but it was tough to make that step. So hard to let go. Football had been my world for so long.

When I'd lost Evelyn, football had still been there. It had kept me moving forward so I could be the father I needed to be for Brodie. Maybe it was time. My spine certainly thought it was time.

I couldn't deny I was tired, and sick of waking up in agony every morning. My body would thank me for the rest, even if my heart hadn't caught up to the idea. I couldn't let Calverdale down now I'd signed, but I could start the accreditation process. I could give them this season. Maybe it would have to be my last.

"You'd be so good at coaching. This conversation has made me feel better."

Had it? Great. It felt good to put a smile on this woman's face, even if she wasn't the player I was supposed to be coaching here. Lana was incredible. Maybe she couldn't see it because she hadn't had enough people telling her.

"I'm glad if I've helped."

"You have. I suggest you go down the coach route. It's either that or retrain as a firefighter. I'm sure you've got what it takes for that, too."

I tore my eyes away from her flirtatious smile. This wasn't the time or the place. I had to have some resolve with this woman. Even if she wanted to hook up again, it wouldn't go anywhere.

"I'll look into it."

Her voice filled with teasing. "The firefighting?"

I rolled my eyes. "The coaching."

She smiled to herself. "Disappointing. I'd like to see you in all the gear, but Coach McAllister has a nice ring to it, doesn't it?"

A smile crept onto my face.

Coach McAllister.

I could get used to it.

Chapter 20

LANA

We walked through the playground full of boisterous kids. A little boy bolted out of nowhere and wrapped his arms around Alex's middle.

"Brodie, this is my friend, Lana." Alex beamed and squeezed the boy tight. "Lana, this is my son, Brodie."

Brodie stood at Alex's side. His face lit up with an infectious grin. "I remember you. You got into a fight at the stadium."

I felt Alex's questioning gaze burn into me. Heat stole into my face. "It wasn't a fight, exactly."

Brodie balled his hand into a fist and threw a punch into his palm. "It was the coolest thing I've ever seen." He cocked his head and appraised me. "Who's your second-favorite pirate?"

Alex flashed an indulgent smile and transferred his gaze to me. "You don't have to answer questions about pirates. We'll be here all day. We have to go." Alex smoothed his son's wild curly hair and steered him back in the direction of the school office. "I'll see you tonight."

"I actually know a lot about pirates."

Alex raised a bemused eyebrow. "You do?"

"My mum used to read me stories about Gráinne O'Malley. She was the pirate queen of Ireland."

Interest flickered in Brodie's eyes. "A girl pirate? Girls can't be pirates."

"Of course they can. Anything boys can do, girls can do too."

Alex rocked back on his heels. "Lana plays for Calverdale. Some people used to think that only men should play football."

Brodie dug his hands into the pockets of his smart blazer. "Are you my dad's new girlfriend?"

Alex shot me an apologetic glance. "Lana is my friend."

"But you don't have friends that are girls." Brodie looked between us with excited eyes. "I'm glad you have a girlfriend. I have three girlfriends." He ticked off on his fingers. "Molly, Jessica, and Olivia. I might ask Imogen next week and then I'll have four."

Alex's laugh was rich. "And to think I was worrying about this kid settling in at a new school."

I couldn't help but laugh too. "I like your style, Brodie. Keep those options open. Don't let yourself get tied down."

Alex shook his head and squeezed Brodie's shoulder. "Lana is my friend, who happens to be a woman."

Brodie shrugged. "If you want her to be your girlfriend, then you just have to ask her. That's how I got all my girlfriends."

Alex shot me a rueful smile, but his eyes were dark and unfathomable. "Thanks for the tip, pal."

"You were amazing in there. You're a natural."

I laughed off Alex's compliment as we walked out of the school gates. Compared to him, I hadn't had a clue what I'd been doing. Alex had stayed in goal, larking about and letting the kids score past him. He had the perfect mix of fun but sensible. I'd hardly been able to concentrate on anything other than watching him. It was getting harder to deny the obvious attraction. Alex McAllister was definitely a DILF.

"I'm not a natural, not like you. I'm terrible with children."

"Are you kidding me? Don't sell yourself short. You were great. Those kids were hanging off every word. I think we're going to see a few of those girls in the club in ten years' time."

"The girls were great. They had fire. You need fire on the pitch."

"Right, and discipline." His velvet-edged tone held me enthralled. "You need fire and discipline."

Warmth spread through my body. Fire and discipline. The fire part came naturally to me. The discipline was a work in progress. Alex thought I was good in there? Once I'd loosened up, I'd enjoyed it. It had been fun playing with the girls. They'd thrown themselves into it. Everybody had been laughing and messing around. I had a sense that I'd done something meaningful. I'd made a difference, even if it was small.

"I still don't think I'm good with kids. You're just being nice to me."

His expression became serious. "No. I'm not. I mean it. You were great. The kids loved your energy. You should keep doing this. It's good for children to have a role model they can look up to."

I rolled my eyes. "You're being so unserious. I'm not a role model."

"Of course you are. Everything you said was right. You're a woman in a man's world. You're an inspiration."

No one else had ever thought that. Everybody had their own ideas about me, and none of those ideas were good. "Try telling Claire that."

"Claire hasn't seen this side of you. Keep up this good work and no one can deny your commitment. This is bigger than the team. This is about doing something good for these kids. Maybe some of those girls will remember your words this afternoon for the rest of their lives."

I leaned into him. I'd never had a conversation like this with anyone. Alex gave such sensible advice, and I had so much to think about. I'd expected him to laugh at my ambitions or doubt my commitment like everyone else, but he had taken my goal to play for England seriously. Everything inside of me buzzed at the new possibilities to prove myself. Football had always been a way to have fun and express myself, but Alex was right, I needed to step up and really show myself on the pitch. It was time to demonstrate my commitment.

"You think this will impress Claire?"

"Maybe, but does it matter? Do it because it's good to help these kids. Anything else is a bonus."

"You're really leaning in to this whole Coach McAllister thing, huh?"

Humor glinted in his eyes. "You made a great case. I've been thinking about it. It might be time."

We rounded the corner, and he stopped next to a huge shiny silver minivan. What was it about being a parent that made you feel you needed to drive around in a tank?

He opened the passenger door for me. "I'll give you a ride back to the club."

No. This was too easy. Alex was so easy to talk to. He was so kind and encouraging. I'd tried to be Mel in that bar, but Alex hadn't been impressed by any of that stuff. He claimed to like the parts that had been me. As much as that made my heart sing, it also terrified me. Alex was the kind of man you could fall for and lose yourself over. If I wasn't careful, he'd get under my skin. I didn't do serious. Nobody had ever wanted serious from me before. I had no idea if I was even capable of it.

"No, thanks. I'll walk."

He hesitated as if he was going to say more, then shut the car door with a gentle click. A light drizzle misted my face. A crack of thunder pierced the sky.

Alex angled his face upward and peered at the gray clouds rolling overhead. "Are you sure you don't want a lift?"

Yes. I wanted a lift. I wanted Alex to tell me all the ways he thought I was good. To tell me again that I was a role model and inspirational. Everybody looked at me and saw a problem, but Alex didn't seem to.

Alex watched me with an unreadable expression. He was so handsome. My fingers itched to touch him again. To fall into his powerful embrace. To feel the heat of his body against mine. Oh God. Really? This man was sending me soft. This was bad. Really fucking bad. I couldn't catch feels for Alex McAllister just because he'd been nice to me and I'd seen him larking around with kids. He didn't want me anyway. Alex had a kid, for goodness' sake. I might have been able to win a bunch of girls round for an hour of football, but I was hardly stepmother material. Why was I even thinking about this?

Get a grip.

The rain picked up, pounding the hood of my jacket.

"Get in the car, Lana." Alex's voice was full of concern. "You're going to get soaked."

"No. Thanks. I'll see you later." I took off down the road.

Chapter 21

Lana

One week later

It was a perfect day for a wedding. A few wispy clouds laced a calm, pale-blue sky. A rose-scented breeze drifted to my nose. Birds sang from the neat hedgerows at the front of the pretty stone chapel. I turned my face up to let the sun warm my cheeks. Skylar clutched her bouquet of pastel tulips and peered up at the soaring bell tower. Those bells would ring soon, and my best friend would be married. A pang pulled at my heart.

I leaned in next to her to snap another selfie while Miri returned to the limo to greet the flower girls and hand them their bouquets.

I fluffed Skylar's bridal train. She ran a hand over her cascading blush-rose waves. "You look incredible."

She squeezed my hand. "I'm so nervous, I think I'm going to puke."

"It's not too late if you want to back out. I subbed for you as captain. If you need me to sub in and marry the doc, I'll do it."

Her eyes sparkled with humor. "Don't you want to wait until after the divorce? I thought you preferred my exes."

At least we could laugh about Sean Wallace. I was lucky to have a friend as forgiving as Skylar.

I cupped her cheeks. "You look beautiful. This is your day. Enjoy every second."

Organ music drifted from the stone-arched entrance to the chapel.

Skylar's dad coughed and stepped closer. He held out his elbow. "Ready, love?"

Skylar grinned and rolled back her inked shoulders. "I'm so ready."

◆　◆　◆

From the edge of the dance floor, I watched Skylar and Reece's first dance. They swayed together slowly, sharing smiles and kisses. In the corner, Gabe bounced his little boy up and down on his lap and mouthed along to the music. Miri hovered behind them smiling, with a hand on Gabe's shoulder. I felt a warm glow seeing my friends so content, but at the same time it gave me a horrible emptiness inside. Everyone was moving on with their lives. All my friends were leaving me behind.

My gaze fell on the tall, imposing figure of a man at the other side of the dance floor. Alexander. Even in a crowd, his formidable, masculine presence was compelling. A smart double-breasted jacket hugged his broad shoulders, and he wore a blue tartan kilt with white knee socks. He'd been dressed the same the night we'd first met. His gaze landed on mine and my heart turned over. His kind smile warmed me from across the room. We shared a secret look. Just the two of us.

Alex was the first to look away when a blonde woman sidled over to engage him in conversation. Had he brought a date? The horrible emptiness I'd been feeling shifted swiftly to jealousy. It shouldn't have mattered. He was free to date whoever he wanted. The band switched to a livelier song and couples filtered onto the floor. I kept my gaze fixed on Alex to see if he'd be dancing with the mystery blonde, but they were too involved in their conversation.

"You're not dancing?"

I turned to see a tall, muscular, dark-haired man. Miri's other brother—the hot ballet dancer one. He shot me a sidelong glance. "I'm Elliot. Miri's brother."

I kept my gaze fixed on Alex. "I know who you are."

He offered me his hand. "I'm looking for a dance partner."

He stood so close, his aftershave invaded my nose. It was nice, but it wasn't Alex's tantalizing scent. "I don't trust myself to dance with a professional. I'd only embarrass myself."

He smiled. "Maybe I could teach you a few things?"

Laughter and music rattled inside my skull. It only made me feel worse to be surrounded by so much joviality.

It would be so easy to lose myself for a night in the arms of Miri's beautiful brother, but it wouldn't change anything. A tangle in the sheets never got rid of this hollow ache inside, no matter how many times I tried to kid myself that it would. I couldn't help my gaze from drifting back to Alex. The blonde woman at his side leaned in to whisper something in his ear. My jaw felt tight and painful. Silly to be jealous. Alex wasn't mine. We weren't even a thing. We'd hooked up twice. So what?

What was wrong with me? I should have been enjoying this. I needed some air.

I gave Elliot a polite nod. "Excuse me."

He opened his mouth to say something, but I was gone before he could finish.

Chapter 22

ALEXANDER

It was the song that threw me. There was always some moment at a wedding that took me back: a fork tinkling on glass before the speeches, the organ's joyful notes, the scent of roses. This time, it was a perfect velvet baritone. The band struck up "The Way You Look Tonight", and the happy couple took to the floor. I tried to focus on them. They looked good together. I didn't know Skylar or Reece well, but they'd been kind enough to invite me. The whole club was here. I supposed they didn't want anyone to be left out.

Guilt nagged at me that I hadn't brought Brodie. He would have loved to be around all these footballers, but Rachel had convinced me to go alone. As much as I loved being a dad, sometimes I needed a night off-duty to enjoy a pint and chat with adults about non-pirate-related topics.

The happy couple swayed together and shared tender looks. Evelyn had made me go to dance lessons before our wedding. Not that it had helped. We'd been in hysterics the whole time. As a goalie, I should have been swift on my feet, but dancing was not my forte. Warmth filled me at the memories. There had been a time when memories only brought pain.

My eyes drifted back to Lana. She stood at the other side of the dance floor, chatting with a tall, dark-haired man. He was standing too close to her, his smile too bright. I had to fight every urge not to fling myself across the dance floor and elbow the handsome-looking bastard out of the way. I had no right to be jealous. I dragged my attention back to Skylar and Reece. It was a constant battle to stop my gaze from roaming again.

What would Evelyn say if she saw me getting all twisted up about a woman so young? She'd probably find it hilarious. Evelyn had been a teacher. She would have liked Lana after seeing how good she was with those schoolkids. She would have liked her sense of humor, too. Evelyn had always appreciated down-to-earth people who didn't mince their words. They would have got on well.

Lana looked beautiful—her red hair twisted in an elaborate braid, and a pretty dress clung to her incredible physique, but then, this woman always looked beautiful. That was just the surface. I was old enough to know that the surface was the least important part. It was the reading she'd done in the church that had held me transfixed. I couldn't remember a single word, something about earthquakes and roots, but there had been a tremor in her voice that made me want to go up to the lectern and stand next to her, just so she didn't have to get through it alone.

I'd watched Lana chatting with everyone here. She'd played with all the children, her laugh always carrying the loudest in a group, but underneath there was . . . something else. Lana was sad. If other people couldn't see that, they were blind. Sometimes she had this look in her eyes that made me desperate to pull her into my arms and hold the world at bay.

I had the sense that Lana wasn't the things that people said about her. Even I'd thought she was like Logan when I'd been on the wrong end of her temper, but she wasn't. I could see how much it meant to her to play for her country. She was serious about football, and fiercely loyal to her team. This woman had a huge heart, but people only saw a party girl.

I fought to tear my gaze away from her for the hundredth time. Reece twisted Skylar in his arms and pulled her close. I couldn't keep my mind from drifting back to that day in that little church in the Highlands. I'd kept my vows to Evelyn. Every one. I'd promised to love her until death parted us, and I had, with all my heart. In her last weeks, Evelyn had asked me to make a promise. She'd wanted me to find someone new to move on with. Even when she was in so much pain and sick from chemotherapy, she'd put me first.

Be happy, my love. Don't spend your life alone. Promise me you won't.

I'd held her hand, and I'd promised, but the words had been hollow. I'd never intended to try. All that had mattered was being a dad. I'd faced my grief head on for Brodie's sake. I'd poured out my heart on therapists' couches. I'd sat in dusty church halls with other widowers, drinking weak coffee and crying until I had nothing left. It had been awful and painful, but I'd done it for Brodie. Nothing else had mattered.

I'd never looked at another woman. Never even found another woman attractive until meeting Lana in that bar. It had been a jolt to the heart. A sudden rush of nerves, and excitement, and desire. All the things I'd thought long gone. She'd come at me like a hurricane, and instead of running away, I'd drawn closer.

The band struck up a livelier song, and relief made my shoulders slump. Good. I didn't want to drown in memories. Every wedding had its moments like these, but I had to focus on the happy times. My wedding day had been wonderful. Every minute I'd had with Evelyn had been a gift. She'd been a wonderful wife.

Evelyn had wanted me to be happy, not just for my sake, but also for Brodie. Now I'd had a taste of all these feelings I'd thought long dead, I wanted to be happy, too. Brodie was amazing company, and he kept me busy, but sometimes I wished I had a partner to watch TV with in the evenings. Someone to confide in at the end of the day. A woman to wake up with so my bed wasn't always empty.

My eyes drifted across the dance floor, but Lana had disappeared. So had her handsome companion. A sick disappointment and yearning assailed me. Even if I could admit to myself that I was ready to move on, it didn't mean Lana was the right choice. She'd stirred my heart again, but there were reasons not to pursue her. If I chased this woman, then I had to accept that it could only ever be casual. Lana didn't want more than that, and I wouldn't let Brodie get attached to someone who would leave us.

If I wanted to find a serious relationship, I wasn't just picking a girlfriend. I was picking a potential stepmother. Whoever I brought into our lives had to be the best choice for Brodie. A flash of teal caught my eye, and I watched Lana escape through the patio doors at the back of the hall. She was alone. A wash of relief went through me.

Every instinct told me not to follow. It was pointless. I didn't want casual, but I needed to see if Lana was alright, because I'd seen the shadows that had darkened her eyes during that reading today, even if no one else had. I wanted to be the one to chase those shadows away. Heart hammering, I skirted around the dance floor to find her.

Be happy, my love.

Chapter 23

Lana

Weddings did something crazy to your brain. All these people were trying to convince themselves that love didn't always end in despair. That you didn't always end up having to say goodbye to the people that mattered most.

I found my way onto the patio at the back of the fancy stately home. A white moon gleamed bright in the inky night. My throat ached with tears, and I didn't even know why.

My small silk clutch bag vibrated. I pulled out my phone to see Karen Delaney's face on the screen. For goodness' sake. I had to answer it. The call could be about Dad, but this was too much to deal with. Not here. Not when I was losing my best friend. Not when everyone was so happy. I had to go back in there and join in, for Skylar's sake. I didn't want her to catch me looking miserable, but first I had to deal with the problem at hand.

My thumb hovered to answer the call, but some reckless impulse made me swipe it away. The phone stopped buzzing. Relief flooded me. I'd deal with it tomorrow.

"I've been looking for you. What are you doing standing out here alone?" The low Scottish voice, so full of concern, sent a tremor through me. "Here." Alex presented me with a champagne flute.

I made no move to take the glass. "No. Thanks. I don't drink alcohol."

"You don't?" Alex's eyes were tender as he surveyed me. "The booze is flowing in there. The rest of the women on the team are very . . . merry."

That was an understatement. Things were bound to get raucous tonight. Skylar and Reece were hopping out early to start their honeymoon, and I didn't blame them. I liked to party. The tabloids assumed that was fueled by something, but I didn't need drugs or booze to be the last one on the dance floor—just a good vibe.

Alex looked incredible in his kilt, but I didn't want to be caught staring. He placed the champagne flute on a ledge. A waiting silence built between us as he surveyed the dark tree line. The night air kicked at my flimsy bridesmaid dress.

A great shiver wracked me. "It's cold. You should go back inside."

Before I could protest, Alex wrapped his smart blazer around my shoulders. The material swamped me, but the warmth instantly soothed me like a hug. His familiar cologne was a drug to my senses.

"Thanks." I pulled the jacket tight.

"You make a beautiful bridesmaid." He held out his hand. "Will you come inside and dance with me?"

"I don't want to go back inside."

"Why not?"

Because I'm sad.

Because my best friend is getting married and I should be happy for her but all I can hear is goodbye.

131

I turned to face him. "How will your date like you dancing with another woman?"

"My date?"

"I saw you in there talking to a blonde."

"That's Lauren from the press office. She was trying to sign me up for a podcast interview."

"Oh." A strange relief washed over me and my shoulders loosened. "Right. Well. Good for you."

Alex cleared his throat. His eyes shone bright in the pale light of the moon and a faint smile pulled at his lips. "Dance with me out here if you don't want to go inside. This is my only chance. I can't dance at home. Brodie always laughs at my embarrassing 'dad dancing'."

He held out his hand, and I let him pull me toward him. One large hand rested at the small of my back and the other clasped my palm. A faint pulse of music drifted from the party inside, and we swayed together in the moonlight. Alex's enormous feet shifted from side to side. I rested my head against his chest. The height difference made it awkward.

"I turned down a professional dancer for this."

"You're not impressed?"

"I think your son might be onto something."

He chuckled at my teasing. I relaxed against him and a deep, warm peace filled me. What was this feeling? Like fear and safety at the same time—half nerves, half delight. It was the point at the top of a roller coaster when the terror and thrill of the plummet could be rationalized by knowing the bar would hold me in the seat. Being close to him made me afraid, but I couldn't ignore the deep sense in my gut that Alex was a good guy. The best I'd known. He wouldn't hurt me on purpose. It didn't mean that he wouldn't hurt me. Sometimes, we hurt people without meaning to. It wasn't as though Mum had ever wanted to say goodbye. She was taken from us. Claire's voice rang in my head.

Who said life was fair?

"Everyone likes weddings. I don't."

He twirled me in his arms and pulled me back into his embrace. "Why?"

"They always make me feel like a side character in someone else's perfect life. Love is bullshit. It always ends in tears."

He drew his lips in as we swayed together in silence. "Does it always?"

"Yes. There is always a goodbye, and that part hurts too much." I tilted my face to his. "I'm not going to fall for you, if that's what you're thinking. You can show up here looking sexy in your kilt. You can keep wrapping me in your coat when I'm cold, and having that accent, and asking me to dance like this, but you should know I'm immune to your charms."

He raised a bemused eyebrow, but stayed silent.

Laughter and frivolity drifted from the party. Alex was so different to the men I'd been with before. He was kind and considerate—always checking in with how I felt. Always offering me a lift somewhere.

There was something so soothing about being able to relax with another person and knowing that he wanted to take care of me. Alex was stable and dependable. He was the kind of guy who would want to be in charge of the passports at the airport and bring you soup when you got sick. This felt safe . . . and right, but I didn't do this. There was no such thing as safe. I'd said I wouldn't fall for him, I couldn't lose myself over a guy.

But what if this is what I need?

A line appeared between Alex's brows. "Did Sean Wallace do this to you?"

My heart jolted. Did he know I'd told secrets to Karen Delaney? "What?"

"Is this why you have so many defenses? I heard the two of you . . . dated. Did Sean Wallace break your heart?"

I couldn't help my indignant laugh. "Sean Wallace? No. And I wouldn't date that arsehole in a million years."

"Then, what? What made you build all these walls?"

Life.

Alex's voice was hoarse. "I have defenses, too. I'm scared to take a risk. I loved my wife with all my heart. I still love her, even though she isn't here physically. The memories that we shared are always with me. Sometimes I feel like I won't ever be ready to start something new. It broke me when I lost her, but it doesn't mean it wasn't worth loving. I think this pain is the price you pay for love."

A faint smile curved his full lips. "If you don't take risks with your heart, then you miss out on wonderful things. I'd never trade what I had with Evelyn while she was here. Just because you say goodbye doesn't mean love ends. The pain you feel is the love you shared. You keep it with you."

How did he do that? How did he talk about his grief with such grace? It was so painful to talk about Mum. Nobody in our house dared speak her name.

I cleared my throat. "I'm sorry for your loss."

I realized for the first time that we'd stopped dancing. Alex held me in his arms. His huge frame like a giant redwood, standing tall and firm. Strong. Protective. Caring.

I swallowed past the lump in my throat. Alex's grace gave me strength. I wanted to tell him about Mum. About all the ways that life had wounded me over the years since we lost her, but the words wedged in my throat.

No. I can't do this.

"You can talk to me, Lana. You can trust me—"

I covered his mouth with mine to shut him up. He held perfectly still, then his lips moved in response. His huge hand rested

134

at the side of my neck. My heart sang as he kissed me. It was a kiss full of sweetness, not the breathless, hungry, devouring kind that I always craved from him. His tongue glided against mine, and I drank in his gentleness. His solid, soothing presence grounded me.

I broke away from his mouth to whisper into his ear. "I want you to come home with me tonight. No strings. Just fun and done. Will you?"

"Aye, sweetheart," he whispered against my lips. "I told you, I'll give you anything you want."

Chapter 24

Lana

We kissed in the dark hallway of my apartment. Alex's large hands explored the curves of my hips through my silk dress.

I broke away from the kiss. "I have to take a quick shower." I'd been on my feet all day at the wedding, and I needed to freshen up.

He pulled me back into his arms. "No. I'm not letting you go."

Laughing, I broke free of him. "Do you want me to get you a drink while you wait?"

He pulled me back into his arms for another breath-stealing kiss before he released me. "Be quick."

"I will." An idea sprang to mind. "Unless you want to join me?"

His gaze dropped over my body. "I can't say no to that."

I took his hand and led him upstairs. I said a silent prayer that I'd tidied my apartment before I left for the wedding. Inside the cream marble bathroom, Alex leaned against the tiled wall, watching me as I stripped. I turned on the shower and stepped in. Hot water beat a delicious rhythm on my bare skin.

"Aren't you getting in?"

A smile curved his mouth. "All in good time."

I lathered myself, smoothing soapy bubbles all over my hips and stomach, and caressing my breasts with silky foam. My nipples firmed into hard pebbles under Alex's heated gaze. "Do you like to watch me, Big Mac?"

"Aye. I like to watch." The rough edge to his voice made my heart pound.

I swiped my palm through the steam that misted the shower door, giving him a clearer view through the glass. An ache pulsed between my thighs. I couldn't resist slipping my fingers down to relieve it. A shiver rippled through me as the hot water pounded. I surrendered to Alex's intense gaze and the delicious pleasure at my core, building to a desperate peak.

I could open the shower door and drag him inside, but I liked him like this, intense and eager. Alex's voice and the way he looked at me as though he'd never be able to look away was enough to push me toward the edge.

I positioned myself so that Alex had a better view. "Do you like this? Knowing that you can look, but you can't touch."

His gaze fixed where my fingers worked between my legs. "I can't touch?"

Pounding water enveloped me in satisfying heat and steam. "No."

My breath came in sharp gasps as I moved my fingers faster. The torturous need inside of me intensified.

Alex cleared his throat; his deep, soothing voice was raw with need. "You like teasing me, don't you?"

"Am I teasing you?"

"I know your game, Lana Sinclair. You know you have the most incredible body." He stepped closer to the steamy glass. "You know full well seeing you like this would drive anyone wild."

"What if I like being wild? The papers call me a wild child. Don't you know that about me by now?"

"I know. I also know what wild girls need."

"What do I need?"

He looked me squarely in the eyes. "A firm hand."

A ripple of pleasure went through me. He pressed his palm flat against the glass. "You're going to bring yourself to the edge and then stop."

"Stop?"

"If I'm not allowed to touch, then you're not allowed to come until I say so. You're not the only one who likes to tease. Do you understand, sweetheart?"

I bit down on my lip. His rough words made pleasure spark under my fingers. I kept my hand still, fighting every urge to keep up the delicious friction. My orgasm teetered out of reach, calling me like a siren to smash and fall apart in a stormy sea.

Alex licked his lips. "Are you on the edge?"

The word was more a moan. "Yes."

"Turn off the shower."

I did as he commanded. The pounding water had been so loud, I hadn't realized until the heavy silence swept in. Cold air made my bare skin prickle, but my muscles were still deliciously loose and heated. The desperate throb between my legs was unbearable as my orgasm began to slip away. I pressed my thighs together, desperate to reclaim it.

"Again. Bring yourself to the edge and stop."

Shit. What was he trying to do to me? He cocked his head to watch me, and I let my hand slip down between my thighs again. A moan left my lips at the relief of attending to the divine pulse. My fingers worked frantically. It only took seconds to reach a peak again.

I slapped my hand on the wall. "Oh. Ah. Ah, I'm going to—"

"Stop. Put your hands by your sides. Don't move a muscle."

My fingers froze. A strange cry of frustration left my mouth. My orgasm hovered so close, behind a veil, taunting me.

Slowly and methodically, Alex began to strip. His sure fingers worked the buttons of his shirt and the socks until he only wore his kilt. His impressive torso rippled with muscle as he removed the heavy woolen fabric from around his middle, leaving him completely bare. My gaze dropped to his impressive erection, standing thick and hard against his toned abdomen. A seductive smile played on his lips.

A sensuous rush made my body flash with heat. "Let me come now. I need it."

"Ask me nicely, and I'll think about it."

Another rough groan escaped me. "Please. I need you to come in here. Enough messing about."

Cold air engulfed me as he swung open the shower door. In one forward motion, I was in his arms. His lips crashed down onto mine, claiming my mouth in a hungry kiss.

He pulled away. His breath fanned my face. "One more time, sweetheart. Bring yourself to the edge and stop. It drives me wild seeing you like this. I promise I'll make it worth your while."

He didn't need to tell me twice. My fingers found my sensitive nerves, and a groan left my lips. Alex's mouth captured mine again, smothering my moans of pleasure. Icy air licked my rapidly cooling skin. Shivers wracked my body.

"Oh God. I'm too close. I can't do this anymore . . . I can't. Please. I'm nearly there—"

"Stop."

A tormented scream wedged in my throat. Hot, pulsing need made my body ache in exquisite agony. "No. Please."

"Turn around. Put your hands on the wall."

Every nerve in my body willed me not to stop, but somehow I forced my palms flat to the cubicle wall. Alex stepped behind me.

His lips grazed my ear and his erection prodded my back. He bent down to whisper into my wet hair. "I don't know what's going on here. You want me to suffer. Look, but don't touch? You don't get to do that to me."

He swatted my ass playfully with his huge palm. A gasp escaped me. Stinging pleasure raced across my backside. The unendurable throb between my thighs intensified. Once, we'd been strangers in a bar. Now, I couldn't imagine a time when I hadn't known Alex McAllister.

"I want you to be mine. All of you. I want these to be mine." Alex reached around me. His large hands slid over my soapy breasts, caressing them and pushing them together. "Just for me. I don't want anyone else touching you."

Shivers of delight shot through me. His hands slid over my hips and around my stomach. "I want every inch of you as mine."

The aching need between my thighs was driving me wild. I groaned and pressed my thighs together, desperate to relieve the ache.

"No. You don't." Alex's knee nudged in between my legs, separating them. "Not until I say so."

He took my hands and held them high over my head. He wrapped one hand around my wrists and pinned me in place. With his other hand, he grabbed my wet hair in his fist, pulling me back lightly, making me arch for him.

"Are you going to behave?"

"Yes."

He released my hair, but kept my hands locked high above my head. Blood coursed hot and excited through my veins. My whole body sang with desire.

Part of me wanted to sass him, and wind him up, but I was so desperate to come my knees shuddered. This was too much. No more teasing or sparring. I needed him to put me out of my misery.

140

Alex's tight grip around my wrists forbade me from slipping my fingers to my throbbing core. Desperation gripped me.

"No. Please. I can't do it anymore."

Instantly, he released me. Twisting me to face him, he dropped to his knees.

"Spread your beautiful legs for me."

My soul almost left my body at the first firm press of his hot tongue against my pulsing flesh. He held my weight up with his hands as my legs quivered uncontrollably. I squirmed, and rocked back and forth against his mouth, desperate for relief. Just when I couldn't take another moment, he grabbed my hips and filled me in one hot thrust. The instant he entered me, I shattered around him.

An agonized cry left my lips, and the siren call of my orgasm finally claimed me in a pure, explosive release. My body clenched and gripped him greedily. I cried out and clawed his strong back and slippery shoulders. He kept working me in smooth thrusts, until every last wave of ecstasy coursed through me. My body sagged, and he caught me in his arms.

Drunk on my orgasm, I could barely stand. Alex guided me out of the shower and wrapped me in a warm, soft towel. He carried me to my bedroom and laid me down on the bed, pulling the duvet over me. Blood still pounded through my body, and my skin tingled with heat and pleasure. He planted a kiss on my forehead. Water soaked his hair and dripped onto my bedroom floor.

He stroked my wet hair back from my face. "You rest now. Are you okay? Was it too much?"

"No. Not too much." Fatigue pressed my soft muscles into the bed. "Never too much . . ."

Alex's whisky eyes lingered in the folds of my mind as sleep claimed me.

Chapter 25

ALEXANDER

"Morning, sweetheart." I put a tray laden with toast and eggs onto the side table next to Lana's bed.

She pushed her red hair behind her ear and reached for a glass of orange juice. "Look at this. Nobody has ever made me breakfast."

"Really?"

She propped pillows behind her back and sat up. A wry smile ghosted her lips. "I usually kick them out before they get a chance. No one stays over here. It's one of my rules. I've never spent the night with anyone before."

No one ever stayed, but she'd let me stay. Not that she'd put much forethought into the decision. Still, it had to mean something.

She stretched her slender legs and munched on her toast. "What are you doing this weekend?"

"I'll take Brodie to the park. Little boys need airing out or they go stir crazy. What are your plans?"

She shrugged. "Not much."

She nibbled her toast and fell silent. The same sadness crept into her eyes that had lingered last night. I was no stranger to loneliness. I knew it, intimately. The last thing I wanted was for Lana to feel lonely. I could invite her out with me and Brodie, but that felt like a leap too far.

Although, perhaps it didn't have to be a big thing. Brodie had met Lana at the school. For all he knew, Lana and I were just friends. It wasn't as though Brodie hadn't met friends of mine before. Lana wasn't a girlfriend. She'd broken one of her rules by letting me stay. I could break mine and introduce her to Brodie, as long as I kept things casual.

"You could come round to mine tonight? I'll cook you dinner."

The words were out of my mouth before I could mull them over properly.

She frowned and stared at me. An old ache burned between my shoulder blades. My heart pounded as I waited for her response. The obvious issue whispered in my mind. Maybe Lana didn't want to spend the day with a man and his kid. Maybe it was a step too far for her as well.

She smoothed a hand over the duvet with studied disinterest. "What about your son?"

"He goes to bed around 8 p.m. If you want to say hi to him, come a little earlier and I'll tell him you're my friend. If not, come after he's gone to bed."

I'd kick the ball back to her side of the pitch. She had the chance to back out if this was too much for her.

"A friend? I suppose that sounds better than telling him I'm your fuck buddy."

I couldn't help my laugh. I'd never met anyone so direct. "We definitely don't tell him that." I held my hands up in mock surrender. "It's fine if it's too much. Come after he's gone to bed. This doesn't have to be a thing if you don't want that—"

"No. I want to . . . I mean, not that I want this to be a thing . . . It's definitely not a thing . . . but I'd like to see Brodie again." Her curious gaze flickered to mine. "I didn't think you'd want me to."

"I do." I moved to the door. "My sister has an appointment. I can't be late. I'll text you my address."

Throwing back the duvet, she patted the spot next to her. "Are you sure you have to rush off?"

The smoldering heat in her eyes made me stiffen. Damn it. This woman was divine. What I wouldn't give to climb back into that bed. Rachel would roast me alive if I was late. I'd already dropped Brodie on her for the wedding. It took every effort not to get back into the bed.

I kissed the tip of her nose. "I'm sorry. Daddy duties."

"I understand. I like it when you're Daddy." She gave me a seductive smile that turned into a chuckle. "And you never need to apologize for being a good dad to your son." She cupped my cheek. "You're sure about later? You're happy for me to spend time with Brodie?"

She held her smile in place, but vulnerability lurked in the green depths of her eyes. Did this matter to her? What were we doing here, exactly? This couldn't end up anywhere good. Lana had joked about fuck buddies, but I'd never done casual. Lana didn't want to open up or get close, but I couldn't deny how much I wanted her. It wasn't just sex. I wanted to be around her—to take care of her. I wanted to put a smile back on her face when that sadness crept around her beautiful eyes.

There were so many reasons to put a stop to this. We were at different stages in our lives. This couldn't end up anywhere but heartache, but every scrap of time I spent with her left me craving more. It didn't have to be heavy. That wasn't what Lana wanted. Maybe it didn't have to be a big thing with Brodie, either. I couldn't risk him getting attached and then abandoned, but I was allowed to have friends. Brodie had met my friends.

I drank in Lana's tangle of wild red hair and her bright green eyes. We could keep it casual. My priority had to be protecting Brodie, but maybe it was time I had something light in my life. Someone like Lana.

Chapter 26

LANA

Alex's immense stone house dominated the surrounding countryside—huge and impressive, like its owner. I cursed under my breath as my heeled boots crunched over the sweeping gravel driveway. This place must have cost a fortune. Male Premier League footballers got paid astronomical wages, while the women who played the same game got a fraction. I'd kick up another fuss about it next time I saw Gabe. To give him his due, Gabe paid us better than most of the other women's teams in the country, but I wouldn't be happy until we could all afford bloody castles too.

I had to deposit the bags of presents I'd brought for Brodie on the floor in order to ring the doorbell. A sudden surge of nerves held my finger frozen over the doorbell. I'd met Brodie for five seconds in that playground. He might not like me, and then what? Alex wouldn't want to see me again if his son didn't want me around. What did it matter? It wasn't as if I wanted anything serious with Alex anyway. This was fun and done. Apart from the fact that I'd let him stay over and now I was here playing happy families. Shaking the nerves away, I rang the doorbell.

After a moment, the door swung open. Alex's heated gaze traveled downward over the camel shift dress and court shoes I'd borrowed from Mel's wardrobe, and when I say borrowed, I mean swiped the last time I'd visited her apartment. Dressing more like Mel had seemed like a good idea at the time. I had no idea how to make a good impression on Brodie, but a chic outfit had to be a good start, right?

A smile pulled at Alex's lips. "You look . . . smart."

"Good smart?"

He stepped aside to let me in. "You always look good."

I peered past Alex down the hallway. "Where is Brodie?"

"He's glued to his games console. I'll have to send a team of stampeding horses to drag him away."

I passed him the box with the chocolate cake.

He raised an eyebrow. "What's this?"

"It's a chocolate cake . . . homemade."

"I hope you didn't go to any trouble."

I shrugged. "It was nothing."

Lies. It had taken all day. This was the third attempt, and it still looked terrible. It had been so bad, I'd been tempted to call Skylar, but I doubted she'd appreciate an international call on her honeymoon just to explain how to coax a cake to rise higher than a centimeter.

"I also brought Brodie some things."

I passed Alex the bag of stuff I'd bought from the kids' section in the supermarket. I'd played it safe and filled the shopping cart with books and games that the assistant had deemed suitable for a seven-year-old.

Alex peered inside the bag.

"What is it? Did I get the wrong stuff?"

"No. Nothing is wrong." He wore an uncertain expression as he studied my face. "You didn't have to buy all this. Is everything

146

okay?" He held out his hands to take my coat. "Is this worrying you? If it's too much, you can come around later once Brodie has gone to bed . . ."

I slipped off my coat and passed it to Alex. "I want to make a good impression with Brodie. It's important to me."

"It is?" His eyes clung to my face.

Yes. That must have been why my heart had pounded all the way over here. This mattered to me. It mattered way more than I wanted to admit, but it definitely mattered. Shit. Why did it matter?

Alex hung up my coat and turned back to me. He cupped my face with one huge palm. "Just be yourself. You're great, Lana. Anyone can see that you're great."

My skin tingled under his touch. I couldn't help but lean into him, like a puppy seeking affection. If I hadn't been here to meet Brodie, I would have been dragging Alex up the stairs to the bedroom.

Alex called up the stairs. "Brodie? Are you joining us?"

"I'm still playing." The shout rang down the stairs.

Alex shook his head and pinched the bridge of his nose. "Kids, eh? Sorry. I'll fetch him."

Alex strode up the stairs and disappeared around the corner. A muttered conversation drifted to my ears, then Alex appeared with his "mini-me" behind him. My heart pounded with every step until they planted themselves in front of me.

"Brodie, you remember Lana?"

"Yeah." Brodie stood at his dad's side. His golden curls gleamed in the bright hall lights as he inclined his head to regard me. "Do you still like pirates?"

"Always. Obviously."

An excited grin lit Brodie's face and he shuffled from side to side. The kid was fizzing with energy, as though he'd been unhooked

147

from charge on a docking station. "You can be the pirate queen. I'll be Blackbeard."

Before I could reply, he darted up the stairs and skidded out of sight.

I shot Alex a glance. "What's going on?"

Alex sighed and rocked back on his heels. "You shouldn't have told him you know about pirates. You're in trouble now. Swashbuckling is the key to his heart."

Brodie raced back down the stairs two at a time so fast in his socks, it was a miracle he didn't slide down. He thrust a plastic sword into my palm and his soft hand wrapped around mine to drag me down the hallway. "Come on, then."

"Where are we going?"

"We're playing pirates. When that gets boring, we'll do the floor is lava. You can decide what to play after that. This is going to be fun."

Chapter 27

Lana

I moved around the enormous kitchen collecting plates and tidying while Alex was upstairs putting Brodie to bed. Brodie made almost as much mess as my dad.

"That went well."

I turned to see Alex leaning in the doorway with a warm smile on his face. "Brodie wouldn't stop talking about you. I didn't think he'd ever fall asleep."

A shaft of light from the kitchen window struck his hair. The dark gray around his temples gleamed like polished silver. Alex had been so caring and even-tempered with Brodie. I'd never met a man that felt so . . . safe. Maybe because I'd wasted so much time on boys. Alex was a real man. Responsible and in charge. Every match, Alex's team relied on him to save the game, and his son depended on him and him alone. He carried his responsibilities so effortlessly.

I plunged another bowl into the hot, soapy water. Alex crossed the kitchen, took the wet bowl from my hand and put it on the drying rack.

"No washing dishes for you." His hands curved around my waist and he spun me to face him. "You don't have to lift a finger here."

"I like to help."

"You're the guest. I'm taking care of you." He planted a kiss in the hollow of my neck. "I like taking care of you."

"You do?"

His hands locked against my spine and he pulled me into his strong arms. Alex was all man, but his smile was boyishly affectionate. "Yes. I do. When you'll let me."

"I'm independent." I wound my arms underneath his woolen sweater and around his back. "I don't need a man to take care of me."

"I know you don't need it. It doesn't mean I don't like being there for you."

I rested my head against his hard chest. It had been a fun day. We'd played football outside together most of the afternoon. It had been difficult playing in Mel's tight dress, but I'd kicked off her heels, and we'd still had fun. Alex had clowned around, letting Brodie kick a couple of balls past him into the net.

I shot him a teasing look. "You let that goal in earlier, didn't you?"

His laugh reverberated through his chest. "No. I'm too competitive for that. It was all you."

"There's something about scoring against one of the best goalkeepers in the Premier League that turns me on."

A flash of humor glinted in his eyes. "*One of* the best?"

I laughed. "Do you really need me to massage your ego?"

His hands slipped up my bare arms. "No. I know I'm the best."

My skin tingled under his huge palms. "You're the best at a lot of things."

"Oh yeah?"

I dropped my hands to the button of his jeans. "Yeah."

He grabbed my hands and held them still. A frown creased his brow. "Brodie hasn't been sleeping well lately." He shot a wary glance toward the kitchen door. "We could watch a movie together?" His lips pulled into an uncertain smile. "Is that okay? It doesn't feel right when Brodie is upstairs. I can call you a cab if you prefer . . . ?"

It wasn't what I'd been hoping to get up to tonight but snuggling up on the couch with Alex's huge arms around me sounded pretty good. I couldn't remember the last time I'd cuddled with a guy just for the sake of it. Touching always led to sex, but this was nice too. Just touching because it felt so good to be touching.

"Do you have popcorn?"

"Of course."

"Then I'll stay."

"Good." He pressed his face into my neck and murmured, "I don't think this could have gone any better."

His lips seared over my skin as he planted kisses up my neck and his mouth found mine. My body molded to the contours of his. Fine, so we couldn't have sex, but kissing was still good. Alex was an incredible kisser. He kissed the same way he did everything—with intensity but also with care and purpose. My heart hammered wildly, and he tightened his grip around me. He pressed hot kisses against my throat. My head fell back and I raked my hands through his soft hair. A moan escaped my lips.

"Daddy?"

Alex couldn't have sprung away from me faster if I'd spontaneously burst into flames. Brodie stood in the hallway, blinking and rubbing sleep from his eyes. The little boy's tired gaze swept between us and he frowned. A grim expression darkened Alex's handsome face, and he smoothed his smile into something neutral. Was it so bad that Brodie had caught us? Why was it so terrible?

It shouldn't have mattered to me that Alex was so horrified by the prospect, but it did. It really did, and that bothered me.

What if we wanted to keep this going? We couldn't sneak around and hide it from Brodie forever, but this look on Alex's face told me everything. He'd never be okay with this. Of course his son would always come first, but did that mean he'd never want to date anyone? Or just me? I'd shown up looking as good as I could in Mel's fancy clothes, with a ton of presents for Brodie, and it still wasn't enough for Alex. I'd tried so hard. I'd even made a disastrous attempt at a cake, and he didn't want me.

"Couldn't sleep, pal? Come on. Let's get you back to bed. We can read more *Matilda* . . ."

Brodie twisted in Alex's arms. He smiled shyly and held out his hand to me. "Can Lana read to me?"

Chapter 28

Alexander

Soft green light from Brodie's nightlight spilled through the open door of his bedroom out onto the landing. I crept, as quietly as I could, to peer inside. Brodie lay snuggled in Lana's arms in his small bed. They were both fast asleep and snoring softly. The book was still in Lana's loose grip on her lap. I crossed the room to wake Lana, but something stopped me. I couldn't help but take a moment to study them when both their faces were smooth and relaxed by sleep.

In the dim light, Lana's beautiful face was both delicate and strong. She'd been so nervous about being around the kids in the school and meeting Brodie, when she had no reason to be. Lana had a charm and warmth about her that couldn't be faked. Kids saw straight through adults to the truth of a person. They all loved Lana.

I pulled the duvet over the pair of them. I couldn't wake Lana when she looked so peaceful. Instead, I sank down to sit on the other side of the room on the floor with my back against the bookcase. The dark stillness of Brodie's bedroom wrapped around me. The rows of teddies and action figures that lined the shelves watched me as though willing me to answer questions I wasn't prepared to think about.

A permanent sorrow had taken root in my heart ever since I'd lost Evelyn. Nothing could ever soothe it or make it better. I'd loved my wife with every fiber of my being. I'd always carry her with me. There was no such thing as moving on. There was just learning to live with loss because life went on whether you wanted it to or not. At the start, I hadn't wanted it to, but I'd kept going for Brodie.

For the first time in a long time, a flame had kindled inside of me that I'd thought long extinguished. I'd never wanted to fall in love again. Evelyn had been the woman I wanted to spend the rest of my life with. She'd been my world. Loving another person after such a deep love had always seemed impossible, but loving again didn't mean I didn't still love Evelyn and carry her with me. I always would.

I couldn't tear my eyes away from Brodie wrapped in Lana's arms. A thread of a whole new future spun out ahead of me, gauzy and dangerous. If I reached to grab it, it could so easily fray and disappear. I didn't dare imagine it. What if this was how it could be between us? Could this woman love us like this? Would she take us both? She'd have to. We came as a package deal. Me and Brodie. How could a twenty-six-year-old woman accept that? Lana was wise beyond her years, but it was asking too much. She had her whole life ahead of her. I couldn't saddle her down.

I tried to snuff the glow inside. My body ached with the longing. I didn't just want Lana in my bed, although heaven knows I liked her there. It wasn't enough. I wanted her like this. I wanted a family again. Not just for me, but for Brodie. My eyes filled with sudden tears. It had been so long since I'd cried. Something vivid had come to life in my head, which I'd never even dared imagine. There were so many reasons that it couldn't be. It was too much to hope for.

But for now, I could imagine.

In the dark stillness of my son's room, I could sit, and, watch, and dream.

◆ ◆ ◆

Pain radiated along my spine. The shrill chatter of the birds filled my ears. I opened my eyes. A line of toy soldiers stared down at me. My back ached as I pulled myself up to sit. Rob would throw a fit if I missed training. My eyes flew to Brodie's soccer ball digital alarm clock. My shoulders dropped with relief. Sunday. Of course. Thank God. A groan escaped my lips as I stretched my arms above my head. I was too old for a night sleeping on a hard floor. Lana's eyes flickered open and met mine. She smoothed her hands over her hair, which gleamed with gold tones in the morning light.

"What time is it?"

I pointed to Brodie's alarm clock. "Eight a.m. You fell asleep last night reading to Brodie."

She covered her yawn with her hand and peered down at the sleeping boy in her arms. "You should have woken me."

"I meant to, but you both looked so peaceful. I sat down here, and I must have nodded off too."

"I should go."

"You don't have to rush. Let me make you breakfast."

She lowered her voice. "We said dinner. You don't want Brodie to know I stayed over, do you? I don't want to make things weird for you."

"It's okay. It's not weird."

But it could get weird. If my heart insisted on this path, it could get dangerous for me and Brodie. Last night, he'd seen me and Lana kiss. What was going through his head? I'd have to talk to him about it. I'd had a moment of weakness. I'd let myself think

155

that this thing with Lana could be a possibility. Brodie's needs still came first. How could this be the right thing for him?

The doorbell rang out from downstairs. My knees creaked as I got up and moved to the window. I poked a finger through the blind and caught sight of Rachel's car. Strange. Usually, she'd text first.

"It's my sister. Excuse me. I'll just be a minute."

I went downstairs, smoothing my crumpled T-shirt and flattening my unruly hair as I went. I'd seen Rachel yesterday. Hopefully, she wouldn't notice I was wearing the same clothes. I swung the door open to greet her.

"Everything okay? Why aren't you ready?" Rachel's shrewd gaze swept over me, and she hitched a brow. "Don't tell me you forgot."

"Forgot what?"

She held up a carryall stuffed with towels. "The water park?"

The realization slapped me in the face. The water park. We'd arranged it weeks ago. It was in the next town. Rachel had wanted to get an early start so we could get a full day there.

Rachel sighed. My sister had always been a stickler for punctuality. "We agreed to set off early. You know I hate being late. It gets too busy."

"Are you talking about Splash Zone? Is that today?"

Brodie's excited cry rang out from the top of the stairs. He sprinted down so fast, it was a miracle he stayed on both feet. He practically buzzed with excitement as he planted himself eagerly in front of Rachel. "We're going, aren't we?"

I smoothed my fingers through his soft curls. "We're not ready. You haven't even had breakfast. Auntie Rachel doesn't want to wait around. We might have to go next time."

Brodie's bottom lip trembled. "I can eat in the car. Lana can come too if she wants." He put his hands together in prayer. "Please, Daddy."

Rachel's eyes widened. Her voice rose in surprise. "Lana?"

My mouth clenched tight. How could I explain this one? There would be too many questions. I couldn't help but dart a glance upstairs. Lana hadn't come down to introduce herself. I didn't know whether to feel disappointed or relieved.

"It doesn't matter." I tried to shove Brodie back behind me. "I promise I'll take you another time."

Brodie stood firm, resisting my attempts to budge him. "But I want to go. Let's ask Lana. She'll want to come."

"Go upstairs and get dressed, please."

Brodie threw his hands up at the injustice, shot me a poisonous look, and raced upstairs.

Rachel made a shockingly poor attempt to keep the excitement from her voice. "Who's Lana?"

"A friend."

Rachel peered over my head up the stairs. "She's here now?"

I twisted to check Brodie was out of earshot and kept my voice low. "Lana was reading to Brodie last night, and we all fell asleep. I know what you're thinking. It's irresponsible. It's too soon to have a woman stay over. I shouldn't be introducing her to Brodie, and even then I don't know how I would ever do that. He's been through so much—"

"Stop." She reached for my hand and squeezed it. Her tone was gentle. "Don't do that. You don't have to explain yourself."

I dared a glance into my sister's eyes. "She really is just a friend."

"Fine, and if she wasn't . . . if you met someone and you wanted more than that . . . that's fine, too. It's okay. Evelyn wouldn't have wanted you to be alone forever. She told you that herself. I'll always have Brodie, if you ever want to go out or you want the house to yourself."

She glanced up the stairs. "Why don't I take Brodie today? Give me his swimming shorts and a towel. We'll get out of your hair."

157

No. Three kids would be hard work alone at a water park. "I wouldn't ask you to do that."

She hitched the carryall high on her shoulder. "It's fine. Rae and Amber are strong swimmers. I'll keep an eye on Brodie, don't worry." She raised a suggestive eyebrow. "I'd take the offer if I were you. You can have the house to yourself for the rest of the day."

Would Lana want to stick around? I didn't want to crowd her, but the idea of a whole day alone together made my heart pound with excitement.

Rachel shot another curious glance up the stairs and whispered, "What's she like? This Lana?"

Divine. Delicious. Far too young.

"She's . . . nice. She plays for the women's team."

"A football player?" Rachel beamed. "That's wonderful. It's so great that you have that in common. Do I get to meet her?"

I swallowed. It was amazing enough that Lana had been so keen to spend time with Brodie; I couldn't imagine she'd be interested in meeting my sister. "Maybe not yet."

"Okay." Rachel clapped her hands together with childish delight. "This is great. I knew the move down here would do you good."

Please don't get too excited, Rachel. Lana was incredible, but I still couldn't reconcile how to do this and protect Brodie. Still, my heart swam with everything—sorrow, excitement, fear. I let it all move through me. Rachel had said that I could hold all of it, and maybe she was right. I could mourn my wife, and still hope to meet someone new. Evelyn had wanted me to find someone. I could almost hear her words in my head.

Be happy, my love.

Rachel tapped her watch. "It's decided. You're going to have a fun day with your new woman, and I'm going to have a day wrangling three kids at Splash Zone." Her eyes grew openly amused. "Never say I'm not good to you."

Chapter 29

LANA

Brodie's laughter drifted upstairs before the slam of the front door rang out. I moved to the bathroom, finally safe to hop in the shower. My mind drifted back to when Brodie had wanted me to snuggle next to him to read the story. I'd been reluctant at first. Perhaps it was crossing a line that would make Alex mad, but it had felt natural. It had felt wonderful, actually. It reminded me of the times Mum had read to me in bed. Just the two of us in a peaceful little cocoon.

I caught a glimpse of my reflection and braced my hands on the sink. I couldn't help but laugh incredulously at the woman who stared back. This wasn't me. What the hell was this man doing to me? I'd never been this mushy over a guy before. This was how other girls like Miri and Skylar acted. They'd fallen hard. Sure, it was all good for now, but later down the line, when the shit hit the fan, I'd be the friend picking up the pieces. There would always be pieces to pick up. Nobody had loved and not let it destroy them.

I wrapped a towel around myself and drifted to Alex's bedroom in search of a hairdryer. A huge double bed dominated the space. Silver-framed family photographs covered the walls. A dark-haired woman in an ivory gown beamed at me from a host of wedding pictures. I brushed a finger over a photo of Alex. He stood in front of an elegant stone chapel. His hair held no trace of gray and his eyes were bright and youthful, with none of the lines that crinkled the corners now.

"What are you doing in here?" The rough edge to Alex's voice startled me.

My neck warmed with guilt. I turned my back on the wedding photos. "I'm sorry. I was looking for a hairdryer."

His gaze slid to the photos that crammed the walls. "I don't have one."

I pulled my towel tighter around myself. It was strange to be half naked with him in this room with all these happy photos of his wife. Had Skylar's wedding reminded him of his own special day? Was it hard for him to be there? It had been five years, and Alex had only just been intimate with someone again. I'd always kept things casual with men, but maybe this was a big deal for him. To my shame, I hadn't really considered it.

"Your wife looks lovely in these photos."

He stood next to me. "Yes. She was." He let out an audible breath and gazed at the image. "The first couple of years, I was walking around in a daze. I was trying not to drop to the ground like a toddler every five minutes and weep. I had to carry on for Brodie, but I thought the pain was going to kill me."

His voice cracked, and he turned his face away. "Evelyn would want me to be happy again. Not just for me, but for Brodie too. I moved down here because I want to heal. I made a decision that I don't want to be this sad, grief-stricken dad forever. When you lose love, it makes a hole in you. You never know, when you walk around in this world, who is doing everything they can just to hold things together, but I want to be happy sometimes, too. I want that for Brodie's sake. Evelyn will always be with me, but I can only move forward, not back."

His eyes were full of sadness, but also warmth, and life. Alex was so open. I owed it to him to give him something in return. "It's nice that you have all these photos on display." I took a breath and swallowed past the lump in my throat. "Dad took all the photos of Mum down and hid them away. I don't think he could deal with seeing her."

"How old were you when you lost your mother?"

Memories battered my brain. *Mum's green eyes, like sunlight dappling leaves. The warm brush of her fingers through my hair.* The pain in my heart had lessened over the years, but it was still enough to wind me if I dwelled too long.

"Fifteen."

"I'm sorry. It must have been a terrible time."

Silence swept in. Alex kept his gaze fixed on the photograph in front of us, and I was glad of that. I couldn't look him in the eye and hold myself together. Now that I'd started talking about her, words I hadn't meant to say poured from my lips.

"A car knocked her off her bike. It was so sudden and unexpected. The worst part was that nobody ever spoke about her anymore. Not even the teachers at school. Nobody knew what to say or how to deal with it. Even now, nobody speaks about her. Not my dad or Mel."

Alex nodded, sagely. "Everybody deals with grief differently. Some people go quiet. I understand the urge. I keep talking for Brodie's sake. Maybe if it wasn't for him, I would have been the same as your family."

"Dad moved us all down from Scotland. I think he missed her so much he couldn't even bear to be in the same country as her memory. But I missed our old place near Loch Shiel. Mum used to grow these beautiful pale-yellow roses in the garden. Whenever I see yellow roses, I think of her. She's buried at the church near the house. I miss it. I go back to visit her when I can, but not often enough."

He offered me a kind smile and moved his finger to brush the back of my hand.

I dared a glance at him. "About the day we met in Gabe's hotel . . . what made you decide you were ready to . . . you know . . . again."

A wry smile twisted his lips. "I had a devastatingly beautiful young woman whispering in my ear. I was hardly thinking with my brain at that point."

"It must have been a big thing for you . . . to be with someone again after so long?"

His expression grew somber. "It was a big deal. All of it. Talking. Touching. Holding hands. Laughing. Kissing. It's all *still* a big deal."

He wrapped his hand around mine. His gentle touch seared heat up my wrist. I held perfectly still. Standing together in the quiet, talking about Mum, in this room stuffed with memories, made my throat burn. I gazed up at Evelyn. Alex had loved her and she'd loved him. I could see why she'd loved him. He wasn't like any man I'd ever met. How wonderful that they'd had that together.

It had meant something to Alex when we'd hooked up. It had meant nothing to me, beyond an exciting tangle in the sheets, but all of this was meaning something now. That was the part that terrified me.

"I can't fall for you, Alex."

He hesitated before he spoke in a soft voice. "Why not?"

Because I'm scared.

Because one day you'll say goodbye, and I can't take that.

Alex's hand wrapped around mine. "This scares me too, Lana. I know loss. Profound, terrible grief. I know what it is, and I know

162

that somehow life goes on, because it has to. I haven't let anyone close. Then I saw you sitting in that bar and for the first time in a long time, I wanted to get swept away by a beautiful stranger. We're not right for each other. I can't date. My life has to be about Brodie now, and still . . ."

He swallowed. "Still I want you. I want to be your protector. I want to do whatever it takes to look after you and make everything right for you. I know you're too young—"

"The age gap is the least important part."

"It's the most important, because of what it means for the future. We're at different stages in our lives. Your twenties are about having fun and making mistakes. You don't want to settle down and have a family. I'm not out partying. I like quiet evenings and routine. The most important thing to me is keeping things stable for Brodie. I can't bring a woman into our lives who will walk away from us. He's been through too much." His thumb brushed lightly over the back of my hand. "Me and Brodie have *both* been through too much."

"I've partied enough in the past couple of years to last my entire twenties. Maybe I'm tired of it. I don't drink, anyway. It doesn't give me what I'm looking for."

"What are you looking for?"

"I don't know. I didn't think I was looking for anything, but maybe I was wrong. Maybe I'm looking for something . . . nice."

"Nice?"

"Someone kind. Stable. Someone who will stick around." A surge of anxiety went through me. "And that scares the shit out of me, because I've never felt like this. I didn't realize how terrifying it all is, because as soon as you realize you have feelings for someone, you have to live with the fear that they might not love you back the same . . . or they might go away—"

"You don't have to be frightened with me. If you give me your heart, I will keep it safe." His large hands cupped my face and held me gently. "You have my word. I'll look after you. This life is so short and precious. I want to find some joy, for my sake, too. You give me joy, Lana. You've brought that back into my life. But I need to know that I'm doing the right thing for Brodie."

"I'd never hurt him. No matter what happened between us. I'd never make things difficult for you and your son. He always comes first. Whatever you need—"

"Come." He pulled me out of the room and onto the landing. He gathered me in his powerful arms, holding me snugly, and the last traces of my resistance faded. I stood on tiptoe until my lips found his. The caress of his mouth set my blood on fire. His sweet kisses left me weak and confused. This wasn't me. Still, I wanted to give myself to him. I craved anything he had to offer.

He led me into another bedroom with bare white walls and a double bed. In silence, we stripped each other and he pulled me down to the bed. I straddled him. His hard length prodded my stomach, and I welcomed him inside of me. With my palms on his chest, I rocked over him, riding him.

He gazed up at me in awe, his hands smoothing a path over my hips, leaving electricity in their wake. His lips hardly left mine, and when he wasn't kissing me, he was looking so deeply into my eyes that I could feel every wall I'd ever built crumbling. Sex had always been a physical release, but this was something different. It made me wonder if I'd been doing it wrong all this time.

"Just like that." His lips brushed my ear. "This feels amazing. You're so beautiful."

The words alone made heat rush through my body. I wanted to please him, to satisfy him, because for once I was thinking about how this felt for him. Sex had always been about performance, or about my pleasure, but this wasn't about me. It was about the two

164

of us, moving together in a perfect harmony. A way to communicate something deeper than we could with words.

I couldn't be close enough. I wanted to mold my body against his, to melt into him, and crawl under his skin. Alex had said he wanted to make me his, and I wanted that too. I never wanted to be separated from this man again, because it felt so good to be this connected to him. I'd made myself vulnerable. I'd told him things I'd never told anyone, and he'd shared himself with me, too. I'd never had sex from a place of trust and raw emotion.

His fingers interlaced with mine as I rode him slowly, grinding and rocking. His eyes on me were intense and worshipful. For the first time, I couldn't care less what I looked like on top. I'd never felt so comfortable or admired. With Alex, I had no scrap of the self-consciousness that I often felt under a man's gaze. This was me. Laid bare. I wasn't trying to perform, or position my body in a certain way to look sexy, or make the noises I thought he'd enjoy. None of that mattered. This was just a moment for us that was truly genuine.

I flattened my body over his. His praise was a gentle whisper in my ear as he held me tight, his hands roaming over my back.

"You're so beautiful. So perfect."

He moved inside of me slowly, his lips hardly leaving mine. I didn't even try to hurry his slow, deliberate thrusts. It felt too good at this pace—slow and intimate.

I clung to him to stop myself from drowning in need. My climax had been building for so long that when it finally claimed me, it left me crying out and clawing his back. I expected Alex to stop, but he kept working inside of me. Neither of us willing to let go of such a divine connection.

He rose to meet me, and my breasts crushed against his firm chest. "I think you've got another one for me, sweetheart."

He was right. Just those words in that low Scottish tone pushed me closer. After the third orgasm, we both collapsed. Alex pulled me into his powerful arms and tucked me against him, our bodies glued together and our legs tangled. His divine sweat filled my nose. That was how bad things had gotten. Even his sweat smelt like expensive cologne.

He moved to face me in the bed. His eyes solemn and earnest. "Do you remember I asked you for a date when we first met?"

"I remember."

"Why did you look so confused?"

It felt like a hundred years ago. "Because I wasn't expecting it. The guys I meet don't ask for a second date."

He traced a finger along my jaw. "Then they're idiots."

We lay like that, breathing hard and coming down. My eyes flickered shut, and I drifted into dreams of dark waters in an ice-cold Scottish loch and pale-yellow roses climbing stone.

Alex's low voice roused me from my slumber. "What about now? What if I asked you on a date now? What would you say?"

I could have teased him, or thrown up walls, or played games—a warning voice still nagged me to do that and keep my heart safe—but I wouldn't, not after what had come to pass between us this morning.

"What do you think?" I kissed the tip of his nose. "I'd say yes, of course."

Chapter 30

LANA

I dropped my bag into my locker. My phone vibrated in my jacket pocket. I pulled it out to see Karen Delaney's number. Shit. Not good. I resisted every urge to throw the phone to the ground and stomp it into pieces.

"Phones are meant to be on silent in the locker room."

Claire stood in the doorway. She folded her arms. The rest of the team hadn't yet arrived for afternoon practice. I'd been getting here at least fifteen minutes before everyone else. I'd kept it up. Still Claire only noticed the things I got wrong. I'd just stepped through the door. Of course I'd forgotten to put my phone on silent.

The phone vibrated loudly again with a call and green light illuminated the dark locker. Claire rolled her eyes, and her gaze darted to the clock.

"Sorry." I switched the phone off and shoved it into my carryall.

Claire's gaze swept over me. "Everything okay?"

"Everything's great."

I shut my locker door, but it slammed too loud. The clang of metal on metal rang out in the empty room.

Claire studied my face. "If something's up, you can tell me. I might be able to help."

There was nothing I wanted more than to tell Claire what was going on, but it wouldn't help me. Claire didn't want to understand my situation. If I wasn't careful, my fate would be much worse than benching. If Claire knew I'd sold out Sean, she'd kick me off the team. I couldn't blame her. That was one instance where she really would need to make an example of me.

"Nothing's wrong."

Claire fingered the shiny whistle hung around her neck. "I'm here if you need to talk."

Chatter and footsteps drifted from the corridor outside. The team would be here any moment. I tried to drag my attention back to getting my kit ready, but Karen Delaney played on my mind. Why get back in contact now? Would she threaten me again? If I didn't produce the goods, would she post that article about Dad? I couldn't allow someone to blackmail me, but I couldn't let that article come out. Either way, this journalist was screwing me.

Sophie dumped her kit bag next to me. Grimacing, she sank down onto the bench.

I perched next to her. "What's the matter?"

"It's that time of the month." She spoke through gritted teeth. "I'll be okay once I get moving."

I put my arm around her shoulder. "That's rough."

She leaned into me, and I held her, stroking her hair back. Uneasiness crept into my bones. I'd taken the last pill in my packet a couple of days ago, and I still hadn't bled. It wasn't a big deal. Sometimes, it didn't happen straight away. Still, a little voice nagged me. These things weren't always a hundred percent. I'd had a friend who got pregnant on the Pill because she'd had a cold and it hadn't worked properly. I'd have to take a test. It was the only way to set my mind at ease.

Despite the churning in my gut, I adjusted my smile and gave Sophie a squeeze. "Can I get you anything? Painkillers? Emergency chocolate?"

She smiled. "I'm never going to turn down emergency chocolate."

◆ ◆ ◆

Later that day, at the school, I put the girls through a set of new drills. I'd been excited about trying something different with them, but now my heart wasn't in it. Alex's gaze had burned into me all session. He checked in twice to ask if I was okay.

I really wasn't okay.

It was hardly a conversation we could have in a school hall full of chattering primary school children. At the end of the session, I led the children through a routine of cool-down stretches on the mat while Alex gathered the equipment together. The children filed out of the hall in a neat line.

Alex held the door open and eased into a smile. "That was fun, wasn't it?"

I ducked under his arm and through the door.

He fell in step next to me; his formidable frame loomed more imposing than ever in the small school corridor. "Is everything okay?"

"Why wouldn't it be?" My voice came out sharp.

Alex held the main entrance open for me, and we stepped out onto the playground. A warm breeze, carrying a faint odor of hot tarmac, hit me. Snatches of laughter from the children playing in small groups around us raked through me.

"You've hardly said two words to me today." He came close, looking down at me intensely, and lowered his voice. "Are you upset about yesterday? I'm sorry I didn't ask you to stay. I thought it might have been too much for Brodie . . ."

A pulse beat in my temple. "Everything's fine."

My mind drifted back to yesterday. I'd spent the day in bed with Alex and left before Brodie got back from the water park. The afternoon with him had been like nothing I'd experienced before. Sex had always just been a physical release, but yesterday afternoon was something I couldn't explain. For once, I hadn't just wanted to ride him in a blind, galloping passion. It had been tender and sweet. A genuine connection. Something peaceful. I liked the rough, exciting sex we'd had before, but the slow, tender, soulful stuff was incredible too. I hadn't realized there was a possibility of both.

We left the school through iron gates and walked the leafy suburban street back to Alex's car. The low rumble of traffic from the main road filled my ears.

Alex stilled me with a hand on my arm. "Something's wrong. What is it?"

"Why do you think something's wrong?"

He offered me a faint smile. "I was married for a long time. I know that when a woman says 'everything is fine' in that tone, it's anything but fine. If I've upset you, then you can tell me." He looked around and lowered his voice. "Yesterday was so . . ." His dark eyes glimmered with shades of amber. "I loved spending time with you. I thought we were making . . . progress."

Progress? Progress to where?

"It felt . . . right between us, that's all." Alex's smile faded a little. "For me, anyway."

Would it still feel right when I landed this news on him? Alex was an amazing father to Brodie, but no man would be thrilled at the prospect of a baby with a woman they hardly knew, would they? I'd have to do this test as soon as I could. It was messing with my head. What if the test was positive?

This wasn't the right time in my life for a baby. In fact, there couldn't have been a worse time. Some women managed to balance motherhood with playing, but not many. It would end any possibility of playing for England. Dad would be so disappointed in me. Maybe Calverdale Ladies wouldn't keep me around. Miri had held on to her spot on the team, but she was shacked up with the director. I had no such assurance.

The way Claire had been acting with me lately, she'd probably be relieved to have an excuse to get rid of me. Then there was Mel. My sister would be furious at the timing. I was supposed to be helping her get Dad back on track, not introducing another mouth to feed. Having a baby wasn't something I could even consider.

I tried to paste on a smile but my lips trembled too much to hold the shape. The words I tried to dismiss Alex with all wedged in my throat. What if I was pregnant? What the hell would I do? If the test came back positive, would I even tell Alex? I'd have to tell him. It wasn't something I'd keep from him. Besides, this was his responsibility too. Not just mine.

I wanted to press myself into his enormous arms and let his scent wrap around me like a warm blanket, but I had to hold firm. Alex might not react well.

"I'm late."

He glanced at his watch. "I'll make sure you get to training on time."

"No. My period hasn't come. It's normally regular."

Alex's steady gaze traveled over my face. At least he hadn't run away. Most of the men I'd been with would have been halfway up the road by now.

"You said you were on the Pill."

Like this was my fault? "I am. These things aren't always one hundred percent reliable."

"Have you done a test?"

171

Was he freaking out? Alex was always so calm and measured. His demeanor was unchanged.

He's going to walk away.

"I only realized this morning. I'll test today. You don't have to be involved. I shouldn't have even said anything—"

"I'm taking you to the pharmacy. Right now. We'll get a test."

"Not now. I can't be late for training."

"I'll meet you afterward. The minute you finish, I'm taking you." His voice was firm, final.

Why had I even told him? This would have been easier to handle alone. "I'm perfectly capable of going to a pharmacy. You don't have to be involved—"

He paled, and the muscle in his jaw jerked again. "You don't want me to be involved?"

I folded my arms tight across my chest and shrugged. "Not if you don't want to be."

His frown deepened. "Why wouldn't I want to be?"

"We've had sex a handful of times. This isn't your problem. I don't expect anything from you, and you don't owe me anything. I'm going to handle this."

"This is my responsibility. Whatever happens, I want to be involved."

I bit my lip until it throbbed like a pulse. I was so used to Dad's indifference and Mel's agitation that it was hard to deal with someone who was always so unfailingly good-natured.

"How do you know it's your responsibility?"

I didn't even know why I'd said it. I hadn't been with anyone else, but where did Alex get off assuming we were exclusive? We'd never had that conversation. It wasn't something either of us wanted. I didn't want to get attached, and Alex wouldn't want anything heavy in case it affected Brodie. Alex's words rattled in my head.

We're making progress.

Progress to what?

"It doesn't matter either way." His voice held a kind tone. "I'll be here, whatever may come."

He reached out, lacing his fingers through mine. My heart pounded, but the touch of his warm hand soothed me.

"You'd help me even if this isn't your problem?"

"Yes."

A sudden heat pressed behind my eyes. I could barely look at him without breaking down. I couldn't do this alone. It was so hard to trust and rely on someone, but with Alex, maybe it was worth the leap. He pulled me toward him. I melted into the strength and warmth of his embrace.

"Whatever you need." His voice was a tender murmur. "I've got you."

Chapter 31

LANA

Later, after training, I sat on the edge of the bathtub in my apartment. My hands shook as I fumbled with the pregnancy test kit box and pulled out the white plastic stick.

"Come out as soon as you've done it." The bathroom door muffled Alex's voice.

I studied the smooth white stick in my hand. Weird that my life could take a completely different path within the next five minutes.

"Whatever happens, we'll figure it out. Don't worry."

"Of course I'm worried. I'm not ready to be a mother."

A pause. "You might feel differently once you have the result in your hand. I didn't think I'd ever be ready to be a father. Being a parent is the hardest thing I've ever done, but it's also the best. Sometimes, it drives me up the wall, but Brodie is my world. You don't have to do anything you don't want to do. There are . . . options. I'm here, whatever you want to do."

Alex might have loved being a parent, but it wasn't something I'd imagined for myself. Not anytime soon. My hands felt clammy on the plastic stick.

"Have you done it yet?"

"Not yet."

A sudden rush of emotion went through me. Alex was still here. He'd driven me from training to the pharmacy and back to my apartment. It was strange to have someone with me. I was so used to doing everything alone. I moved to the door. The wood was cool against my cheek.

"You should know that I haven't been with anyone but you."

He could walk away. A pause. My heart pounded.

"Okay, sweetheart."

I took a breath. This had to be done. Alex would help me. The sooner we knew, the better. I moved to the toilet and pulled down my leggings and knickers. A flash of red against white cotton caught my eye. My period. Relief washed over me, but it was swiftly replaced by a heavy, sinking sensation.

I put the pregnancy test stick on the side of the bathtub with a gentle click. A cramp gripped my belly. For a moment, my imaginary future life had split like a river forked in two and carved out an entirely different and unexpected channel. If this test had been positive, how would this afternoon have played out? If I'd decided to keep the baby, Alex would have been in my life forever. No doubt he would have been a wonderful father to our child. He was so good with kids. Would we have given a relationship a shot? Maybe we would have tried for the sake of the child. That would have meant inheriting an entire family in one fell swoop. Could I be a stepmother to Brodie?

"You've gone quiet. Is everything okay?"

I adjusted my smile and swung the door open. "It was a false alarm."

A shadow of some indefinable emotion flickered in Alex's eyes. "That must be a relief."

I nodded, but my voice sounded dull. "It is. Such a relief."

I found myself studying his dark profile on the silent landing. This could have been so different. Everything could have changed for us in this one moment. My stomach cramped again. I couldn't help my wince.

Gently, he brushed his thumb along my cheekbone. "Are you okay?"

"Just cramps."

Alex opened his arms to me. I pressed myself into him. Heat emanated from his solid chest, and the faint, clean scent of his cologne filled my nose. "Come on. Let's get you a hot-water bottle and a cup of tea. Everything is more manageable with a cup of tea."

Chapter 32

ALEXANDER

Lana held my gaze as she peeled out of her football kit. She bent over the massage table, waiting for me. Anticipation made my heart race.

"Do you like the view, Big Mac? Are you just going to watch or are you going to—"

"Daddy. Daddy!"

Brodie's terrified scream pulled me from my filthy dream. I shot out of bed and stumbled blindly down the landing in darkness to his bedroom. The nightlight painted Brodie's slight frame in a green glow. He sat up in his narrow bed, wide-eyed and trembling. He held the duvet tight under his chin.

I dropped next to him. "You okay, pal? Another nightmare?"

He nodded. I held the back of my hand against his cool forehead. That was a relief, at least. There was nothing worse than a sudden fever in the middle of the night. These were the parenting bits that were the most difficult alone: the fever at two in the morning, the tears after school over a broken friendship, the rash that might mean something terrible. All the decisions came down to me and me alone. Evelyn had always known what to do. When Brodie was in distress, she could comfort him with a soft word and a cuddle. I tried to do the same, but how could it ever be enough? Sometimes, I was flailing in the dark, trying to guess what to do next. Actually, not sometimes. All the time.

Brodie's eyes were wide and pleading. "Will you stay with me, Daddy?"

"Of course I will."

He threw back his duvet and patted the cool space next to him. I lay down on my side, twisted and cramped, with my legs hanging off the tiny bed. Pain seared the length of my spine. Whenever we fell asleep like this, I always woke up with a backache. Brodie snuggled into me, and I pulled him tight, savoring his warmth and the soft brush of his hair on my cheek. The faint strawberry tang of his shampoo wafted to my nose.

Sleep thickened his voice. "What did you do today?"

My mind drifted to this afternoon. I should have been nervous as I'd waited outside the bathroom for Lana to tell me the news, but I hadn't been. A strange sense of calm had come over me. Clearly, she was relieved at the outcome. I understood. Lana was so young. She was also an elite athlete. She didn't want to be tied down with a baby and a family. For me, it had ignited a hopeful possibility I hadn't considered. Another child. A sibling for Brodie. A chance at a future with Lana Sinclair. Whatever Lana had wanted, I would have supported her. For one afternoon, my life had looked different, and it should have worried me, but it had made my heart sing with the possibilities.

I'd been trying to keep things casual with Lana because I knew I couldn't have her, but this had made my longing for her concrete. It wasn't just that I was ready to move on and have a relationship. I was ready to move on with Lana. It had to be her. No one else.

"I'll tell you tomorrow. It's bedtime now."

"I had fun at Auntie Rachel's house." In the dim light, his beautiful eyes gleamed with expectation. "I like it here in England. I want to stay."

I held him tighter. Thank God. If Brodie was happy, then it was all worth it. I could put up with all of it: the aches and pains, the team full of arrogant kids who thought I was washed up, the absolute arsehole of a captain, the thugs in the stadium shouting shit at me because I let a goal in. I could even put up with these confusing feelings for Lana, a woman who was driving me wild with need. Not just need but longing, too. I wanted her to be mine. As unlikely as a relationship between the two of us was, I couldn't deny that I'd fallen for her.

If Brodie was happy, then I'd put up with anything. I'd walk through hell and back to put a smile on his face. The trouble was, it was too much to ask of her. Lana was at a different stage in her life. She had big dreams for her football career, and she was single and carefree. We couldn't possibly want the same things. I wanted a family and stability. I doubted Lana wanted that too. All I could do was focus on Brodie for now. I'd have to work the rest out somehow. I kissed the top of his head. "I love you, Brodie."

His heart beat a steady rhythm against my chest. "Love you too, Dad."

Chapter 33

LANA

Karen pulled her recording device out of her briefcase and twisted it on the table that divided us. She smiled blandly. "I'm not turning this on yet. This is all off the record."

I took a sip of lava-hot tea and tried not to grimace. A garbage truck rattled down the street outside and rain hammered against the café window. This wasn't a part of town I frequented, but we'd agreed to meet somewhere low key and far away from the stadium. I couldn't risk anyone seeing me with Karen since the story on Sean had broken. I'd seen him stomping around in the gym. By all accounts, he wasn't a happy bunny. Guilt made my throat tight, but I swallowed past the feeling.

Better Sean than Dad.

Karen tapped a sharp red nail on her notebook. "My editor wants more."

She spoke as though this outcome was obvious. Perhaps it was. Perhaps this was the plan all along. Keep stringing out the threat. I'd been an idiot to think I could get out of this.

I wrapped my hands around my mug, searching for some small, warming comfort. I kept my voice as level as I could. Better not to show weakness. "Tough luck. I don't know anything else. The men's team talk among themselves. They don't tell me anything."

"What about Zack Sutheran? There's a rumor he likes to powder his nose . . ."

It was one thing talking about Sean. It was another ruining the career of a guy I hardly knew. "I don't know anything about that."

She cleared her throat. "Aiden Thwaite? He's quiet. What's he up to?"

Absolutely not. Aiden was dating my teammate Sophie. He didn't talk much, but he was a great guy and he made Sophie happy.

"There's nothing. You won't get anything else out of me." I leaned in and lowered my voice. "I'd stop all this bullshit if I were you. This is blackmail."

A chill silence stretched between us. A waitress passed by with a tray laden with fish and chips. The vinegary aroma made my stomach turn.

Karen sighed and her face relaxed. "That's a shame. Looks like we'll have to go back to the original article."

"You can't do that. I gave you Sean."

"It's not enough."

"What do you want from me? I can't feed you secrets for the rest of my life. You got your article."

She stood and smoothed her skirt.

I leaped up with her. "My dad is in recovery. Addiction is a disease, you know. Something like this will hurt him. Don't you care about that? If you have a conscience, you wouldn't do this."

She flashed a bleak smile. "A conscience is a luxury I can't afford. My family need to eat. This is the way the world works. You chose a career in the spotlight."

"No. I didn't. I chose a career in professional football." My breath came in quick, shallow gasps. I couldn't let her walk out of here and do this. "You're not sorry. Not in the slightest. You'll ruin a man to sell papers."

She twisted her gold pendant between her fingers. "What about the new goalie? Alexander McAllister. Any dirt on him?"

No. Not Alex. I'd never give her Alex. I rolled my shoulders back in a display of nonchalance. "I don't know him."

"Not at all? He transferred from Rangers."

"Yes. Of course, I know *of* him." My voice came out shakier than I would have liked. "I just don't know him."

Her eyes gleamed with interest. "There must be something. In my experience, it's the squeaky-clean family men who have the worst skeletons in the closet. I bet there's something juicy."

I fought to keep my expression neutral despite my racing heart. I couldn't have her sniffing around Alex. "There isn't. He's a good guy."

"There's no such thing."

I hadn't thought so either, but then I'd met Alex. There *were* good men in this world. The kind who communicated, who didn't want to play games, and who stepped up to raise their kids well. Alex was a great man. I wouldn't hurt him.

She studied my face. For an instant, her gaze sharpened. "Now, wouldn't that be a story? The single dad and the wild child half his age. My editor would jump at that."

Heat climbed my neck to the tips of my ears. "Are you that desperate that you'll make things up?"

Her cynical eyes impaled me. "It's true, isn't it? I've been doing this job long enough to sniff out a story." She sat back in her chair and regarded me. "He's almost old enough to be your father."

Of course she would exaggerate the age gap. Anything for a good story. "There's nothing going on."

"I want the story first-hand from you. All the ins and outs." She ticked off on her stumpy fingers. "How you met. What dates you've been on. What the kid thinks of his new stepmother—"

"We're not together." A whoosh of steam from the coffee machine filled my ears and made my heart skyrocket. "I'm consulting a lawyer. This is blackmail. You can't bully people like this."

"By the time you get anywhere with legal action, we will have printed the story. It would pay you not to forget who holds the power here, Lana." She held her simpering smile in place as she rapped her knuckle against the table. "I need to put an article on my editor's desk. It's you and Alexander, or it's your father."

Panic spiraled through me. Karen had me over a barrel as long as I was frightened of her. If I told her things about Alex, then what next? She'd want the next story, and the next. I couldn't spend my life selling out my teammates, but this could send Dad back to the bottle, and maybe this time it wouldn't just be a slip. At his worst, he'd spent nights sleeping on park benches. It had been hell.

I can't go through it again with Dad.

I can't put Mel through it again.

An idea came hurtling into my consciousness. I'd told her what I knew about Sean, but it wasn't everything I knew.

"Wait. What about Sean? He's more famous than any of the others. I'll tell you one last thing about Sean, but then you need to promise that this stops. You can't keep doing this to me. I want it to stop, and we need to shake on it."

She narrowed her eyes. "What have you got?"

This was low. Guilt weighed horrible and heavy inside. Being a lousy shag was one thing, but the things I knew about Sean would tank his career. It would ruin him. If it ever came back to me, then Skylar would know I'd betrayed her trust . . . again. But if someone had to take the fall, then Sean Wallace was the last person I'd lose sleep over. Skylar's words drifted back to me.

He's a bully. He hurt me all the time.

"You need to promise me that this is the last time you ask me to do this."

She studied me for a moment, then inclined her head in a nod. Was this tidbit juicy enough? What other choice did I have?

"I suspect Sean is taking performance-enhancing drugs."

"You suspect?"

"I don't know for certain. It's a rumor."

"I want facts, not rumors."

"Since when did the truth matter to the gutter press?"

She flattened her lips and packed her briefcase. "Take care of yourself, Lana. I'll see you again soon."

No. I couldn't let her go like this. I grabbed her wrist. "Are we done? Are you printing the story on Sean? What about my dad?"

She flinched and pursed her lips. I dropped her arm. "Please. I'm begging you."

She turned on her heel without a word.

Chapter 34

LANA

Mel busied herself restocking the fridge. Dad sat at the table watching her. Dark circles ringed his eyes, and a vape dangled from his mouth. The sickly strawberry scent of the steam seared my nose, but at least it wasn't a cigarette, and at least it wasn't alcohol.

I slid into the chair opposite him at the small foldout table. "How are you doing?"

He flashed a weak smile and hitched a shoulder. "I'm fine."

I scanned the neat kitchen. In silence, Mel moved from the fridge to the sink.

"Can I do anything to help?"

Mel kept her back to me at the sink. "I've got it under control."

The ticking clock that hung on the yellowed wall grew deafeningly loud. This is how it went with us. Sometimes grief brought people together, but for us it had driven in a wedge of pain and silence. Nobody wanted to talk about Mum. We'd walked our own lonely paths, until so much had been left unsaid that it was impossible to start talking.

Dad leaned back in the chair, closing his eyes as steam from his vape poured out of his nose. My throat felt tight. I wanted to talk the way Alex and Brodie talked. I wanted the pictures of Mum on the walls, the way Alex had his wife so lovingly displayed. Mum had been here, whether anybody wanted to talk about her or not. We couldn't erase her existence. She'd been the beating heart of this family. I couldn't keep pretending that the wounds weren't still open and bleeding. Maybe we could change. Maybe I'd have to be the one brave enough to take the leap.

I took a deep breath. "You've done a good job tidying, Mel. You must have inherited Mum's cleaning genes. I don't think I did."

Mel grunted and kept wiping the counter. Dad sat still, his eyes narrow. My mouth felt suddenly dry, but I'd started this thing now so I wouldn't stop.

"I remember in the old house, when I was little she used to let me stand on the upright vacuum and she'd vacuum with me on it, pretending we were on a ride. I used to love that. Do you remember the time when—"

"We've run out of dishwashing liquid again." Mel turned stiffly away from the sink. Her eyes were cold, and her expression was tight with strain. "If you want to be helpful, then go get some."

Mel was always the same. My hands balled into fists and I stood. Fine. Mel could send me on a pointless errand because she couldn't do the decent thing and talk to me.

"Eleven years." Dad's hoarse voice startled me.

My body froze in surprise. Dad nodded woodenly and put the vape on the table. His gray eyebrows slanted in a frown and his eyes took on a dim, faraway look. "I was walking around Sainsbury's and they were playing a song . . . Your mother's favorite . . . Something snapped in me . . ." He rubbed his chest as if it ached.

Mel planted her hands on his shoulders. "Stop, Dad. Don't upset yourself like this."

"No. Let him talk if he wants to."

Dad shot me a grateful glance and patted Mel's hand. She snatched her hands away and retreated to stand by the sink.

He drew a shaky breath and continued, "I left the shopping cart in the aisle and walked out of the door. I meant to go to my car, but I found myself in the pub. It was like I'd sleepwalked there." Dad raked a trembling hand over his grizzled face. "I want to be better. It's so hard . . . It won't happen again. I'm determined this time. I'm keeping up with the therapy. The guy says I need to keep talking. I need to talk about her, I think . . ."

I covered his hand with mine. "That's good. Talking is good."

My heart hurt, but this was positive. Dad was talking about why he'd relapsed. We'd learned enough from AA to know that was the important part. You had to understand the trigger.

A tear slipped down his cheek. "It was my fault, you know. I didn't treat her right. I loved your mother so much."

I dashed to him and wrapped my arms around his neck. "It wasn't your fault. She loved you too, I know she did. We love you as—"

"Look what you've done." Mel's voice hardened ruthlessly. "You've upset him now."

I held my father while he cried. Mel turned and watched us from the sink. Her brows set in a straight line, but her normally aloof eyes held an imperceptible note of pleading. The truth hit me like a punch in the gut. Maybe it wasn't that Mel didn't have emotions. Maybe she cared, but she'd buried the pain so deep, it had got stuck.

This is too much for her.

I held out my hand to beckon her. "He needs to let it out, Mel. We all do. There's nothing wrong with crying. We miss her. It's okay to miss her . . ."

Mel's bottom lip trembled, and she took a step toward us. My hand brushed hers. Discomfort clouded her expression. She snapped her hand away and shook her head. Her brittle voice rattled through the kitchen. "I can't. I'm sorry."

She walked out of the room.

Chapter 35

LANA

"Have you heard any more from that journalist?" Mel descended the stairs slowly.

She'd disappeared for a couple of hours after she'd walked out on us. Now, as usual, she would pretend that nothing had happened. I slipped my coat on in the hallway, ready to go back to my apartment. My shoulders ached so much from the burden of carrying this mess with Karen Delaney.

"I've given her two stories on Sean Wallace. Now she's asking me about Alex. She won't drop it. This is not going to end. You don't beat bullies by caving in to their demands. We accept that it's coming and deal with it. Sean Wallace is one thing, but I won't sell out Alex, or anyone else on that team."

Mel leaned back against the kitchen door frame and closed her eyes. "The timing couldn't be worse. Look at the state of Dad. He's sitting at the table sobbing."

"Maybe he needs to sob. Maybe that's a good thing. He's going to AA, and he's talking about Mum. This is how people heal. What if he's stronger than we think? There will never be a good time for Dad to get dragged through the gutter press. This shitstorm is coming. We have to put up our umbrellas and wait for it to pass."

She frowned, and spaced each of her words out evenly as though talking to a child. "Fine. It's coming. I know, but the relapse is still fresh. You need to buy us some time. Even if it's a couple of weeks . . ."

I flung out my hands. "Are you listening to me? I can't keep doing it. There's nothing left for me to tell her. She wants a story about me and Alex. I won't do it."

She sighed heavily. "I thought you were handling this, Lana. You told me you had it under control. I can't keep doing this with him. I'm tired." Her voice was so quiet, I had to lean in to listen. "I just need him to be okay. It's me here doing all of this. Always me picking up the pieces." A choked laugh escaped her. "Not that it matters. Whatever I do, you're still the favorite."

Me? The favorite?

"That's the most ridiculous thing I've ever heard. You're the one who kept this family going. You're so perfect, and sensible, and put-together."

Her mouth opened in dismay. "Right, and it's not enough. It doesn't matter what I do. I've looked after Dad, and this house. When there's a leaky tap, who do you think calls the plumber? When the garden overgrows, who cuts the hedges back? I've carried this family for so long and now I'm tired. I've given up so much to be back here. This isn't the life I was meant to be living. I wanted to work in fashion, not be stuck at a football club."

Her words stung. Of course Mel had given up so much, but I didn't realize how much she resented us because of it. "I got you that job because I thought you'd like it."

She threw her arms up. "I don't like any of the jobs I've had to do. I went into law because it was the only course at the local college with places, and it would make us enough money to keep

189

going. Why have I even bothered? I can't kick a ball around a pitch, so Dad will never be proud of me the way he's proud of you."

She drew a sharp breath. "I can't fix things this time. The truth is, I don't want to. Haven't I done enough for this family already? When do I get to breathe? When is any part of my life about what I want to do? I'm not a robot, Lana. I loved Mum, too. Just because I don't run wild or drown myself in booze doesn't mean I haven't got problems. It's your turn to step up. I'm done. This is on you to make right. If you care about this family, you will do everything you can to stop us from breaking. I can't do it anymore."

"Of course I care about this family."

"Talk is cheap. Show us." She covered her face with trembling hands. "Tell this journalist whatever you need to tell her. Keep her off our backs. Buy us time. Wait until Dad is stronger, and then we'll all put up our umbrellas and deal with a shitstorm. Alex is strong. He won't bat an eyelid about a story in the press. It won't affect him the way it affects Dad."

The pain in my heart became sick and fiery. I'd never seen Mel like this. It was awful to see her crack. I kept my voice as soft as I could. "I can't do that. You can't ask me to throw Alex under the bus."

She gave an impatient shrug. "He's just another notch on your bedpost. What does it matter?"

No. He wasn't. A swell of panic hit me with the realization. It was different with Alex. It might have started as fun and done, but it was so much more than that. I couldn't lose him. Alex kept his name out of the papers to protect Brodie. A story in the press would drive unwanted interest in his direction.

I kept my tears rigidly in check, and for the first time in a long time, Mel and I had swapped roles in our dance. I was the mountain, cold and composed, and Mel was the waves breaking around me. Mel could help me, but she didn't want to. Maybe she was trying to punish me. She'd given up her dreams for me and Dad. No wonder Mel treated me like a screw-up. I'd always felt guilty for messing up her life, but I'd never known the depth of resentment she was harboring over her sacrifices.

"I love Alex. I won't hurt him on purpose. He'll never forgive me."

Mel's face was pale and drawn. "Then you need to make a choice, because if you let that story about Dad go to the press, then *I'll* never forgive you."

Chapter 36

LANA

Soft blue light from the TV illuminated the room in a cozy glow. A fire crackled in the hearth. Brodie lay over us on the couch. His head rested in my lap and his feet stretched across Alex. A soft snore drifted from my lap. I craned my neck to watch Brodie's peaceful form, and smoothed my fingers through his soft curls.

Sometimes, when it was the three of us in these quiet moments, I understood how it was to feel content. There was nothing to chase. Nothing to improve upon. Everything was just . . . how it should be. I'd never felt like that before. I'd trade all of it—the partying, the late nights, the one-night stands—for a moment like this. Being here made me whole. I'd walked into this thing with Alex with my heart shut tight, and he and his little boy had blasted it wide open.

Everything about us was cozy, but I couldn't shake Mel's parting shot. She wanted me to choose between this and Dad. How could I? How could anyone? Alex leaned across and pressed a kiss to my temple. His smile warmed me, despite my distress.

"You hardly ate any dinner." Alex kept his voice low so as not to wake the sleeping boy laid across us. "Are you okay?"

Okay? I hadn't been okay for a very long while, and now I was in pieces. I couldn't even eat any dinner because I felt too nauseous. I had to tell Alex what was going on, but if I did, I'd have to betray my dad's trust. Dad wouldn't want his former teammate knowing his problems. I'd also have to tell him I'd leaked the story about Sean. I got the impression that there was no love lost between Alex and Sean, but Alex was still fiercely loyal to his team. There was no telling how disappointed he'd be with me.

Don't be a coward. Tell him.

Tell him everything.

I opened my mouth, but the words wouldn't come. If I told him, then I'd made the decision. I'd chosen Alex over my family. How could I do that when I'd spent a lifetime trying to do right by Dad and Mel? This was the worst possible timing for Dad. I had to hold the faith that he could get back on track, but that would be more difficult if he was being kicked while he was on the floor. Alex raised a questioning eyebrow. "You're so quiet. Is something wrong?"

He knew there was something off. He'd known before, when I hadn't wanted to tell him about the pregnancy scare. A part of me wanted him to wheedle it out of me. It would be so much easier than having to confess.

I cleared my throat. "No. Nothing's wrong."

I held my breath, waiting for him to push me on it, but he smiled and rested his head back on the cushion. His eyes flickered shut. Alex looked younger asleep, before the weight of the world settled on him. He'd been through so much. He'd lost his wife, and he'd had to raise a child on his own while grief-stricken. A goalkeeper lived their life under pressure—always in defense. When you played in attack, you got all the attention. A good goal would see you lifted on your team's shoulders and paraded around. A goalkeeper didn't get that glory. They just did their duty and protected the net. If it went wrong and they let in a goal, they got all the shit in the world thrown at them.

Alex had been under pressure all his life, and he'd weathered it. He'd stood tall and firm, like a mighty oak. He'd stepped up when his heart must have been breaking in two, and he'd raised a beautiful child. How could I possibly betray him? Alex would hate me. I'd hate me, too. If I chose my dad and Mel, I would lose the man I'd fallen in love with. I couldn't hurt him. I couldn't hurt Brodie, either. It was an impossible choice.

Another snore drifted from Brodie. I slid out from underneath him like a ninja, careful not to wake either of them. Brodie's limbs were limp and heavy as I lifted him into my arms and carried him upstairs to bed. I tucked Brodie in. A small smile graced his lips.

"Night, Lana-Banana. Love you."

He loves me?

My lips parted in surprise and my eyes filled with tears. I loved him too. I hadn't meant to get attached to this little boy, but how could I not?

"Night, Brodie." My voice sounded thick and uneven. "I love you too."

I went back downstairs and watched Alex sleeping. Pain speared my heart, and it hurt so much I wanted to weep. This is why I didn't do love. I reached out to wake him, but my hand hovered by his shoulder. All I had to do was squeeze Alex's shoulder and tell him everything.

Don't be a coward.

Do it.

I bit my lip until it throbbed like a pulse. I needed time to think.

Alex's eyes flickered open. Fatigue had painted dark circles under his kind eyes and for the first time I noticed how tired he looked. Memories of Mum drifted to mind. When things went wrong, it tore you apart. I had no idea how to survive it. What would Alex think of me if he knew how badly I'd let things fall apart? Everything was unraveling—Dad, my chance to play for England, my relationship with Mel. If Alex knew the depth of what was going on, he'd see me the same way as everyone else did, like a screw-up.

Alex was the only person who bothered to look deeper. He'd told me he was worried about the age gap between us. He thought I was young and irresponsible. Being responsible and in control was easy for Alex. If I confessed the mess I was in, it would confirm his suspicions about me. I couldn't let him see me at my worst. Better to handle this and make it go away. That was the only way to show people that I could be mature. I needed to prove myself through my actions, just like Alex had told me. I had to get out of here and think about what that action should be.

He yawned. "It's late. Stay with me tonight?"

I tried to keep my voice casual despite my pounding heart. "No. It's really time to go."

Chapter 37

LANA

Later, at Dad's place, a knot of hunger in my stomach woke me. I'd been too sick with stress to eat at Alex's place and now my body screamed for food. I pulled on a robe and crept downstairs in pursuit of something to eat. Light spilled from underneath the kitchen door and a faint shuffling sound drifted to my ears. My teeth gritted.

Please don't let it be Mel.

I paused at the door and listened. This wasn't the time for another argument. I'd have to just do my best to ignore her, make my toast, and get out. I pushed the door open to find Dad sitting at the kitchen table. Relief made my shoulders slump. Good. Not Mel. Dad wore his usual threadbare red dressing gown over boxers. Dozens of photographs and old pieces of paper littered the kitchen table. Dad's eyes widened when he noticed me. He scrambled to gather the scattered items together and sweep them into a shoebox.

"Wait." I pinned a photo to the table with my fingertip before he could remove it. "What are these?"

His eyes slipped away. "Nothing. You don't have to look at them if you don't want to."

I scanned the display of old family photos. Mum's face smiled back at me and knocked the air from my lungs. I hadn't seen these photos in so long. They'd covered the walls of our old house before Dad had taken them all away. Nobody had dared ask for him to put them back. It had always upset him so much to mention them. I'd assumed we had lost them over time, along with most of Dad's stuff.

One painful, beautiful memory after another caught my attention. My fingers hovered over Mum standing proudly with a younger Mel and me. We stood in front of the magnolia tree in our old yard. Mel must have been around fourteen. She had her arm around my waist, and her grin dazzled with affection. Strange to see her like that. It had been a long time since I'd seen her smile. I couldn't remember much about the photo, but I could guess why my eyes shone with delight. Mel was giving me attention. It was all I'd longed for as a child—my older sister wanting to spend time with me.

Once, we'd been close. Now, I didn't know how to talk to her. Since Mum died, my sister and I had become two magnets polarized in opposite directions. We couldn't connect. The more I tried to get close, the harder she pushed away. In my weaker moments, I wanted to hurt her with my words, but only because I needed the reaction. I needed something back from her. These days, snark and bickering was all I could get.

I traced a finger over the younger me. My long red hair fell in tangles around my mud-splattered face. I'd been so innocent then. I wanted to go back in time and grab that little girl by the shoulders, and warn her about the things to come, but what good would it do to know? She'd still have to survive. I'd been surviving for so long. Life had turned into a slog, like running around a muddy pitch in torrential rain with no shots on goal. With Alex, life didn't feel like survival. It felt like winning.

"I'm sorry. You don't have to look at these." Dad's hoarse voice broke me out of my reverie.

"You don't have to say sorry. I want to see them. I didn't know you had kept them."

He inclined his head in a nod. "Aye. Of course I kept them."

"We could put them back up around the house if you wanted?" I spoke tentatively. I had a feeling like I had a tiny bird in my hands and if I moved too quickly, it would fly away.

Dad shifted in his seat. "No. I don't think . . . I'm not ready . . ."

"That's okay. Don't worry."

Dad's raspy breathing filled the silence.

"I came to get some toast. Do you want a drink or—"

"I'm not doing so well, Lana. I don't want to be like this anymore." His eyes shone with tears. "I'm really trying."

The tremor in his voice made my heart ache. I rested my hand on his shoulder. "I know you are."

He fixed his teary gaze on a faded photo of Mum blowing out the candles on a birthday cake. "I want to be better for my girls. I can get back on track. You have to know that I'm trying. I'm really trying." He patted my hand on his shoulder. "You're a good girl, Lana. You never give up on me." He tapped his finger on the photo of Mum and a faint smile lifted his lips. "You look like her, don't you? Your mother never gave up on me either. I've messed up a lot in my life, but I'm lucky, I have you."

"And Mel. You have both of us."

He nodded absently. Tears found their way down his cheeks, and he bit his lip trying to hold back his sob. I held him tight while he wept. At least Mel wasn't here this time to tell him to stop. Dad's soft sobbing filled my ears. He'd been struggling on like this for a while, but Mel and I had been too busy to notice. A grim realization settled over me. Mel was right. Alex would survive whatever the tabloids threw at him. Alex was a redwood built to endure any weather. My dad's branches were so thin and worn, they'd snap and break at a breeze.

I had to put Karen off with this article until Dad was stronger. Alex would be so mad with me, but this family was my team, and life had tackled Dad to the ground. I'd never leave him behind. You had to help your team members. I had to help get my dad and Mel back on their feet. How could I throw my father out into the cold when he was already on his knees?

I sat with Dad and held him while he wept. When I'd finally helped him upstairs and to bed, the sun was rising outside, coloring the sky a faint orange. A new day. I tucked Dad into his bed and brushed back the gray hair from his forehead.

He flashed a thin, grateful smile. "You're good to me. I don't deserve you."

I tried to manage a feeble answer. All I wanted was to be good. To fix my family and make us better again. Mel was right. The only way I could repair this family was to buy Dad time, even though the cost was hurting the man I'd fallen in love with.

When Dad started snoring, I found my way back to my room in a daze. Faint birdsong filtered through my bedroom window. I'd always loved that sound, but at this ungodly hour the chirrups rang sharp and accusatory, as though the birds knew the despicable act I had to commit. Their incessant twittering echoed with the word *betrayal*. Guilt gnawed at my belly as though it might devour me from inside.

I'd lose Alex. Nobody could forgive something like this. A betrayal is a betrayal. There were no good answers. There was only hurting the person who was better able to withstand it. Either way, when you loved, it always ended in goodbye. My breath came in sharp pants and my heart ached as though someone had kicked a football directly at my chest. It had to be done. I took a deep breath. With sweaty fingers, I texted Karen Delaney. I hit send before I could change my mind. Before I could give in to the screaming voice in my head telling me to stop.

Keep my dad out of the press. I'll tell you about me and Alex.

Chapter 38

ALEXANDER

Lana's phone diverted to voicemail for the hundredth time. I fired off another text. What was going on? She'd been distant for a couple of days. Something was wrong. I'd seen her four nights ago and ever since she'd made excuses not to be with me. I'd had a feeling like something was off when I'd seen her, but I didn't want to push her. She could be prickly sometimes.

I'd opted to give Lana space, but maybe I should have gone deeper with it. She hadn't touched a bite of the meal I'd cooked that night. Now, she was always busy with practice, and she'd hardly sent me more than a two-word answer every time I checked in. Whenever I bumped into her at the club, she always had an excuse to run in the opposite direction.

Maybe she wasn't feeling well. I had no time to dwell, I just had to speak to her. She'd agreed to watch Brodie while I played a match this morning. I'd checked in last night and she'd confirmed she'd be here. If she wouldn't answer her phone, I needed to find someone else, or I'd be late.

I knelt down next to Brodie's bed. "Wake up, pal. We need to get moving."

Brodie opened his eyes and yawned. "Is Lana here yet?"

"Not yet."

Disappointment shadowed Brodie's face as he rubbed sleep from his eyes with his fists. "I wanted her to get here early. I like it when Lana makes my scrambled eggs. She's better than you."

"I know, pal."

"When is she coming?"

I kept my voice level despite my rising agitation. "I don't know, pal. She said she'd be here."

I rushed around the house getting Brodie's clothes together. I hadn't prepped the night before like I would usually, because I'd assumed Lana would be around to watch Brodie while I got everything organized. What had happened? Was she okay? If something had happened, I needed a back-up plan.

I sent off a quick text to Rachel. Any chance you could take Brodie today? I've got a match in less than an hour.

Rachel's reply pinged back. At the office. Sorry. Is there anyone else?

Who else could I call at the last minute? Worry made my jaw clench. Lana wouldn't let me down unless something was seriously wrong, would she? A little voice niggled in my head. I'd brushed off her lack of messages as her just being busy, but what if it was more than that? Was she having second thoughts about this relationship? Brodie appeared at the kitchen door, still in his pajamas. Damn it. We were going to be late. Late to a bloody league match! I was never late.

"What are you doing? Why aren't you dressed?" My voice came out harsher than I'd meant it.

Brodie's eyes widened, and his bottom lip trembled. "I wanted breakfast."

Guilt stabbed me. I never snapped at Brodie if I could help it. The poor kid had been through so much. He needed gentle and calm. This wasn't Brodie's fault. I dropped on my knees on the cold tiled floor. "I'm so sorry, pal. Your old man's stressed. I don't like to be late. Do you think we could get going?"

He nodded and stepped into my embrace. After a hug, he ran off to get dressed, and I scrambled to get my kit ready. I'd have to take him to the game with me. It wasn't great, but I'd find one of the crew to watch him.

How could Lana leave me in the lurch like this? Was this it for us? She'd run out on me after every encounter. She'd looked as though I'd slapped her around the face the one time I'd dared to suggest we were making progress toward something more solid. Had things got too heavy for her and caused her to panic and run? I'd have to find her, but first I needed someone to look after Brodie. I could only pray I made it to the stadium before kickoff.

Chapter 39

LANA

"Come in."

Claire called me into her office. I hadn't been able to shift the sick fluttering inside since she'd texted me and asked me to come to the training suite. I pulled out my phone to switch it off. There were a dozen missed calls from Alex. I didn't bother to read them. I'd hardly responded to his messages the past couple of days. The guilt wouldn't allow it. I had to speak to him and give him a heads-up, but every time I tried to think of the words, I couldn't do it. I had to find the right time.

Coward.

I'd have to deal with Alex before the story broke, but first Claire wanted to talk to me. I switched my phone off, took a deep breath, and stepped inside her office. She gestured for me to take a seat. She scrolled her phone and passed it to me. I stared at the screen, my brain unable to process the headline: *Exclusive—My Love Affair with Sugar Daddy Alex Mac. The Wild Child of Women's Football Tells All.*

I scanned the story. It was even worse than I could have imagined. I'd given Karen the truth. I'd told her that Alex was the first man I'd ever loved. Maybe some part of me had thought he wouldn't be so mad if he saw how much I cared about him, but this article was sensationalist bullshit. It focused on the age gap, and the ongoing scandal with Sean Wallace. It looked terrible for the team. After this, everyone would know it was me that had been leaking information. No one would ever trust me again.

Claire's exasperated gaze met mine. "What were you thinking?"

"She's twisted everything. This wasn't my fault. I didn't even want to talk to Karen Delaney. The press department made me do it."

"PR wants you to talk about women's football and paint the team in a good light. You've made this place sound like a den of iniquity: bed-hopping, drug-taking, kickbacks, affairs."

"She's made it all up. My private life is private. I didn't ask for any of this. The media hounds anyone in the public eye. You know what this is . . ."

"The press can be awful, but I need to ask you a question, and I want you to be honest. Have you been leaking information about the team to the press?"

Shame stole my words.

Her voice hardened. "The men's team suspended Sean Wallace pending results of a drug test. Karen Delaney knows every detail. The test has come back negative. Sean is in the clear but understandably annoyed that he's had to go through the indignity. He's pointed the finger at Alexander McAllister as the leak."

Not Alex. Anyone but Alex. "Sean Wallace is a liar. No one will take him at his word, will they?"

Claire's eyes narrowed. "Sean says Alexander is the only one who saw him injecting. It was vitamins, apparently. The club will need to investigate the allegations. The men's team can't function with a leak."

I couldn't let Alex take the blame. Hadn't I already caused him enough pain?

"It's not Alex."

Claire's eyes clung to mine. She knew. Of course she knew. Despair thrashed in my gut like a wild beast. This was too much. I couldn't lose my spot on the team. I loved this club. If they kicked me out, I'd lose my dream to play for England. First Alex and Brodie, and now this. I'd have nothing left. There was no way back from this, but I'd fall on my sword if it meant protecting the man I loved. I wouldn't let the blowback from any of this affect him.

"Alex knows nothing about this. I might have mentioned something to Karen about Sean, but I didn't know she'd print all this nonsense."

A chill, brittle silence smothered the office.

Claire watched me warily. "Why would you talk about Sean?"

The despair inside dug its claws deeper. Telling the truth about Karen's threats would mean exposing my dad's struggles. He'd hate that. I wouldn't betray him.

Claire raised a questioning brow. "You sold out a teammate. Are you going to tell me why?"

My heart sank. Claire wouldn't give me the benefit of the doubt. I'd been trying to win her approval for so long. It was pointless. The same way that it was pointless to try and impress Mel. The wild party girl narrative in Karen's article was the one Claire had always bought into, too, and no matter what I did, I couldn't shake it. I was Logan Sinclair's daughter—the girl who pulled stupid pranks and turned up late one too many times. The girl Claire had made captain as a way to get her to take her career more seriously. Why couldn't they see how serious I was about football?

They couldn't have got me more wrong. Football was my world, and this club meant everything to me. The fact that everyone was constantly questioning that made my heart ache. Fine. If that was the way Claire wanted to see me, then I couldn't change her mind. Maybe it was better for everyone if she believed that. Better than the truth. The real Lana had been drowning for so long.

The real Lana was a broken teenager sitting on the steps listening to a police officer explaining to her dad why her mum wasn't coming home. The real Lana was trying to carry on as normal and convince everyone she was fine while her dad tried to drink himself to death. Claire wanted a wild child. She could have one. It was easier, and far less painful than the truth.

Rain lashed the office windows and thundered a harsh drum inside my skull. I took a deep, unsteady breath. "Because Sean Wallace is a prick. He deserves everything he gets. Don't pretend you don't know it."

Claire shook her head, unimpressed. "I've tried with you, Lana. I've really tried. We made you captain on Skylar's break because we thought the responsibility might settle you down. Clearly, it hasn't worked. What more can I do with you?" Her eyes slipped away, and she turned her back to peer out of the window at the training pitches. Her voice was sad and hollow. "This is the end of the road. You're off the team."

"You don't mean that . . ."

"Clear out your locker. We're done." Claire kept her back to me. "Goodbye, Lana."

Tears blinded me as I dashed out of the training suite. She'd meant it. Claire had let me go. My life had revolved around playing for this club for so long, and everything I'd built here had crumbled around me. What was I supposed to do if I wasn't playing here? How could I play for another team? This team was my family. That was supposing another team would even have me. What team would want to take me on after that article? My reputation would be dirt.

Before, I'd been a wild child, now I was a player who had sold out her team to a journalist. That article had shattered my dreams of playing for England. This wasn't just destroying my relationship with Alex and Brodie. I could only imagine what my friends and family would think. Dad and Mel would be so embarrassed. Tears blinded me but I pressed on down the narrow corridor, past the swimming pool, past the gym, past the offices. My head reeled and nausea gripped my gut. I just needed to get out of this bloody building before I threw up.

"Lana?"

The small voice held me in my tracks.

I twisted to see Brodie at the vending machine. He held up a coin in his hand. "Gabe gave me money for a slushie."

Cold panic overwhelmed me. If Brodie was here, then Alex was here.

I flashed a glance down the hallway to Gabe's office. "Gabe? Why are you with Gabe?"

Brodie scanned the vending machine contents with eager eyes. "Because you didn't show up."

I tried to follow the conversation despite my pounding heart. "I didn't show? What do you mean?"

"Dad has a match. You were supposed to look after me."

Oh God. That was right. Alex had a match this morning. I'd been so stressed, I'd forgotten. I threw my hand to my forehead. "Shit."

Brodie's eyes widened, and he giggled. "You said the *S word*."

"Did I? Oh, shit . . . I mean, sugar . . . Oh God . . . I'm sorry. I shouldn't have said that. I'm sorry I didn't come to look after you."

Poor Alex. He must have been so stressed, trying to arrange childcare before a match.

"It's fine. Gabe's staying with me. I can come with you now, though?"

"Come with me?"

He hitched a shoulder. "You can look after me now you're here. Gabe's okay, but you're more fun."

No. Brodie couldn't come with me. As much as I wanted him to, Alex wouldn't want me to take him now. Heat pressed behind my eyes as the realization settled. I hadn't just lost Alex. I'd promised Alex that I wouldn't hurt his son, but that was what I was doing. Would Alex still let me spend time with Brodie?

I dropped to my knees. "You're going to have to stay with Gabe. I'll see you later."

"When?"

A tear escaped, and I brushed it away. "I don't know."

"After the match?"

"I don't know. I don't think so." Another tear fell down my cheek. "Your dad and I need to talk."

"Why are you crying? You're still going to be Dad's girlfriend, aren't you? Why don't we—"

"Brodie?"

The masculine voice made my heart contract. I straightened to see the tall figure of a man at the end of the corridor. The bright corridor lights glinted from Gabe's chestnut hair. Relief flooded me. Good. Not Alex. I would have to face him soon, but not yet. Not that I wanted to see Gabe either. If Claire was pissed off with me, then no doubt Gabe was too. I hadn't said a word about him to Karen Delaney, but she'd taken the opportunity to lay the boot into him. The media had always hated Gabe. Now they'd had an opportunity to have another shot at his beloved team.

I turned Brodie by the shoulders and angled him gently back down the corridor. "Go back to Gabe now."

He wrapped his arms around me and kissed my cheek. "Love you, Lana-Banana."

There was no hope for me and Alex after this. How could there be? Alex wouldn't forgive me. This would hurt him so much.

I swallowed past the lump in my throat. "I love you, too."

He twisted in my arms. "When will I see you again?"

Tears ran down my cheeks and I tried so hard to smother them, but I couldn't. A pulse beat in my temple. I'd said goodbye to Alex, and to my club. I couldn't say goodbye to Brodie. Endings were too painful. That was why I left before it got to that part.

"I'll see you soon." I kissed Brodie on the cheek. "Now, go back to Gabe."

I watched Brodie skip back to Gabe at the end of the corridor. Gabe lingered a moment before he escorted Brodie into his office and shut the door. Gabe was another person on the list I'd hurt today. Skylar and the entire team would be reeling. On trembling legs, I walked out of Calverdale Ladies for the last time. I should have gone home, but I couldn't face Mel. I couldn't face any of this.

Instead, my legs carried me to the train station.

Instead, I did the thing I'd been doing for years.

I ran.

Chapter 40

ALEXANDER

Lana's cheery voicemail message rang in my ears again. Where was she? I swung by Gabe's office after the match to pick up Brodie. Gabe had spotted us walking into the training suite this morning and volunteered to watch Brodie. He wouldn't have been my first choice, but only because I'd assumed he'd be too busy. He had a kid of his own, so at least I knew I could trust him.

Brodie sat in Gabe's huge reclining chair, slurping a blue slushie through a long straw. Football cards lay strewn all over Gabe's huge, immaculate desk.

"Thanks so much for watching him. You're a lifesaver."

Gabe smiled and ruffled Brodie's hair. "We've been looking at this football card collection. I'm bringing out a range next year for the women's team. It's only fair."

Brodie rocked back in Gabe's fancy white leather chair. The slushie hovered dangerously in his hand. "That's great. Come on, then. Let's go."

Brodie leaped to his feet, and I braced myself to catch the slushie. Miraculously, he didn't spill a drop.

"Gabe has a boat. He's going to take me on it. We're going to be pirates for the day."

I raised a rueful eyebrow. "Go steady on the pillaging though, won't you? Superyachts weren't built for that kind of thing." I transferred my attention to Gabe. "Are the women training today? I haven't seen them around."

Gabe swept a handful of football cards together and stacked them in a neat pile. "Lana was here this morning. She had a meeting with Claire."

"Lana? Oh? Did she?" I tried to keep my voice from sounding unduly interested.

"Lana is Dad's girlfriend," Brodie said, matter-of-factly.

"Lana is my friend. Not a girlfriend."

Brodie took a long, loud slurp of his slushie. His wide eyes shone with innocence. "You had all those sleepovers, and you were kissing in the kitchen. I don't kiss my friends. Lana was supposed to look after me this morning, but she's run off somewhere, and now we can't find her."

Gabe darted a glance at Brodie and pulled out a five-pound note from his smart suit jacket. He passed the money to Brodie. "Why don't you go to the vending machine at the end of the hall and get yourself a Coke."

Brodie's face lit with eagerness and disbelief. "You already got me a slushie?"

"Well, you can have two overpriced sugary drinks. Off you go."

The last thing I needed today was a kid with a sugar rush. I opened my mouth to protest but Gabe's emerald eyes gleamed with purpose. He must have had a reason to send Brodie away.

I moved to the door, so I could keep an eye on Brodie. "Fine. Make sure it's a sugar-free one."

Brodie beamed and skipped down the corridor. Gabe reached into his jacket and pulled out his phone. He scrolled it and passed it to me.

My mind reeled as I scanned the article. *Exclusive—My Love Affair with Sugar Daddy Alex Mac. The Wild Child of Women's Football Tells All.*

Lana had sold me out? She wouldn't, would she?

"I'm sorry about this, mate. Better coming from someone inside the club."

Gabe was still talking, but I couldn't take any of it in. His voice faded to a drone as I watched Brodie at the vending machine down the hall. It didn't matter what the papers said about me, but what about Brodie? This would affect him. How could she do that to us? Brodie's footsteps echoed in the corridor, muted and sharp at the same time. My guts churned.

Gabe ran his tongue over his lower lip. "The tabloids have hounded me my whole life. This is mild compared to the stories that have been printed about me. They will have blown everything out of proportion. Try not to take it personally."

How could I not take it personally? The woman I'd fallen in love with, and trusted, had sold me out? For what? What reason could she possibly have for doing this to me? To Brodie? It didn't make any sense. I wouldn't have believed her capable of it if I hadn't read the article and seen with my own eyes. There were things in there that only Lana knew.

This was completely out of character. She wouldn't have spoken to the press voluntarily. Nonsense like this wouldn't just push me and Brodie away, it would jeopardize her chances of playing for England. I'd seen how seriously she took that. Something must have happened for her to get caught out by the press like this.

If she'd been having trouble with the press, why wouldn't she come to me for help? Why would she sit on something like this? I'd thought we were building something stable. I'd tried to be there for her. I'd trusted her enough to let her into Brodie's life, so why couldn't she trust me enough to ask me for help if she was struggling?

Gabe's emerald eyes held sympathy rather than their usual humor.

Brodie skipped back toward us. Oh, Brodie. The poor kid would be devastated. He'd got so attached to Lana. This was my fault. I'd let it happen, knowing full well it wasn't the best thing for him. Lana wasn't ready for any of this. The foundation of a stable, committed relationship was trust, but Lana hadn't trusted me enough to come to me with whatever she was dealing with.

Lana had always only wanted to keep things casual. I'd thought we were making progress. After the pregnancy scare, I'd supported her. I would have been there for her whatever, but it wasn't enough to prove myself. She didn't trust me enough to open up. I'd uprooted Brodie from our old lives because I'd thought a new start would help us heal. My focus had to be Brodie. I'd been a fool to think I could get involved with Lana. We were always too much for her. I'd lost track of the game and let a goal get past me.

Somehow, I forced a smile onto my lips. "Are you ready to go, pal?"

Brodie nodded and slipped his soft hand into mine. I straightened. All that mattered was defending Brodie from the fallout. I'd let him down. I wouldn't make that mistake again.

Chapter 41

LANA

Pebbles crunched underfoot as I traversed the beach that edged the secluded loch. Sunlight sparkled diamonds on the flat, mirrored surface of the water, dazzling me. I threw a hand up to shield my eyes. Everything was so bright. Of course, I hadn't thought to bring sunglasses.

These clear, warm days were so rare. An endless expanse of wild countryside unfurled around me, beautiful and rugged. The occasional bleating of sheep drifted over the hills, but it was so quiet and still you could almost hear the clouds rolling across the sky. Long-forgotten memories hit me one after another.

Me and Mel splashing through puddles in wellies and raincoats while Mum tried to negotiate with us to carry our umbrellas. Mel spinning in a circle and laughing as I chased her.

The bright day only made my mood sourer. Even sunlight and devastating beauty couldn't stop the grief that consumed me. Everything had gone wrong. I'd betrayed Alex, and I'd run away. It was what I'd been doing my whole life. I'd been running. Not committing myself too seriously to anything. Not getting close to anyone. The truth was, I'd been running from this feeling. Most days, I felt like I was on a moving walkway and my legs were just carrying me along whether or not I wanted to go.

Alex and Brodie had been a light in the darkness. A sunbeam that had pierced a small shard in the armor that I'd built around my heart for the past ten years. Now, I'd lost them. I'd run, rather than attempt to explain myself. How could I ever go home? I had no job to go back to. No team.

My phone had died the minute I'd got off the train, and I hadn't even remembered a charger. It wasn't as though I'd been thinking straight when I'd packed the bag. Alex had probably seen the story by now. He wouldn't forgive me when he realized what a mess I'd made of things.

I couldn't forgive myself either.

Chapter 42

ALEXANDER

Brodie nibbled his ice cream. The freckles on his nose bunched. "You should have invited Lana. She loves this place."

It felt like a punch in the ribs to hear her name. "Lana's busy today."

"But Lana always hangs out with us after you play a match. Why didn't she want to watch you?"

I'd have to tell him. I just had to think of the right way. "Do you remember when you had that argument with Oliver about the football cards?"

Brodie nodded. "He stole my Haaland card."

"Right. Well, Lana and I had a falling-out. We're still going to be friends, but we might not spend time together anymore."

Brodie eyed me suspiciously. "Does that mean she's not your girlfriend now?"

"She never was my girlfriend, pal. She was just my friend."

"But I don't kiss my friends." Brodie jabbed at his ice cream. "Why did you fall out?"

Better to be honest. We'd have to have a discussion. No doubt the kids at school would be talking about it on Monday. "Lana told a journalist some things about me. It hurt me that she would go behind my back."

Brodie wrinkled his nose. "Lana wouldn't say mean things about you on purpose."

No. I didn't think so either.

"I bet it's because you're so boring. It wasn't Lana's fault. The papers had to make things up about you to make you sound interesting."

I sighed. No doubt some of it was exaggerated, but there was no smoke without fire. There were facts about our relationship in the article that only Lana knew. It was definitely her. Lana shouldn't have breathed a word about private matters. There had to be something deeper to it. A dollop of ice cream slipped off Brodie's spoon onto his white sweater. I passed him a napkin and tried not to cringe. That wasn't going to be easy to get out in the wash.

"If any of the kids at school say anything to you, tell me. I can talk to the teacher about it."

"They can say what they want. I'm not bothered." He shoved another spoonful into his mouth. "They're all just jealous because my dad is the coolest."

"You think I'm cool?"

"I mean, not really. You're not good at *Mario Kart*, and when you try and dance it's cringe, but you played in the World Cup. No one else's dad has done that."

I couldn't help the smile that pulled at my lips.

Brodie blew out a breath. "Can I still see Lana?"

I picked at a crack in the table. "Sure. We can still watch the women's team play if you want to."

"It's not the same. I want her to come round to the house. Can't you make friends again? I made friends with Oliver."

"We are friends. It's just going to be . . . different now."

"Can't you talk to her? If me and Oliver made friends again, then you can."

"It's not that simple, pal. I wish it was."

Brodie's face dropped. "Why not?"

Because I have to protect you. Because this conversation is exactly the kind I didn't want to have.

"This is for the best. If I have girlfriends, and they don't stick around, everybody gets upset."

Brodie straightened in the chair. "But Lana wants to stick around. She told me. One night, she whispered it to me. I don't think she thought I heard it, but I did."

"What did she say?"

"She told me her mum read to her when she was little. That she missed her mum so much, but nobody ever talked about her like we talk about Mum. She said she's lonely all the time even though she's got lots of friends. She said she always wants to be around to make us happy.

"Oliver only stole my card because he thought I'd stolen his. I didn't even know that was why. That's how we became friends again. He didn't mean to upset me. I bet Lana didn't mean to upset you either. If I hadn't asked Oliver why he stole my card, we still wouldn't be friends."

The noise of the ice-cream parlor filled my ears. That was the part that made no sense. She must have known how this would upset me. Why had she done it? Lana had never been interested in celebrity or making a name for herself in the media. Did she need the money? She could have asked me, and I would have helped her.

My phone buzzed in my pocket. I pulled it out to see an unknown number. I swiped the call away. This wasn't the time. A message popped up.

This is Mel. Lana's sister. Is Lana with you?

I texted Mel back. I haven't seen her since yesterday.

She's missing. She got kicked off the team. She's not answering her phone. I'm worried. Let me know if you see her.

I glanced down the row of tiny houses. Neatly trimmed hedges and flowerpots bursting with color lined a tiny patch of garden. I pulled out my phone and checked the address that Mel had texted me. At the height of his career, Logan Sinclair had been the captain of the Scottish team. He'd been so rich, he'd lived in a castle up by Loch Shiel. Trouble had always followed Logan, but how had he ended up here?

I knocked on the door. A siren screamed in the distance and shredded my nerves. Brodie jumped, pressing himself close to me. Mel swung the door open.

I peered past her into the narrow hallway. "Have you heard from her yet?"

Mel folded her arms. Dark shadows haunted her eyes and her normally sleek red hair was pulled into a messy ponytail. "She texted to say she needed some space and not to worry, but now she's not answering her phone. She's not at her place or the club. They sacked her this morning. How can I not worry?"

The club meant everything to her. This would devastate her.

Mel hugged herself. A tremor touched her lips. "Maybe her phone ran out of battery . . ." Her voice cracked and her hand fluttered to fiddle with the fine gold chain around her neck. "She's fine. I'm sure she's fine. She has to be."

She shook her head and her shining eyes came to rest on mine. "This is all my fault. I take it you've seen the article?"

"How is any of it your fault?"

She chewed her lip and stepped aside. "You'd better come in."

Chapter 43

Alexander

It had been ten years since I'd seen my old captain. We'd lost touch when he left Scotland. Logan's hair, which had once been lustrous, had all but vanished apart from fuzzy patches above his ears. Deep lines etched his haggard red face. Eyes that I remembered as brightly lit and full of laughter were now bloodshot and glassy. Logan Sinclair was a shadow of his former self.

Logan stopped short with dismay when I entered the compact but neat kitchen. He tightened the rope around his threadbare dressing gown and weaved his head from side to side like a snake trying to focus. His confused gaze fell on his daughter. "You didn't tell me we'd have visitors?"

Logan frowned, and then he let out a bark of laughter. "Alex McAllister? Big Mac!" He opened his arms wide and pulled me into his embrace. His sour citrus scent enveloped me. He pounded his fist against my back.

"I watched you play the other day. How did you miss that save?" Logan's eyes fell on Brodie. "And who's this wee chap?"

"This is my son, Brodie."

Logan shook Brodie's hand. "He's got a firm handshake, this fella." Logan transferred his gaze back to me. "Good to see you, pal. Can I get you a drink? You want a beer?"

Mel raised an unimpressed eyebrow. "I'm making tea."

Logan poked absently at a raised pink scar on his forehead. "How's things? What have you been up to these past years?"

I've been sleeping with your daughter.

She sold me out to the national press.

We have no idea where she is.

All that mattered was finding Lana. "I need to know what's going on."

Mel weaved with brusque efficiency around the kitchen, wiping the surfaces. "Alex isn't here for chitchat, Dad. He's here about Lana."

"Lana?"

The hiss of the teakettle raked through me. How was he going to take this news? I didn't have time for this. I just wanted to know that Lana was okay.

"Lana is Dad's girlfriend," Brodie announced proudly.

I coughed, awkwardly. "That's not quite true, pal."

Logan's confused eyes met mine. "What?"

"I know I'm older, but . . ."

I love her.

The words stuck in my throat. Not because I didn't mean them, but because of what it would mean to speak them out loud. Brodie looked up at me with keenly expectant eyes. The damage was done. The worst had come to pass. Brodie loved Lana, too. I had to be honest with him. We'd cope with the heartbreak together—the way we'd always done. I couldn't stop life from happening to Brodie. Life would keep coming, and with it, pain. I couldn't stop him from getting hurt. I could only be with him and stand firm when he needed me to help weather it.

"I've fallen in love with your daughter."

A muscle jumped in Logan's jaw. He drew his lips in then flashed a wry smile. "Well, good luck with that one, pal. Lana can be a lot of trouble. All I care about is that you treat her right . . ."

"You love Lana?" Mel put a steaming mug of tea on the table in front of me.

I couldn't turn my feelings off like a light switch, even after the article. We were too much for Lana, but I'd still fallen for her.

Brodie's face split into a wide grin. "We both love her."

My heart dropped at the same time as a small smile played on my lips. Brodie was always so happy around Lana. She'd brought him so much joy, even if now she'd brought us pain. That was the price we'd paid.

"Yes. I love her. Now, do you want to tell me what's happened?"

Mel sighed. She cast her weary gaze over her father and smoothed her smart shift dress. "Lana was being blackmailed. Some nasty journalist was threatening to print a story if Lana didn't give her dirt on the team. She's been trying to hold it off by feeding her information about Sean."

A frown creased my brow. "Lana was the one leaking stories to the press?"

Mel slid into a chair at the table, her thin fingers tensed in her lap. "Sean Wallace is a nasty piece of work. He deserves whatever he gets. In the end, the journalist was out for blood. Lana had no choice. She either told the story of the two of you or . . ." Mel bit her lip, and her eyes slipped away. "The journalist had some stuff on Dad."

Logan paled, his dull eyes blazing brighter. "What? What stuff?"

Mel swallowed, and her gaze rested on Brodie. "Private stuff. Now's not the time. Suffice to say, it was damaging. I told Lana that if she didn't keep the journalist off our back by giving her the story she wanted . . ." A swift shadow crossed Mel's composed face. "I wouldn't forgive her."

The color drained from Logan's grizzled face. "You did what?"

"It was an impossible situation. I thought Alex could weather something like this better. What does it matter to him? It's flattering, isn't it? A beautiful young athlete has fallen in love with you and wants to tell everyone about it. It's hardly the end of the world. I knew you'd be able to cope."

"What private stuff?" Logan's voice had a strange soft edge.

"Not now. It doesn't matter," Mel said quietly.

Logan slammed his fist so hard on the kitchen table it made his newspaper jump. "Of course it matters. If it's about me, then this was my responsibility, not yours or Lana's. You should have come to me with it. I would have handled it."

Mel shot him a dubious look. "We were trying to protect you."

He rubbed a sparse gray eyebrow with a trembling finger. "I'm a grown man. Whatever it is, you should have come to me."

Lana had been backed into a corner, and she'd tried to protect her family. I could understand. All that had ever mattered to me was protecting my family. Brodie hopped up to sit in my lap. "But where is she? We can't just sit here. We need to find her."

Mel's expression was stony. "She loves you, too. I think this is the first time she's ever opened herself up to anything since . . ." Her gaze flashed to her father and she looked away. "For a long time."

I thought she'd been opening up too, but she hadn't trusted me to help her. Silence swirled around us. A memory drifted back. Lana had told me once about the place she'd lived before.

Yellow roses climbing the walls. A loch, the bluest blue you've ever seen.

It was a long shot, but we'd have to try. "I have an idea of where she might be."

Mel swallowed, and her eyes met mine. "Me too."

Chapter 44

ALEXANDER

Brodie sat on a booster cushion in the passenger seat next to me. He lifted his head from his comic to address Mel in the back seat. "Who's your second-favorite pirate?"

"Pirates are criminals. I don't like any of them. We shouldn't be glorifying them."

"Lana said your mum used to tell you stories about girl pirates."

Mel didn't reply. I watched her in the rearview mirror. She turned her face to watch the countryside whizz by outside.

Brodie twisted in his seat and eyed our reluctant passenger warily. "Do you like Pokémon?"

"No."

"Dinosaurs?"

"No."

Brodie scowled. "What do you like?"

"Quiet car journeys."

The faint sound of Lana's voicemail message drifted to my ears as Mel tried her sister's phone again.

"When we find Lana, is she still going to be your girlfriend?" Brodie shuffled his deck of football cards. "I'm sure she'll come and do sleepovers again if you ask her."

Lana didn't want to be my girlfriend. Who knew what was going through her head? I just wanted to bring her home, safe and well. An awkward heat suffused me, and I avoided Mel's stern eyes in the rearview mirror. "I don't think we'll be doing any more sleepovers."

"She didn't want to hurt you. I know she didn't," Mel piped up from the back. Her voice was softer than usual. "How would you feel if Lana *is* your dad's girlfriend?"

My hands clenched on the steering wheel. I kept my eyes fixed on the road ahead as we crossed the border to Scotland. "You don't have to answer that, Brodie. I don't care about girlfriends. You know you're my number-one priority."

Brodie shrugged. "I'd love it."

"And what if one day Lana didn't want to be my girlfriend anymore? If she left? Wouldn't that make you sad?"

"No. Just get another girlfriend. When Bella said she didn't want to be my girlfriend anymore, I asked Lizzy, and she's my girlfriend now."

In the rearview mirror, I caught Mel's sardonic eyebrow raise. "There you go. Problem solved. Just get another one," she said.

I couldn't find it in me to laugh. Not until we found Lana. No matter what had gone on between us, I needed to know that she was okay.

Chapter 45

LANA

Bright buttercups scattered the graveyard in constellations like fallen stars. Weeds covered the weathered stone of Mum's grave.

"Lana?"

Mel's voice made me jump. Taking a deep, unsteady breath, she stepped toward me. Her normally pristine hair was disheveled, and shadows haunted her eyes.

"What are you doing here?"

Mel clamped her mouth tight. "You're not answering your phone. People are worried about you. How could you be so irresponsible?"

Mel was on the warpath as usual. I shouldn't have expected different. "Have you driven all this way to lecture me? That's a fine effort. I commend your commitment."

"Why did you run?"

"Because I don't do this part."

"What part?"

I reached down and brushed Mum's gravestone. The moss was spongy and forgiving under my fingertips. "The goodbye."

A bitter wind whipped around us, and I pulled my cardigan tight.

Mel held perfectly still. "I'm sorry."

"No. You're not. You pushed me into this thing with the journalist. You asked me to choose between you and Alex."

Her face was pale. "And you chose us. Your family."

"I sacrificed Alex for this family, and why? You hate me. You talk to me like shit. Dad is so broken. I can't get through to him, no matter how hard I try. I've thrown away two families that actually care about me: my team, and Alex and Brodie."

"I don't hate you."

"Right. I feel sorry for the people you do hate."

I watched a raven pull a worm from the earth and snap it in two with its sharp beak.

"I've fucked everything up, Mel. Why is life like this? So . . . brutal."

Mel dropped down and pulled some dandelions from the grass around Mum's grave. She was silent for so long, I'd given up on her ever speaking, but then words fell softly from her lips.

"Do you remember what Mum would say whenever we were upset? She used to say, it's always darkest before dawn. We never know what is around the corner. Sometimes, when you think something is the worst it could ever be, it's because something wonderful is about to happen."

"Do you believe that?"

She shrugged. "Not really. Usually what's around the corner is more shit, but I was trying to be reassuring."

I couldn't help my incredulous snort. "You need to work on your motivational speeches. You started off so well."

Her eyebrows lifted. "In my experience, if you feel like life is falling apart, then you're hungry, or tired, or it's PMS. Either way, it will pass. All things pass. What is done is done, but it doesn't have to be over with Alex. That man cares about you. As for football, you're one of the most talented players in this country. You'll find a place to play, and wherever you go, they will be lucky to have you."

Tears welled in my eyes, but I held them in check.

"Alex must care about you, anyway, if he drove all the way up here."

Warmth rushed through me. "Alex and Brodie are here?"

I followed her gaze to the tall trees that edged the graveyard and the two figures standing at a distance.

A rare smile pulled at Mel's lips. "I don't think they came all this way to say goodbye, do you?"

I smothered the urge to run to Alex and throw myself at his feet. He must have been so mad at me. "I thought he'd never speak to me again. I can't believe he came all this way."

"He's not angry, he's been as worried about you as we are. I had to tell him everything. He already knew something was going on." Mel studied my face. "He knows you, Lana. He knows you're not capable of hurting someone on purpose. He knew there had to be a good reason. That the press had forced your hand somehow."

I'd been so frightened that Alex would assume the worst about me, like everyone else.

I looked up to find Mel watching me. "You get through to Dad in a way I can't. You put a smile on his face. That's worth its weight in gold." She rolled her shoulders and gazed down at the dandelions in her hand. "You must forgive me, Lana, because I'm sorry. None of this is easy for me. I've let you down. I know I'm not . . . expressive, but it doesn't mean I don't feel things. I feel . . . a lot of things. The truth is, I'm not good at talking about that, and I'm not good at goodbye either."

The strained tone of Mel's voice held me transfixed. It had been so long since she'd opened up to me. So long since it felt like we were talking and not sniping at each other. I'd given up trying to be honest with Mel. She saw a teenage screw-up and I saw a disapproving older sister. For years, we'd been giving each other what the other expected. We'd been stuck in these molds for so long, whether we liked it or not. But this wasn't the Mel I was used to. This was a Mel waving a white flag. A Mel who was being raw and honest, even though it was difficult for her.

She studied the dandelions in her hand as though they were the most interesting thing in the world. "I wish we could get through this together, not apart. I want to try and be . . . better."

I nodded woodenly and brushed the tears from my cheeks with the back of my hand. I wanted that, too. I wanted Mel to know me. To see the real me. If I was good enough for Alex, maybe I was good enough for her, too. "I'm sorry too. I want things to be better between us. The way that they used to be."

Mel's palm hovered over my shoulder. She frowned and withdrew her hand. It wasn't easy for her, but I wouldn't let her go. I pulled her toward me and into my arms. She held rigid for a moment, then relaxed. Her head rested against my shoulder and she spoke in a soft voice. "If a man says goodbye, then you'll survive it. It's worse not to try and put things right. Imagine if you could fix things and you didn't even try. You can't run like this. You have to stick around and face your fears."

"I'm too scared."

"You're the bravest person I know. You run around on that pitch in front of all those people and the cameras, and it doesn't faze you. I might have a folder full of certificates, but I could never do what you do. Be brave now. You can do it."

I squeezed her tighter. "I'm grateful for everything you've done for this family."

I felt her relax into my embrace. "I needed to be here to take care of my family, but I think it's time I think about what I need from this life, too. The reason I've been so busy lately is that I'm taking some courses after work. Once we get Dad settled again, I want to find some work that I'm passionate about."

"You should do. That's a great idea."

Birdsong filtered into the silence. She patted my back. A teasing note to her voice. "This is nice, but it's getting weird now. You can let me go."

I laughed and released her. "I know, but we had a lot of hugs to catch up on."

It had been so long since Mel had been a sister to me. I hadn't just lost my mum, I'd lost how Dad used to be. I'd lost the Mel that had been like this. It wasn't her fault. She'd been hurting, too. And I'd lost myself. I'd played into the versions of me that everyone else had created because it was easier than being me. I didn't want that anymore. As hard as it was to be me, it felt like a relief. We'd all been hurting so much and for so long. Honesty was the only way forward.

Mel shielded her eyes from the sun and squinted over at Alex and Brodie.

A little shiver went through me. Alex might not have been mad about the article, but he'd still feel betrayed. It wasn't as though things could just go back to how they were. I'd kept a huge secret from him.

"Talk to him. Just be honest. It will be okay. I'll take the kid." Humor glinted in her normally steely eyes. "Do you have any tips on how to make him stop talking?"

Chapter 46

Lana

Brodie launched himself at me, throwing his arms around my waist. I dropped down to his level to hug him.

"You came all this way to see me?"

Brodie gave a vigorous nod. "Are you coming home with us?"

Mel held out her hand to him. "Come on. Let's go for a walk. We can play a game."

Brodie's expression brightened. "What game?"

Her stern countenance held a hint of humor. "Who can be quiet for the longest."

Alex planted himself in front of me. The wind kicked at his dark hair. The gray at his temples looked to have spread a little. Guilt pressed me down like a bar pushing my shoulders. "I'm so sorry about the article, I'm so sorry. I didn't want to do it. I didn't want it to be like that—"

"We can talk about it. I only care that you're okay." He studied me intently. The deep tone of his lilting voice washed over me. "Are you okay?"

No. How could I be okay after what I'd done? "You came all this way. What are you doing here?"

He gazed out at the graveyard behind us and flashed a small smile. "I was passing by."

"In the Highlands of Scotland?"

"I took the scenic route."

The wind whispered among the trees at my back. A shiver ran through me.

"Here." Alex took off his huge coat and wrapped me in it. He took a tentative step closer. "I've been worried about you. We all were . . . Your dad and Mel . . . You didn't answer your phone."

"I'm sorry. It was cut off."

Silence wound around us.

"Claire kicked me off the team."

He nodded. "You'll get snapped up by another team."

"I don't want to play for another team."

"Talk to Claire. Fight your corner. You might be able to sort this out if you explain how difficult it's been. Nobody knows, Lana. We see you bouncing around with that cocky smile on your face and nobody knows that you have any troubles. I understand you want to protect your father, but maybe Claire would be more lenient if she knew what you'd been going through."

"Mel told you about Dad?"

He reached around and rubbed the back of his neck. "I went to his house. Mel told me about the blackmail. I knew you wouldn't do it if you didn't have a reason."

This should never have darkened Alex's door. I'd let him and Brodie down. "How angry are you?"

"It could have been worse." His mouth twitched with amusement. "The article was quite complimentary. I've never been called a sugar daddy before."

How could he be taking this with such good humor? His teasing was affectionate, not malicious. He moved to stand next to me. Side by side, we looked out over the endless rugged countryside.

"I'm not angry about the article, Lana. I'm disappointed that you didn't trust me or anyone at the club enough to open up about it. I would have helped you. You could have gone to Claire or Gabe and they would have helped you too."

"I couldn't face it. I didn't want anyone to know how badly my life had unraveled. I wanted to look like I was coping. You want a girlfriend who is mature and sensible. You kept worrying about me being so much younger than you. I wanted to be responsible and deal with this myself. I shouldn't have run. Everything happened all at once. I lost all the things that mattered to me the most in one day. You, Brodie, my team, my career. I wasn't thinking straight. It was always going to end this way. This is how things go. People meet, they fall for each other, and then they leave. This is why I don't want to get attached to anyone."

He held motionless, but his finger brushed the back of my hand lightly. The slight contact seared up my wrist.

"You could have told me about this. We could have worked through it together. I always knew that this was too much for you. You're young and focused on your career. You didn't want an old man and his kid."

My heart sank. He was talking about us in the past tense. I hadn't realized I had still been holding on to hope.

"You're not old, and you're what I want, Alex. I want you and Brodie. You come together, and I wouldn't have it any other way. Maybe I didn't tell you the truth about all this for the same reason I pretended to be Mel when we first met. I didn't want you to see the real me."

"The real you?"

I held my arms wide and shrugged, regretfully. "This Lana. Not some twenty-something party girl or whatever everyone thinks about me. The Lana who is grieving and struggling. This Lana, who is always messing everything up."

He shot me a sidelong glance. "We're the same underneath. Life has turned us inside out. It doesn't make me want you less. It makes me admire you more. I see you, Lana. I know how much you're hurting, and I know that some people have you all wrong, and they will continue to make that mistake if you don't show yourself."

"I want to. It's difficult to know how to start."

"Just be you. The Lana with a huge heart. The Lana who can hold a whole school hall transfixed with her passion for football. The Lana who is willing to spend a whole day pretending to be a pirate with my little boy and who he won't stop talking about. This is the Lana that we all want. This is the Lana that we all love." His large hands wrapped around mine. "The Lana that *I* love."

An overwhelming relief went through me, and heat pressed behind my eyes. He loved me? What did that mean? He still wanted to be with me? Could we work on this? How could he forgive me? If we were going to try again, then I'd have to be honest about all of it.

"I love you too, Alex. You and Brodie, but you should know that it wasn't just the article about us. I leaked information about Sean Wallace. He's your captain."

A muscle tensed in his jaw. "You did what you had to do."

"This isn't goodbye?"

He put a hand over his chest. "Not if you don't want it to be. We're adults, and we can get past this if we want to. We'll need to work on things. Promise me that next time you get scared, you'll talk to me and not run. I want to be the man who you can trust to have your back when everything seems too much. We need to communicate about everything, and we need to be honest with each other. It's not fair on Brodie if you're not as committed to this as I am."

"I'm committed. I want to be committed. If you give me another chance, I'll always be honest with you. You'll always get the real Lana. I swear it."

He rocked back on his heels. "I don't know how young people do these things these days, but according to Brodie the best thing to do is to ask outright." He raked a hand over the stubble on his jaw. "Lana Sinclair, will you be my girlfriend?"

His earnest expression made me melt. "It would be an honor to be your girlfriend."

His soft eyes sparkled with humor. "Good. If the wild child of women's football wants me for her sugar daddy, who am I to say no?"

Chapter 47

LANA

ONE WEEK LATER

My trainers squeaked on polished marble. Alex was at my side. His towering, solid presence was almost enough to put me at ease. We traversed a long corridor with thick cream carpets. Vases brimming with fresh flowers perched on tall, evenly spaced plinths. A floral scent filled my nose. The huge clinic was more like a five-star hotel than how I'd imagined a rehab facility. It was still hard to comprehend that Dad had agreed to do this, and even harder to fathom how we could accept this help from Alex. It must have been costing a fortune.

Mel was already waiting in Dad's room. She stood at the window, surveying the artfully manicured lawns. Of course she would be here first. Some things never changed. Mel shot Alex an accusatory glance, her smile stretched tight across her lips. "We can't accept this from you. Look at this place. How much is this costing?"

Alex held his hands up and broke into a wide, open smile. "It's fine."

Dad peered into the mini fridge. The bright light illuminated a shelf of mineral water and fancy snacks. Dad scratched the gray scruff on his jaw. "Look at this. This is too much."

They were both right. We couldn't accept this.

I surveyed the contents of the fridge alongside Dad. "How much are they paying you on the men's team? Because they sure as hell aren't paying me this much. This is the gender pay gap in action."

"Right? So, let me balance that injustice in some small way. Let's not talk about money again."

I pressed myself to Alex's warm, muscular body. His steady heartbeat thudded against my ears. Mel averted her gaze. Dad coughed. If it was weird for them to see us together, then tough luck. They'd have to get used to it.

Alex rubbed my back. His deep, lilting voice rumbled through his strong chest. "Let me do this for you. Me and Brodie come as a package, and your family comes with you too."

"But Brodie is cute. My family are . . ."

I pulled away from Alex and met Mel's eyes. She raised an expectant eyebrow, but a hint of laughter twisted her lips.

"My family are . . . older . . . and more expensive to maintain."

Mel snorted. Alex folded his arms. "Are you kidding me? This rehab is cheap compared to Brodie's football card addiction."

Alex pulled me into his arms and whispered low in my ear so my dad and Mel couldn't hear. "Besides, I like treating you well. If your sugar daddy can't spoil you, who can?"

Dad sat on the bed, testing the bounce. "So this is my home for a while. At least the bed feels good. I need a solid mattress with my back." He clapped his hands together and shooed us away. "Go on then. Stop gawking. You can all get out of here. You don't need to fuss."

He hauled his case up onto the bed and started to unpack. I exchanged a look with Mel. I knew we were both thinking the same thing. Neither one of us wanted to leave him here alone.

Mel hovered at his side. "Do you need help unpacking?"

"I can unpack a case."

He pulled out his toiletry bag, and I couldn't help but run an inventory of all the things he'd probably forgotten to pack. "Did you remember your toothbrush?"

"I'm sure I did."

"If you forgot anything, you can call me," I said.

"Or me," Mel piped up.

Dad paused with a sweater in his hand, and turned to face us. "You don't have to worry about me. I'm going to be okay." Dad folded the sweater and put it neatly in a drawer. "I'm ready to do the work. I've been in a lot of bother in my life, but this is rock bottom. You girls have suffered for too long. The last thing I ever wanted was to put so much on you. I haven't been a good father, but I'm here because I want to do better.

"I won't promise you, because I know it won't mean anything to you. My promises aren't worth much. All of my mistakes are my own, and I have to live with them. There have been too many promises before, but it's going to be different this time."

I wanted to believe him. We'd dropped him off at rehab plenty of times, but he'd never looked so earnest before, and we'd never had a place like this. If he was ever going to succeed, it was now. The most important part was that he was taking responsibility. This wasn't up to me and Mel to solve. Whatever happened we'd support him, but now this was about him.

I gave him a hug. "Good luck, Dad."

"Thanks, love."

Claire summoned me into her office and tipped her head to the chair opposite her desk. Skylar stood in the corner with her arms folded across her chest. I hardly dared look at her. She had to be so mad with me. She'd told me private things about Sean and I'd betrayed her . . . again. A shudder of guilt ran through me, but I'd come here to face the music. I drew a sharp breath and sat tall in the chair. Whatever they needed to say, I'd take it. Claire had already decided, and I hadn't come to argue or challenge her on it. I understood. From Claire's point of view, I was a liability. I'd let her down every time I got here late.

"You wanted to see me?"

Claire pressed her lips, thoughtfully. "I've had a call."

A small glimmer lit in my heart. Not *the call*? Surely not. Not after that article. I had no chance.

"It was from Mr. Singh, the head teacher at Daleside Primary. He said how much the kids had enjoyed the lessons with you. They all want to know when Lana Sinclair is coming back. You must have made a big impression. Mr. Singh said you're still welcome to go back to the school whenever, even if you're not involved with the club."

Thank goodness. Not *the call*, but still something brilliant. I didn't want to stop my school visits. My girls were making progress, and I always left with the biggest smile on my face. Alex had started his coaching qualifications, and I couldn't deny how great it sounded. If I couldn't find another team to take me on as a player, then coaching might be an option.

Claire flashed me a faint smile. "Will you go back to the school? It would be a shame if they missed out just because you're not on the team anymore."

"I wouldn't miss it for the world. We've got our future England captain in that group."

I'd messed up my career, but that didn't mean I still couldn't help others. I had to speak to Gabe about this goalkeeper. Maybe Alex and I could do some one-on-one training with her on our visits to the school.

I felt Skylar's eyes burning into me, but I still didn't dare look at her. It hurt too much. I couldn't bear the thought of not coming in to work every day and seeing my best friend. It had been hard enough when she'd been in LA, but at least I'd known she was coming back. I'd let her down. She'd texted me, but I hadn't known how to respond. Alex might have accepted the real me, but this was different. Showing myself to my team had always been so hard.

I searched for the speech that I'd prepared with Alex. I'd rehearsed it with him so many times, but all of those well-practiced words had slipped away. Instead, I fumbled my way through the truth.

"It's too little too late, but I wanted to apologize and explain. I've been struggling with some personal matters."

Claire leaned back in her chair, relaxing. "Do you want to tell us more about that?"

I kept my gaze fixed on a glass paperweight on Claire's desk because I had to say my piece, and it was easier like this. "I came here from rehab. We dropped my dad off this morning. The truth is, my dad has been sober for many years, but recently he had a relapse. Addiction is a terrible disease. Really terrible.

"My sister and I watched Dad struggle for a long time. Things got bad after Mum died. None of us are good at talking about how we feel. Dad tried to cope with booze. Mel shut down and became bitter and angry. I haven't been coping well for a long time, but I didn't want anyone to see that. I was scared that if the truth came out then people wouldn't want to know me."

I looked up at Skylar for the first time. "That my friends wouldn't want to know me."

Tears glimmered in my best friend's eyes, and I transferred my gaze onto Claire so I wouldn't cry too. I had to get through this. I couldn't undo what I'd done, but at least I could try and make them understand why this had happened.

"Everybody looks at me and sees someone wild like my father. I get it. Sometimes, it's just easier to be the person everyone expects me to be. You made me captain because you thought I needed to take football more seriously. It hurts to think about that because this team is everything to me. All I've ever wanted is to play for England. I'm serious about football and this team. I know that nobody can see that, so I gave up trying to prove myself. It was easier just to let you see what you wanted to see."

I glanced up at Claire. A muscle worked in her jaw.

"Every time I was late it was because I'd got in a mess trying to help Dad, not because I didn't care about the team. I'm sorry because I know the example it sets to the younger players, and I want to be a role model. I love going into school and talking to those young girls. It reminds me of me at that age, when that passion for football was so pure, before I had to deal with everything the world piled onto my shoulders. I was too young to cope with it. I got so used to lying to everyone that everything was okay at home, that lying became easier than the truth."

I forced myself to stay calm, despite my rioting panic about being so open. "I didn't want that article to go out. I didn't want a single story in the press about this club, but that journalist blackmailed me, and threatened to expose secrets about my dad. I didn't know what to do. It was an impossible situation. This club has always meant the world to me, but so does my family."

Skylar cleared her throat. "You should have told me. I would have helped you."

"I was scared. I wanted to prove that I'm not the irresponsible screw-up everyone thinks I am. I wanted to take responsibility and fix it myself. I let you all down. I'm sorry. I let you down with this, and I let you down last season. I've been a terrible friend."

Skylar grabbed my hand. "You're not. I told you I'm over that stupid bet, the stuff with Sean. It doesn't matter. I hate to think of what you've been going through all alone. I wish you'd told me. I would have helped you."

I'd make an effort from now on to be a better friend. I'd be honest with Skylar, and hope that she liked this version of Lana as much as the old one.

"Anyway, I've taken up enough of your time. I'm sure you want to get on with training. I needed to come here today to apologize and clear the air. Thank you for the honor of being a part of this team. It's been a privilege to be here, and I wish you all the best."

Claire frowned and straightened in her chair. "You could have told us earlier. I would have been able to help."

"I've always found it difficult to ask for help. I want to be better at my next club."

Claire sighed and shook her head. "I shouldn't have inflicted that journalist on you. I knew she'd give you a hard time, but this is part of the job at this level. That's why I was so keen for you to do the interview. I wanted to give you some practice handling the press. If I'd have known what this woman was capable of, or what you were going through at home . . ."

She leaned forward in the chair. Her voice was softer than usual. "We've all got stuff going on in our personal lives. Life is complicated. I understand that. Your private life is your private life, but if it's going to affect your performance, then you need to be upfront with me so we can do whatever we can to support you. We're a team. We're your family, too. Thank you for being honest with us. It makes it easier to understand what has been going on with you this season. Let's try and find a way to support you better for the rest of the season."

My eyes filled with tears. "What do you mean? I thought I was off the team. You're giving me another chance?"

Claire nodded and transferred her gaze to Skylar. "Yes, I'm not losing two of my best players."

A pulse pounded in my temple. "Two? I don't understand."

Claire raised a sardonic eyebrow. "Apparently if you go, then I lose my captain, too."

Skylar's face was full of strength and determination. She hitched her shoulder and offered me a faint smile. "That's right."

I stared at her, baffled. Why wasn't she angry with me after what I'd done? She couldn't make that sacrifice. This was her career. Her team. Besides, I didn't want to stay if Claire didn't truly want me here.

"You can't do that, Sky."

Skylar's voice was soft. "Mel already told me everything. You don't deserve to get kicked off this team."

"You're not angry with me?"

"I was, but I talked it all out with Reece. I understand that you were in an impossible situation, and you were just doing your best."

Claire's solemn gazed bored into me in expectation. "I want you to stay, Lana. This is nothing to do with Skylar. I won't be blackmailed or coerced. This is me telling you I want a fresh start. This is my decision, but you need to tell me what's going on in your life if it's going to affect your performance on the pitch. I can't help you if you don't talk to me."

I stood taller. "I can do that."

"Good. I go hard on you all because I want you to be the best, and frankly, I don't need the admin that comes with sacking you so . . ." Humor glinted in her blue eyes. She waved a dismissive hand and pointed to the door. "That's enough now. I've got a team to run. Both of you get out of here and do some laps before I change my mind."

Skylar threw her arm around me and guided me to the door.

"Actually, wait. I need a word with Lana in private." Claire's words halted us.

Skylar pulled me into a hug before she left, closing the door behind her.

Claire picked up a paperweight and passed it between her hands. "I've heard we're going to have some scouts watching the match this weekend. If you're serious about playing for England then I advise you to put everything out there on the pitch."

"Nobody is going to want me after that article."

"It will blow over. I've been doing this job a long time, and these things always do. Just ask Gabe. You were caught up in a terrible situation. You could have been honest and handled it better, but . . . I get it."

Claire gave me a nod. "I'll put in a word for you with the scouts. I don't know if it will make any difference, but I'll make sure they know what you're capable of."

Heat burned my throat. I'd wanted Claire's approval for so long. I'd never thought it possible. "You think I have a chance? They might want me?"

She smiled and it was full of warmth. "With your talent and passion? I think they'd be mad not to."

Chapter 48

Alexander

Three months later

Brodie grabbed Lana's hand and dragged her toward the entrance to the trampoline park.

Lana shot me a look. "They really let the adults do this too?"

"You don't have to. Grab a coffee and watch from the balcony."

Brodie wailed. "No. Lana's doing it. She said she wanted to."

She laughed. "I wouldn't miss it. I've been looking forward to this. Who wouldn't want to spend an hour bouncing on giant trampolines? How often do you get to do that?"

Brodie skipped around a puddle. "Wait till you see Dad do a somersault."

"We've talked about this, Brodie. I'm not doing a somersault."

Lana threw back her head and laughed. "Spoilsport."

We entered the chaotic foyer. A barrage of sound from the crowds of kids getting ready to trampoline hit us. I spotted Rachel and the kids over by the counter and gave her a wave. Lana shot me a look of trepidation.

I leaned and whispered under my breath. "She's going to love you."

Rachel came streaming through the crowd of kids. She pulled me into a hug. "Don't worry. I brought us jumping socks from home. I'm not letting us get ripped off with the prices in these places."

I let go of her. "This is Lana. Lana, this is my sister, Rachel."

Rachel beamed. "Hi, Lana. So great to meet you at last." My sister wrapped her arms around Lana. "I'm a hugger."

"I warned her you're a hugger," I said.

Lana laughed, and the two women embraced. When Lana extracted herself from my sister, I was relieved to see she had a huge smile on her face. I'd wondered if this might be too much for her, but Lana had been so keen to meet Rachel. None of the things I might have worried about fazed her. She always volunteered to walk Brodie to school, and she'd been so excited last week when we'd gone together to choose a puppy for Brodie.

"Are you jumping?" Lana asked.

Rachel wrinkled her nose. "God. No. I've had two kids. Not with my pelvic floor. I'm here for a flat white and a rest."

I tried not to cringe. Rachel had never had a problem being herself.

Lana laughed and shot me a teasing look. "Well, I can't miss the trampolines. Alex has promised us a somersault."

I held my hands up. "I've got through my whole career without an injury. I'm not about to push my luck at Bounce Land."

Lana squeezed Brodie, and beamed. "If it's half as much fun as laser tag or go-karting, then it will be great."

A glow lit me. It was great taking Lana out with us. She had so much energy that everywhere she went, she got stuck in and played with Brodie. I couldn't ask for more.

Lana's phone rang, and she rifled around her in her handbag. She glanced at the screen and frowned. "Unknown number." She flashed Rachel an apologetic look. "Sorry, I'd better get this. It could be about my dad."

Lana flashed me a tentative smile and moved away to take the call. Logan was doing so well. He'd committed to the ninety-day program. Lana and Mel didn't want to get their hopes up, which was understandable, but I'd known Logan for many years, and this Logan was different. He was accepting responsibility for his actions. I believed that he wanted to change, and now he had the best facility to try and make it happen.

Rachel waited until Lana was out of earshot. Her eyes sparkled with excitement. "Oh my God. I love her. She's so nice. Brodie never shuts up about her."

"It's because she made him a pirate outfit for World Book Day."

Rachel smacked her hand to her forehead. "Bloody World Book Day. Where do I get a beautiful young woman to make costumes for my kids?"

I laughed. "Well, you can't have this one. She's mine."

Rachel studied my face, and lowered her voice to a whisper. "It's going well, then?"

Better than well. Lana had brought light back into my and Brodie's lives. Every day I wanted to pinch myself because of how lucky I felt. "It's going amazing."

Rachel's smile was full of warmth. "I was hoping for this. I'm thrilled for you, Alex. I know how difficult this has been, but you deserve to be happy. I love that you're moving into coaching, too. You're going to be great."

"Thanks."

Lana planted herself in front of us. The phone trembled in her hands, and her face was pale.

"What is it? Is it your dad?"

She swallowed. "No."

"Then what?"

She choked out a noise that was half laugh and half sob. "It was . . . the call."

Rachel frowned. "What call?"

Lana's eyes glimmered with happy tears. She let out a whoop of excitement. "The call! The bloody call."

A couple of people turned to stare, but I couldn't care less. All that mattered was the joy on Lana's face. Brodie and his cousins ran back over to see what all the excitement was about.

Rachel scratched her head. "I don't understand. What call? A good call?"

"*The* call." A huge smile stretched my face, and my heart swelled. "The best call. We're standing in the presence of an official Lioness." I cupped her face. "I'm so proud of you, sweetheart. You deserve it."

THANKS FOR READING!

Ready for more Calverdale Ladies? Check out the next book in the series! I can't wait for you to get to meet my Welsh mountain man, Geraint.

Have you read the prequel novella, PITCHING MY BEST FRIEND? Sign up to my newsletter here, and get it for free! https://BookHip.com/RVXCHSB I send newsletters once a month with book updates and recommendations of other books you might like. I promise to keep the boring photos of my garden and my dog to a minimum.

LET'S HANG OUT!

All I've ever wanted from life is a crew to hang around with so that we can all wear sunglasses, look cool and click our fingers in an intimidating fashion at rival crews. We can chat all things romance and occasionally you might be called upon to become involved in a choreographed dance fight. I will also be your best friend forever. NB: Dance fighting skills not mandatory (but encouraged).

Join my reader group:
www.facebook.com/groups/979907003370581/
Follow my author page:
www.facebook.com/profile.php?id=61553872688253
TikTok: Sasha Lace Author (@sasha_lace_author)
Instagram: www.instagram.com/Sasha_Lace_Author

Psst! Hang on! I'd love a review if you've got a sec? If you enjoyed this book, please consider leaving a review wherever you like to leave them. Amazon, Goodreads or BookBub. Reviews are the life-blood of authors, and are very much appreciated! Thanks so much.

ACKNOWLEDGMENTS

This is my second run at writing these acknowledgments. The first time, I was a fresh-faced indie author leaping into the unknown. I had no idea if anyone would pick up my story, or whether (more likely) it would be lost in a pile with a million others. What I didn't expect was to find so many people willing to take a chance on an unknown author.

Writing has brought so many wonderful women into my life. Thank you to all the readers who have supported me, whether it was taking the time to message with words of encouragement, leaving a thoughtful review, or shouting about my books. You helped me find my confidence as a writer. You made me feel like my words have value. It means the world, truly.

Thank you to everyone in the Montlake Romance team for all of your hard work on these books. It has truly been such a brilliant experience, and I've loved every moment. I'm so excited to relaunch these books with an amazing team of professionals. Thank you to Victoria Oundjian for giving me this chance, for your passion and enthusiasm for the series, and for making my lifelong dream to be traditionally published a reality.

Thank you to Victoria Pepe for taking this series on and bringing so much energy and enthusiasm to it. I feel so confident that it is in wonderful hands, and I'm so grateful. Thank you to Lindsey

Faber for your brilliant development editing insight, and for helping me to dig so much deeper with these characters. To Jenni Davis, thank you for giving these books such a beautiful polish, and helping me to banish the word 'quirked' from my vocabulary. I don't know how many books it will take before I can rid myself of it completely, but I live in hope.

Thank you to Laura and Clare at Liverpool Lit. You are amazing agents and lovely human beings. It is genuinely an honor to be represented by an agency so committed to breaking down barriers in publishing.

To my beta reader/editor/mentor Angela, I sent out a plea for help with my first story and the universe overshot the net and sent me you—the best friend I've never met! You have always been so accepting, so generous, and so insightful. You understood what I was trying to say with that weird first story (better than I did) and you helped make sense of it. Not only did you help me become a better writer, but you showed me that people can be miraculously kind.

To my lovely writer bestie, Heather G Harris. I have long suspected the 'G' stands for genius. You've always believed in me, and encouraged me, and you've been so generous with your time and knowledge. Thank you for being my very first beta reader, and for giving me the confidence to go for it with this story. I appreciate you.

To Jo, Tamymanne, and Kat. You are a wildly accepting bunch of fellow smut-butts. Thank you for all the laughs, and the log-ins. Jo, seriously, thank you. What would I do without the log-ins!? Please don't ever change your password, or this is all over for me.

To Helen, I'm so grateful to have a lovely friend to share this writing and publishing journey with. I really appreciate your talent for finding the perfect shocked-doll expression for every occasion, and your dedication to uncovering Rhysand fan art. Whatever happens, we'll always have the Willywahs and that street team of Ken dolls from Sainsbury's.

Thank you to my precious friend Katie. You have always brought so much joy into my life. Whatever I'm doing, no matter the hour, I'd always rather be on a boat with you, playing table tennis, and stuffing my face with free sushi and peanut M&Ms at 5 p.m., directly before our five-course meal is about to be served.

To Ruchi, my twin flame, all my literary aspirations began with you. Your West Midlands project spoke to me of beauty. The letter to Thom Yorke helped me to refine my prose. All that time spent doctoring BT phone bills honed my attention to detail. The environmental rap taught me how to dig deep. The hole in the ozone layer isn't even an issue anymore. Coincidence, or the power of rap?

Thank you to my mum for always encouraging my passion to read. Even when we had so little, you made sure I always had books. Thank you for your unconditional love and support. The past couple of years have been tough, but your selflessness and strength leave me in awe. Better times are coming, I know it. Thank you for being you. I love you.

To James, your support makes my writing possible. Your support makes everything possible. You've made me laugh every day for the past twenty years. The best part of writing about football is that I get to talk about these books with you. Why are you so randomly good at plotting? It's like that time we went windsurfing and you just knew how to stand up and do it straight away, and I was covered in goose shit and crying. It makes no sense, but I'm into it. You're better than all the book boyfriends put together. They should make a trope about you.

Last, thank you to my kind, beautiful, bright, funny, smart, wonderful boys. I became a writer when I became a mother. You gave me the will to be the best version of myself. Please know that you are the greatest joy in my life, and I love you more than anyone has ever loved anyone EVER. Now get out of here. Go on. Clear off! Do not read these books. Not even when you're grown-ups. I cannot afford the therapy you will need from reading your mother's sweary, spicy books. I have given you fair warning.

PLAYING TO WIN

Turn the page for an exclusive teaser chapter from *Playing to Win*, the next book in Sasha Lace's Playing the Field series . . .

Chapter 1

Madison

Six months ago

Kentucky, US

Dad surveyed the dirt track ahead and flexed his fingers on the huge steering wheel. "You're sure about this? It's not too late to back out."

His tone was light, but I didn't miss the shadow that crossed his work-hardened face. My family had never warmed to Bryce. They were always polite—their Southern manners wouldn't allow them to be anything else—but I wasn't blind to the way they looked at us together.

I took a deep breath and smoothed my clammy palms over layers of scratchy organza and lace. "Yes. I'm sure. Of course I'm sure."

Dad's jaw tensed, but he held his silence as we rumbled over wide-open countryside in his beat-up old tractor. It was an unlikely wedding car, but Dad's face had lit up like a Christmas tree when he'd suggested it. It would likely horrify Bryce's fancy LA relatives when we rocked up outside the church, juddering and spewing fumes. They'd hear us coming a mile off. No doubt that's why Dad had been set on the idea.

We hit another bump in the dirt track. I snapped my hand to my veil to stop it flying off. Dad flashed me a glance and chuckled. I couldn't help but laugh with him. My family thought it was too fast. I got it. Bryce was so different from the guys I'd brought home in high school. He was LA to the core, dazzling and full of charm. I always got so nervous at the fancy events PR insisted I attend, but none of it fazed Bryce. When the cameras appeared, he'd grip my hand and whisper in my ear, and it grounded me. This wasn't who my parents had envisioned for me, but this is what I wanted. A heavy weight pressed down on my shoulders. I had one life to live. I had to do it my way, even if it meant disappointing my family. Maybe with time, they'd come to love Bryce as much as I did—probably around the same time pigs sprouted wings and took to the skies. Still, I wouldn't lose hope.

The tractor rumbled to a halt. A cardinal's song rang out in the bracing silence. The bright-red bird perched on a branch in one of the many trees that lined the shady path to the church. I'd loved that sound as a kid. Now the low whistle jangled in my ears. A rush of anxiety gripped me. What if the table arrangements got messed up and my warring cousins got seated together? What if I stumbled over my vows and couldn't get my words out? What if Bryce's creepy uncle with the dairy intolerance got served the crème brûlée?

What if this whole thing is one gigantic mistake?

Sweat prickled my top lip in the awful heat, but I took a calming breath. By the end of today, I would start my life as Mrs. Bryce Muller. Everything could begin. After years of pressure, grind, and picking up a dozen injuries, I'd finally get to announce my retirement from soccer and start a family. A thrill of excitement went through me.

"This is it. Ready, darlin'?" Dad's voice was thick with emotion.

This is it.

The low whistle from the little red bird increased in pitch. My heart pounded along with its staccato trill. Dad opened the cab door and held out a hand to help me down. My heels clanked on the rusted metal steps. So much for an elegant entrance. If I could have gotten married in cleats, I would have. Assuming the tractor wasn't enough to knock Bryce's family into a tailspin, the cleats would have sent them over the edge. I fought to take a full breath against the press of my tight dress.

Dad's rough hand closed around mine. "Just breathe and take it all in."

My parents had been married for thirty years. They adored each other. If Bryce and I could be half as happy as my parents, we'd be doing great. Smiling, I closed my eyes and lifted my face to the sun's warmth.

Just breathe and take it all in.

Diesel fumes filled my nose and made me cough. I opened my eyes to see Anna, my maid of honor. She gripped my elbows. Her face was gray and grim. An alarm bell rang in my head. We'd been friends since elementary school. I knew this look. It was the one she'd worn the time she'd taken home the ill-fated school hamster. Poor little Hamilton, God rest his soul.

What had gone wrong? The catering? The band? My crazy cousins in a brawl?

"I'm sorry, Maddie." Tears filled my best friend's eyes. "It's Bryce. He ran. I don't think he's coming back."

ABOUT THE AUTHOR

Sasha Lace used to be a very serious scientist before she ditched the lab coat and started writing kissing books. Sasha lives in the North of England and is a mom of two young boys. Everyone in her family is soccer mad, so she knows way more about soccer than she ever wanted to know. As a scientist and mom, her hobbies include: mulling over the complexities of the universe, treading barefoot on Lego, chipping dried Play-Doh from fabric surfaces, dried flower arranging (because you can't kill something twice), and writing about herself in the third person.

Follow the Author on Amazon

If you enjoyed this book, follow Sasha Lace on Amazon to be notified when the author releases a new book!

To do this, please follow these instructions:

Desktop:

1) Search for the author's name on Amazon or in the Amazon App.

2) Click on the author's name to arrive on their Amazon page.

3) Click the "Follow" button.

Mobile and Tablet:

1) Search for the author's name on Amazon or in the Amazon App.

2) Click on one of the author's books.

3) Click on the author's name to arrive on their Amazon page.

4) Click the "Follow" button.

Kindle eReader and Kindle App:

If you enjoyed this book on a Kindle eReader or in the Kindle App, you will find the author "Follow" button after the last page.